PRAISE FOR
The Secret Fruit of Peter P...

A Barnes & Noble Discover Great New Writers
Selection and Extended Book Sense Pick

"Charming. . . . Sweet, tart, and forbidden in all the right places." —*Entertainment Weekly*

"Honest, sad, and funny." —*San Francisco Chronicle*

"All gay teens bargain with their own bodies, bodies they often feel betrayed by, but rarely is the bargaining and the cover-up so moving or funny. A beautiful story."
  —DAN SAVAGE, columnist of "Savage Love" and author of *Skipping Towards Gomorrah, The Kid,* and *The Commitment*

"Engrossing. . . . Accomplished. . . . Wrenching and humorous. . . . Extreme in its insight and tenacious in its willingness to delve into a tormented youth."
  —*Denver Post*

"Engaging, eminently likable. . . . A sweet, goofy levity, a rare and welcome lightness of touch that serves, rather than compromises, the weight and gravity of its message." —*New York Journal News*

"Bracingly off-center, flirting with lunacy, finally affirming that love must have its way."
  —*Globe and Mail* (Toronto)

The Secret Fruit of
Peter Paddington

The Secret Fruit of Peter Paddington

A NOVEL

Brian Francis

HARPER **PERENNIAL**

HARPER ● PERENNIAL

A hardcover edition of this book was published under the title *Fruit* in the United States in 2004 by MacAdam/Cage Publishers.

A paperback edition of this book was published under the title *Fruit* in Canada in 2004 by ECW Press.

P.S.™ is a trademark of HarperCollins Publishers.

HarperCollins books may be purchased for educational, business, or sales promotional use. For information please write: Special Markets Department, HarperCollins Publishers, 10 East 53rd Street, New York, NY 10022.

First Harper Perennial edition published 2005.

Designed by Dorothy Carico Smith

Library of Congress Cataloging-in-Publication Data

Francis, Brian.
　　[Fruit]
　　The secret fruit of Peter Paddington / Brian Francis.—1st Harper Perennial ed.
　　　　p.　cm.
　　Originally published under title: Fruit
　　ISBN-13: 978-0-06-079244-2 ISBN-10: 0-06-079244-2
　　　　1. Gay youth—Fiction. 2. Teenage boys—Fiction. 3. Overweight persons—Fiction. 4. Fantasy—Fiction. I. Title.

PR9199.4.F725F78 2005
813'.6—dc22　　　　　　　　　　　　　　　　　2005040609

05 06 07 08 09　❖/RRD　10 9 8 7 6 5 4 3 2 1

FOR DAD

ACKNOWLEDGMENTS

Thanks to the Writers' Union of Canada and the Toronto Community Foundation.

Thanks to Jill Schwartzman and the rest of the team at Harper Perennial.

Thanks to Dan Savage for the Q & A.

A very special thanks to Lesley Krueger for the guidance and encouragement.

Last, but not least, love and thanks to Serge, my family—both immediate and extended—and to my friends for continued support throughout the years.

The Secret Fruit of
Peter Paddington

one

My name is Peter Paddington. I just started 8th grade at Clarkedale Middle School. Six days a week, I deliver the *Bluewater Observer* and the other day, my nipples popped out.

I've always had boobs, but not girl-boobs. More like the "I need to lose weight" kind. I'm not thrilled about them, but they're pretty easy to hide under my sweat-shirts, and it's not like I ever jog or anything, so they stay in place. Besides, I know I won't have them for much longer because I'm planning to start my diet any day and be thin and normal by Christmas.

I know that I've got my work cut out for me, because there are lots of things about me that need fixing. For starters, I'm big-boned, which is a nicer way of saying "All my pants have elasticized waistbands." When I stick my finger into my belly button, it goes just past my second knuckle. That's my own test to see if I've gained weight or not. Last year, my stomach only went to my first knuckle, so I've put on a knuckle's worth of weight this year.

There are plenty of other things wrong with my body. Last year, I started growing hair on my legs and in my armpits, which was pretty disturbing. I was already having a hard enough time getting over the new hairs around my

dink. Before that, I had peach fuzz, which I didn't mind at
all because it was soft and blond, like the hairs inside a
corn husk. But then it turned brown and curly and now
the hair looks like the stuff that comes out of the tops of
corn husks, all dried up and burnt by the sun. I thought
about shaving my dink hair off once, but then I read
somewhere that if you shave a part of your body, the hair
grows back thicker and bushier. And then you're really in
a pickle, because even though you're shaving like crazy, the
hair will keep coming back like an angry weed until one
day, you can't even see your dink anymore. That's how
hairy you'll be.

The hair on my legs is softer than the hair around my
dink, but it still grosses me out. I wish my legs were bare
and tanned, like James MacDonnell's. He's adopted and
sits two rows over from me. He has a tan the whole year
through, even in the wintertime. He must be Mexican. Or
maybe Greek. James came to school the other day wearing
a pair of navy blue short shorts and I couldn't stop looking down at his legs. I had to be careful that I didn't get
caught, especially by Brian Cinder. He sits behind James.
So I pretended to study the patterns in the linoleum tiles.
Was that a cow I saw? And over there, wasn't that the face
of Jesus? I chewed my lower lip to look really convincing.

Anyways, I couldn't stop thinking about James' legs
and I was so jealous of them. There he was in his tube
socks and short shorts, not even thinking twice about
what people thought of his legs. I haven't worn a pair of
shorts since 6th grade, mainly because I don't want to
gross anyone out. Maybe my legs wouldn't look so bad if

they were tanned like James' legs, but then, how are they ever going to get tanned if I never wear shorts? And since I never wear shorts, my legs have pimples on them from rubbing against my pant legs all summer long. So my legs have three strikes against them.

The only other boy in my class with hairy legs is Andy Dover, but he's pretty hairy all over. He's the tallest student in our class, too. Even taller than Mr. Mitchell, our teacher. I wonder if Andy is really thirteen, because he looks older. Sometimes, I think that Andy is a spy investigating our school. Maybe he's a secret agent and has to prove that the chocolate bar money we raised last year wasn't for new curtains for the stage. Instead, the money went to Mr. Gray, our principal, so he could buy drugs. Or maybe Mr. Mitchell stole the money to buy a new van for his wife and seven kids.

But the more I think about it, the more I realize that there's no way Andy could be a secret agent. He's pretty stupid and spends most of his recess making fart noises under his hairy armpit. A secret agent would find better things to do with his time.

The morning I noticed my nipples, I was getting ready for school. I couldn't decide what to wear, since it was still hot outside. My gray sweatshirt would be cooler, but I wanted to wear the new black one I got through the Sears catalogue.

While I was standing there in my underwear, trying to make up my mind, something in the mirror caught my eye and I turned to look. My nipples looked like two little cherries.

"That's not right," I thought to myself and frowned. My nipples were round and puffy and not the two pink raisins they used to be. I ran my finger over the left one. It was soft as a rose petal. I turned sideways in the mirror and went from my nipples to my big white stomach to my dink with its burnt corn husk hair to my fat, pimply, hairy legs.

"This is the last thing I need," I said.

Then my mother banged on my bedroom door. "Hurry up or you're not going to have time for breakfast!"

It was hard to pay attention at school. I was afraid that someone might see my nipples poking out from under my sweatshirt. When my pencil tip broke during math class, I should've gone up to the pencil sharpener. But I just couldn't. So I finished off my questions using the broken lead stub, which wasn't easy, and my fingertips were all black by the time I finished.

While I was delivering papers later that afternoon, I kept my fingers crossed that Mr. Hanlan wouldn't see me. He usually keeps a lookout for me from his living room window. But he has to be careful that his wife doesn't catch him or she'll blow up and start screaming at him.

Mr. Hanlan is my favorite paper-route customer. He lives on Evergreen Street and works as an electrician. He's younger than most of my customers and has the brownest eyes I've ever seen. His wife, Mrs. Hanlan, is evil. She tricked him into marrying her because there's no way Mr. Hanlan would ever marry someone as ugly as her. She's so skinny, her arms look like toothpicks and her boobs look like acorns. She's got a very bad perm, too.

Mrs. Hanlan pretends to be all nice to me whenever I come collecting.

"Oh hi, Peter. Is it that time of the week already?" Or, "You must be awfully hot today. Do you want something to drink?"

"Keep your poison to yourself," I think.

I feel bad for Mr. Hanlan because I'm the only bright spot in his day. When he sees me coming up his driveway, I can just imagine the smile on his face. But if he ever finds out that I have a medical condition and my nipple disease might kill me, he'll get so depressed.

"What's the point of getting out of bed if someone has stolen my sun?" he'll ask.

"Shut up and go make some money!" Mrs. Hanlan will scream.

Anyways, while I was walking up the driveway, I noticed that Mr. Hanlan's car was gone, so he still must've been at work. Probably working overtime so that he can afford to get Mrs. Hanlan a new perm. I folded up the paper and stuck it in the mailbox before Mrs. Hanlan had the chance to run out and offer me a cup of bleach or something worse.

Tonight, I had trouble concentrating on my homework. I kept sneaking peeks down my pajama top to see if anything had changed. But my nipples were the same. Maybe even bigger. I snuck out of my room and went to the kitchen to grab some ice cubes.

"Peter, what are you doing?" my mom called out from the living room. She always thinks I'm up to something.

"I'm getting a drink," I said.

"It better not be pop. No pop after nine. You know that."

I put two ice cubes in a Kleenex and tucked them into my hand. Then I made my way back to my room, shut the door, and stuck my desk chair under the door handle, like I always do when I need top security. Then I unbuttoned my top and rubbed little ice cube circles on my nipples. Sure enough, they crinkled right up, like flowers blooming in reverse. So for a few minutes, I thought I might have cured myself. But it wasn't long before they got warm and swelled up again. Cherries on top of two scoops of vanilla ice cream. Thinking that gave me a craving so I went back out to the kitchen and scooped two balls of Heavenly Hash into a bowl and hurried back to my room before my mom noticed.

After putting the chair back under the door handle, I sat down on the floor with my ice cream and leaned back against my bed. I was scared about the future. Eighth grade had just started. How was I ever going to make it through the year with deformed nipples? How was I going to make it without anyone finding out my terrible secret? I was so worried that I almost didn't finish the ice cream.

"Why are you acting this way?" I asked my nipples, but they didn't answer.

• •

My sister Nancy noticed my nipples the other day. I just know she's going to say something to Christine. They're always bugging me, calling me a Momma's Boy and that

I'll end up like Uncle Ed, which isn't true at all because I know how to work a washing machine and the only reason I'm nice to my mom is because she's going through The Change and needs a lot of sympathy.

I could call them names back and say things like "Does Mom know you have a copy of *Playgirl* in your drawer, Nancy?" but I don't because that wouldn't be Christian and if Jesus had sisters who got on his case all the time, he'd still turn the other cheek and pray for their dirty souls. Plus, I'm afraid of my sisters. They're both older than me and once you get on their bad sides, you don't have much of a chance. Like a few weeks ago when Christine caught me in her room. I wasn't snooping. I was only looking for a pen. But she got pretty hot under the collar, calling me a "snoop" and saying "who keeps pens in their underwear drawer so don't even try that with me." The next night, I was in the bathroom, waiting for the tub to fill up. I was naked and bent over, checking the water temperature when I heard a click and then a scream. Nancy and Christine had picked the bathroom door lock with a hairpin and I turned around to see them standing in the doorway, pointing at my dink and screaming their heads off. I started screaming back at them and grabbed the only thing I could—my mom's hand mirror—to cover my dink. Then they raced down the hall and I slammed the door so hard, it cracked down the middle and my dad had to replace it.

"Not so funny now, is it?" he said as he screwed the new door into place.

"Dad, I'm not laughing, am I?"

"Are you sure your mother wasn't behind this? She's been on my back about a new bathroom door for weeks."

If my mother had her way, she'd make my father replace everything in our house. She wants to change the shag carpeting to low-pile, she wants sheers for the living room window instead of curtains, and she wants new cupboard doors for the kitchen.

"We've had these since the early seventies, Henry," she always says.

"So? They still open and close, don't they?"

If my father had *his* way, he'd want everything to stay the same until either it broke or the world blew up. He doesn't even change his washcloth. It hangs off the curtain rod like a sad flag. Every now and then, I'll get a whiff of it. My mom keeps telling him he should wash it, but he says he washes it every time he's having a bath, which is once a week.

"That's not washing it, Henry," my mom says. "You're not washing anything if you're cleaning your butt with it."

Anyways, I know that Nancy noticed my nipples, even though she didn't say anything. We were sitting in the living room. I was watching TV and eating Cheez Doodles. Nancy was eating a row of Oreos, waiting for her boyfriend. André was half an hour late and Nancy was freaking out.

"Are you sure he didn't call?" she yelled. Her teeth were brown with Oreo paste. But no one answered her because André is always late picking up Nancy.

Nancy and I were sitting there and I dropped a Cheez Doodle. So I bent down to pick it up and as I grabbed the

Cheez Doodle, I looked up and caught Nancy looking down my top. She did it really quickly, but I'm pretty sure of it. It takes a lot to pull the wool over my eyes. I was wearing one of my old sweatshirts with a loose neck so she could've seen my nipples very easily. I sat back up and pressed one of the couch pillows against my chest. Nancy coughed, looked at the living room clock, and started working on a new row of Oreos. She wasn't going to admit to seeing my nipples, so I sent her a mental telepathy message.

"I'd watch it if I were you," I said as loudly as I could in my head. "One word and I'll tell Mom how long you and André were parked in the driveway the other night."

Just then, André's car pulled into our driveway and Nancy jumped up.

"Finally," she said, grabbing her jacket from the hall chair. As I watched her and André drive away in his blue car, I got a mental telepathy message back from her.

"Everyone's going to find out your secret sooner or later."

• •

Today after school, I walked to the Shop 'N' Bag and bought some Scotch tape. The Shop 'N' Bag is in the Westown Plaza, which is a five-minute walk from my house. I think of the Westown Plaza as my second home, the one I go to when things are bothering me or a place to go on a Saturday afternoon if there's nothing on television. There's a Rite Aid, a butcher shop called "Ye Olde Butcher Shoppe," a Bi-Way, two empty stores that have had "For Lease" signs in the windows for as long as I can remember, and "Papa Bertoli," the restaurant that Daniela Bertoli's dad owns. There's also a pet store called "Kathy's Kritter Korner." Daniela calls it "Kathy's Killing Korner," because she said that Kathy shoots the kittens and puppies she doesn't sell, but I don't think that's true because Kathy wears a gold cross around her neck. And I've caught Daniela telling lies to me before, like when she told me her dad tried to strangle her mom.

"I had to hop on his fuckin' back to get him off her," she said. "You can still see the bruises on her neck."

So I grabbed my binoculars and spied on the Bertolis' house the next day and when Mrs. Bertoli came out, wearing her Orioles cap and a T-shirt, there was not a single bruise on her neck.

The Shop 'N' Bag is at the very end of the strip. It's a small variety store that sells candy and chips, as well as birthday cards, roach traps, canned vegetables, hair gel, shoelaces, clothing dye, and black velvet paintings of sombreros. The man who owns the Shop 'N' Bag is Mr. Bernard. He has no hair but he's always very nice to me. That's because I'm a preferred customer. When the new 7-Eleven opened down the street, I made my mind up to keep shopping at Mr. Bernard's store, even though the 7-Eleven was closer.

"You still have the best selection in town," I told him one afternoon. He laughed and said "Thank you" and threw a Butterfinger into my bag, which already had a Payday and a chocolate milk in it. "Compliments of the house," he said.

The next Saturday, I told Mr. Bernard I really liked

his sombrero paintings. "They're very high quality," I said. "I'm going to tell everyone on my paper route about them."

Mr. Bernard thanked me again, but didn't put anything in my bag. That kind of cheesed me off, because I spend close to five dollars there every week.

"Don't bite the hand that feeds you, Mr. Bernard," I thought as I walked out.

Today, when I put my Scotch tape on the counter, along with two Milky Way bars, I told Mr. Bernard I was wrapping presents.

"It's my best friend's birthday," I said. I had made up a whole story to cover my tracks.

"Oh, that sounds nice," Mr. Bernard said. "Do you need any wrapping paper? We have a nice selection of birthday cards over there, as well."

"No, I have all that at home."

"Is your friend having a party?"

"Yes. A big one, actually. Everyone from school is going."

"What did you get for your friend?" Mr. Bernard asked, putting the tape and the chocolate bars into a paper bag. He was asking too many questions, as far as I was concerned. I started to get suspicious.

"A bike."

"A *bike?* Well, that's quite an expensive gift, isn't it?" Mr. Bernard leaned across the counter toward me. I noticed he had dry skin on his cheeks.

"My paper route pays pretty well," I said and shrugged. I grabbed my bag and got out of there before Mr. Bernard could ask anything more.

When I got back home, I went straight to my room
with my Scotch tape. I took off my sweatshirt and made
a Scotch tape "x" across each of my nipples. I put my shirt
back on and stood in front of the fan. I thought it was
very smart of me to fake wind.

The Scotch tape isn't too bad, although it makes my
skin crinkle under it. It looks like I have many-pointed
nipples now. They're stars, which are better than cherries
any day.

••

When Mr. Mitchell assigned us our desks for the year, I
kept my fingers crossed that wherever I ended up, I was
a) as far as possible from Brian Cinder and b) as close to
Andrew Sinclair as possible. Andrew is the most fashionable boy in 8th grade and I think we could be friends
some day. But before I even think about asking him to be
friends, I'll have to lose a lot of weight, shave my legs,
change my personality, and cure my nipples.

As it turned out, I got stuck beside Michelle Appleby,
the leader of the Slut Group at Clarkedale, and Jackie
Myner, the ugliest girl in the whole school. Jackie is
obsessed with Adrian Zmed. He's a Hollywood actor who
plays a cop on a television show. She collects photographs
of Adrian and pastes them into her "Adrian Zmed" scrap-
book. She even wrote out his name in thick black marker
on the cover, but she started her letters off too big and by
the time she got to the "e" and "d" in "Zmed," she'd run
out of room. So the cover says "Adrian Zm" with the "ed"
on the inside cover.

On the first day of school, Mr. Mitchell pulled out a copy of *Christian Tales for Modern Youth* and told us he'd be reading us a story every morning.

"You may think that school is only about math and English and spelling," he said, his eyes stopping on each of our faces. "But my job is also to equip you with the spiritual tools necessary to guide you throughout your lives. Think of this," he said, rapping the cover of the book, "as God's utility belt."

Then he opened up the book and read us a story about a kid who keeps the largest piece of pie for himself and later gets a visit from the Devil.

My mom asked me what religion Mr. Mitchell is, but I don't know.

"His wife and daughters can't cut their hair," I said, "or wear pants. I know that much." I've seen them, waiting for him in the parking lot after school. They creep me out a bit because they all look like zombies.

My mom scrunched up her mouth. "Hmm," she said, "Jehovahs aren't hung up about hair, really."

My mom is afraid of Jehovah's Witnesses. When I was younger, the Jehovahs would come to our neighborhood on Saturday mornings, knocking on all the doors. When my dad was working, my mom would sit by the window and watch for them. When she spotted the Jehovahs making their way down the street, she would whisper/scream "Jehovahs!"

Then she would close the drapes, turn the TV off, and make me and my sisters go into the kitchen and hide behind the counter.

"It's not like they're going to break in if they know we're here," Christine would say.

"sssHHH!" my mom would whisper/scream.

It's good to know that Mr. Mitchell isn't a Jehovah. But my mom thinks that he belongs to a cult.

"There's a group of them that meet out on Highway 7," she said. "Under that big canopy tent. And I'd bet my bottom dollar there are snakes involved."

This morning, after we said The Lord's Prayer and mouthed the words to the Pledge of Allegiance, Mr. Mitchell pulled out his *Christian Tales* book and read us a story about a rich girl who gives a poor girl a new pair of patent leather shoes.

"Who can tell me the message of this story?" he asked at the end. He looked at the Indian kids when he asked, like he was hoping they were listening. But the only answer he got was Eric Bird horking into a Kleenex.

"Anyone?"

Mr. Mitchell looked over at Margaret Stone. Her dad is the minister of St. Paul's Church. I don't think Margaret listens to the stories, either, but she must know them all by heart. Before she could say anything, Jackie Myner put up her hand. Mr. Mitchell pretended not to see her because Jackie stutters and it takes a very long time for her to say anything. But she kept waving her arm and twisting around in her seat and making these little grunting noises, so Mr. Mitchell didn't have much of a choice.

"Yes, Jackie?"

"C-c-c-can I g-g-go to the bathroom? I th-think I'm g-g-g-going to throw up."

Mr. Mitchell rolled his eyes and said yes, she could, but to hurry up. Jackie ran out of her seat and out the door.

• •

The more I think about it, the more I realize that I have deformed nipples because of my subconscious. I know about that because my sister Christine told me about it. The subconscious is a very tricky thing, Christine said. She told me that when bad things happen to people, it's because their subconscious secretly wants the bad things to happen.

"Do you honestly think Mom fell off that porch by accident?" she asked me. A few months back, my mom got her first job selling Mary Kay cosmetics. She said it was her idea, but it was really my dad who got after her.

"If you're bored, why don't you get out of the house and find something to do, Beth?" He wasn't angry, but he did sound very tired.

"Well I don't know what to do, Henry. I've been raising three kids for the past eighteen years but I can't put that on a résumé. Can I?"

Then my mom got invited to a Mary Kay party and came home with new lipstick and a new attitude.

"This is it!" she said. "I've found what I'm looking for."

We all tried to sound happy for her, but everyone remembered my mom had said the same thing when she got hired to take the census. She only lasted a day before she quit.

"I just felt I was invading people's privacy," she told my dad.

Anyways, when my mom was leaving her very first Mary Kay house party, she slipped off the woman's porch and twisted her ankle.

"Her subconscious made her fall," Christine said. "She did it because she didn't make her quota at the party. And you know what she's like. If at first you don't succeed, might as well just give up."

I wasn't sure about that. I mean, my mom was crying because she said her ankle hurt so bad.

"How could she make herself fall?" I asked. "How could her unconscious mind make her do something stupid like that? And if she really didn't want to work, why wouldn't she just quit?"

"That's *sub*-conscious, not *un*conscious, you moron," Christine said. "And never underestimate the power of psychological persuasion. Look at me. Do you know how many girls would *kill* for the chance to work for Peoples? But I believed in myself enough to make it happen."

Then Christine went back to filing her nails.

I ignored Christine, the way I always do when she starts talking about her brain or how much she loves her job at Peoples Jewelers. But now, I'm wondering if she's right. What if my mom *didn't* fall off that porch by accident? Maybe we *do* make bad things happen to ourselves because we think we deserve them. Maybe we *need* to be punished for thinking things we shouldn't.

The more I think about it, the more I realize I'm being punished for the Bedtime Movies. I started having them a couple of years ago. No one knows about them. The Bedtime Movies play over and over in my head until I fall asleep at night. Even though they make me feel bad, I can't stop them from coming into my head. They have a mind of their own.

BEDTIME MOVIE #1

I'm Brooke Shields. I'm wearing a shiny pink dress. The hem of my dress is very high. I'm wearing spice-colored nylons over my shapely legs. I'm also wearing white high-heeled shoes.

My car has broken down in front of Mr. Hanlan's house.

I'm Brooke Shields in a shiny pink dress and why can't I start this icky car? Jeez! I hit the steering wheel. Mr. Hanlan is watching me from his living room window. He thinks I've got great hair and comes out to help me. He's wearing a red Speedo.

Unfortunately, Mr. Hanlan can't start my car.

"There's not much we can do about it," he says and slams the car hood down. "She's a goner."

"What am I going to do?" I ask him. I think I'm going to cry. "Now I'm going to be late for my photo shoot."

"Would you like to come in for a hot chocolate?" Mr. Hanlan asks me.

"I don't think your wife would like that," I say. My eyes want to look at his chest, his red Speedo. But I'm stronger than that.

"My wife's dead," Mr. Hanlan says. "She was killed last week in a car accident."

"That's terrible!" I say.

"Not really," Mr. Hanlan says. He's staring at my long, red nails. "I didn't really love her, anyway. I only married her because she forced me to. Besides, the accident was her fault. She ran a red light. Lucky there was no one else hurt."

Mr. Hanlan tells me he's lonely.

"Every day, I just sit in the house with no one to talk to. Sure could use some company, though. I guess I can't change your mind about that hot chocolate, can I?"

"If you insist," I sigh and look down at my wristwatch. "It's the least I can do. But I can't stay for very long. I have a photo shoot, remember."

Mr. Hanlan tells me not to worry, that he won't take up too much of my time. He knows that I'm Brooke Shields and that I'm very busy.

"Besides, you're not going anywhere with a broken-down car," he says and smiles. "When you're done with your hot chocolate, I'll drive you where you have to go."

I sit at Mr. Hanlan's kitchen table while he makes the hot chocolate. He asks me questions about myself, but I'm vague and check my hair for split ends.

Although I don't say it, it's warm and comforting and exciting in Mr. Hanlan's kitchen. It's also a little scary, because then I realize that Mr. Hanlan is wearing a Speedo, his wife is dead, and there's no one else home.

Mr. Hanlan turns to me and winks. "Would you like big or small marshmallows in your hot chocolate?"

Then I fall asleep.

two

My mom is turning forty-nine next week. My dad is nervous because he doesn't know how she'll be on her birthday.

"She's either going to spend the day crying in bed or laughing her head off or screaming at everyone," he said. "Does anyone feel like placing bets?"

I suggested that he make dinner reservations at the Conch Shell, one of the fancier restaurants in Bluewater.

"You think that'll do the trick?" my dad asked me.

I nodded, reminding myself to order the escargot. I've never had them, but you have to start sometime.

"Okay," my dad said. "I'll make the reservations. Tell your sisters and keep your fingers crossed."

I watched my dad walk out of the living room. Sometimes, I feel sorry for him. Not only because he has someone like me for a son, but because he has all of us for his family. Plus, he works in Chemical Valley, which can't be very exciting. Every day, he puts on a beige work shirt with matching beige pants and packs his lunch or dinner in a gray lunch box and drives into the Valley for a twelve-hour shift. Bluewater is famous for Chemical Valley. It stinks pretty bad most days and isn't very nice to look at, even though at Christmas, they put colored lights on all the smokestacks. But I heard once that if there ever was a war, Bluewater would be one of the top three places in the world to get bombed. That scared me, but it made me kind of proud, too.

My dad grew up in the prairies, pooping in an out-house and using the Sears catalogue as toilet paper. Every other summer, we all have to drive out west to visit his family. Most of them are strangers to me so I just watch TV on my grandmother's sofa while everyone goes around being fake-nice.

The truth of the matter is that sometimes, I can't help but think my dad is embarrassed of me. I mean, he isn't fat and none of his relatives are, so how come I am? I catch them looking at me and I know what they're thinking:

"That's not Henry's son."

I bet they think my mom had an affair with a fat man while my dad was at work. That makes me feel dirty.

I don't think my mom ever had an affair, but she's done some pretty stupid things in her life. Last year, she got into an accident in the Sears parking lot. She meant to back out of her spot, but put the car in drive instead. She said it wasn't really her fault because her eyesight is bad. My dad says it's not her eyes, it's her dirty glasses.

"You'd be surprised how much your eyes will improve without having to see through six layers of fingerprints," he said once.

My mom felt very bad about the accident, though, since the car she hit belonged to Mrs. Clarke, a woman from our church. So for the next few weeks, she cleaned her glasses twice a day. But after a while, she forgot to do it and now they're back to their dirty old selves again.

Overall, my mom is a pretty crappy driver. She didn't get her driver's licence until she was in her thirties and only when my dad made her. She drives around the city now, but she's afraid to take the busy streets, even though there aren't any in Bluewater. Instead, she gets out her map and plans her route before leaving.

"I could take Lansdowne and then go right onto Mayfair. No, that won't do because then I'd have to turn left onto Springfield Road."

My mom won't make left-hand turns. Ever. She won't park beside poles in underground parking garages, either. And she never drives on the highway. She says the trucks scare her.

"It's all mind over matter, Beth," my dad told her once.

"I'm sorry I didn't grow up on a farm with chickens and goats, Henry!" my mom yelled.

"What does that have to do with you driving on the highway?"

"Don't act stupid, Henry. You know exactly what I'm talking about."

My dad looked confused but he backed off pretty quickly. I bet he sometimes wishes he'd married a simple prairie girl.

• •

I think my mom is on to me and my nipples. Yesterday, when I came home for lunch, there was a big plate of sloppy joes and French fries waiting for me, so I knew something was up.

"Is there anything you want to talk about?" she asked me just before I bit into my first fry.

"What do you mean?" I squirted some ketchup on the side of my plate and kept my eyes down, thinking that Nancy must've said something to her.

"You seem a little preoccupied lately. Anything going on that I should know about?"

My cheeks were burning and underneath my sweatshirt, my taped star-nipples started to itch. My mom has ways of finding things out. That's because she's very nosy. She snoops through my room when I'm at school. I know this because I set out traps. I take a couple of hairs from Christine's brush, stretch one between two of my dresser drawers and tape it into place. That way, I know that if the hair is broken, my mom opened my drawers. And sure enough, when I get home from school, there are broken hairs about fifty percent of the time.

I get pretty hot under the collar about that because I never feel like I have any privacy. Sometimes, I think about telling my mom I know she's been snooping. But I can't tell her about my traps or else she'd just untape the hair and put it back in its place. Then I'd never know if she was snooping or not, so I just keep my mouth shut.

Every morning, if I have time, I tape more hairs to my dresser. Lately, though, none of them have been broken, so I wonder if my mom has found the trap. She can be pretty smart when she wants to be. So now, I've put notes in my dresser drawers.

In my top drawer, the note says, "What are you looking

for?" The second drawer note reads, "Do unto others as you want them to do unto you." The third drawer note says, "Don't you feel guilty for doing this?" The fourth drawer note says, "Respect people's privacy!" and the last drawer note says, "Drugs are fun!"

I don't know if my mom has found the notes or not. She'd never say it if she did, because then she'd have to admit to snooping in the first place.

"Everything's fine," I said and reached for the mustard jar.

"Are you sure, Peter?" She grabbed my hand. I hate when she does that. "Sometimes, I feel like we don't talk anymore. At least, not like we used to."

Her eyes started to get misty and she reached for the Kleenex box. I had no idea what my mom was talking about, but then, that's nothing new, especially since she started going through The Change. It's been very difficult for everyone in my family.

"You're going to have to be extra-patient with her," my dad told me a while ago. He had just gotten back from the Rite Aid with a big pink box of Kotex pads under his arm. My mom was in the bathroom, yelling at everyone to please give her some privacy, even though no one had even walked by the bathroom door.

"Your Mom is going through something right now, Peter," my dad said. "Some very bizarre female... *thing*. I don't know what it is, or when it started. I just hope it ends pretty soon."

"Get away from me!" my mom yelled from behind the bathroom door.

"There's nothing wrong," I said to my mom. "Everything is fine."

"Are you enjoying school this year?"

"Yes," I lied.

"Making lots of new friends?"

"Yes." Another lie.

"Everyone likes my Peter."

Sometimes, I think my mom is the dumbest person in Bluewater.

• •

What my mom *doesn't* know is that every day for the past three weeks, I've had to tie Brian Cinder's shoelaces. He cornered me after school one day.

"Don't you think you better tie this for me?" he asked and pointed to his shoe.

I thought that was pretty stupid, because even though Brian is a Banger, I'm sure he knows how to tie his own shoelace. But I got down on my knee and tied it for him because I was afraid of what he'd do to me if I said no.

The next day, Brian asked me to tie his shoes again.

"You did a good job last time," he said.

I stood there for a minute with a sick feeling in my stomach. Brian was smiling. I could see the chip in his front tooth.

"I think you know how to tie your shoes," I said to him.

"Yeah, but you do it better, fatso," he said, "so what are you waiting for?"

In my head, I wanted to tell Brian to screw off. But there's just no way I could ever say something like that. So I prayed that Andrew Sinclair wouldn't see me and bent down to tie his shoelace again.

Every day since, I've had to tie Brian's shoelaces. Sometimes, he undoes them himself. Other times, he'll say, "I don't like the way you did it. Tie them again."

"You know," I said to him the other day, after tying his shoelace for the third time, "they make shoes with Velcro."

Anyways, I'm keeping my fingers crossed that Brian will forget about me soon enough and move on to someone else. He's like that. One day, he'll be after me like I'm the only person in the world to bug. The next, he'll walk right by without even looking at me. But most Bangers are like that. They don't have good attention spans.

• •

I'm not the fattest person in my family. Uncle Ed is. I don't know how much he weighs, but Christine thinks he must be around 300 pounds. He slicks back his hair with Grecian Formula and wears Hawaiian shirts, even in the winter. Uncle Ed smells kind of funny some days, too. He's my mother's younger brother and lives in a small apartment above a mechanic's shop.

Uncle Ed works in Chemical Valley too, but he doesn't wear a uniform. He must work in an office. I don't know for sure because I've never asked him. I don't ask Uncle Ed much because once he starts talking, he has a hard time stopping.

"Verbal diarrhea," my mother always says, which makes my father roll his eyes and say that's the pot calling the kettle black.

My mom says that Uncle Ed should go on a diet, but whenever Nancy goes on a diet, my mom tells her it's bad for her.

"Your system goes into shock, Nancy. It's a medical fact."

Nancy is never on a diet for very long, though. The last one she was on was the Hot Dog, Potato, and Egg Diet. On Day One, she only ate six hot dogs. On Day Two, she ate six boiled potatoes. By the time Day Three rolled around, Nancy was the crabbiest person in Bluewater. I think she only managed to get two eggs into her before she caved and tore open a box of Pinwheels.

I think Nancy gets upset because she can't shop at Suzy Shier, like every other girl in Bluewater. Instead, she has to buy her clothes at Suzanne's, the fat women's clothing store in Bluewater.

"Fuller-figured?" the Suzanne's radio commercials ask. "That doesn't mean you can't have the styles you want in the sizes you need at the prices you'll love! Suzanne's Fashion Boutique. Where Fashion is a Plus!"

I think it's Suzanne's voice on the radio ads, although I've never seen her. Maybe there isn't a real Suzanne. Maybe she's like Betty Crocker or Aunt Jemima. Or maybe the real Suzanne is skinny and buys her clothes at Reitman's. If that's the case, then she better stay in hiding forever or else there'll be a lot of angry fat women coming after her.

Once a month, Nancy gets a flyer in the mail from Suzanne's, letting her know that there's a special going on or that all spring fashions have now been reduced up to 70%! When Nancy gets the flyer, she'll pick it up and stuff it into her back pocket before anyone else sees, even though everyone has.

The thing is that Suzanne's doesn't have very nice clothes. At least, not for eighteen-year-old girls. I went in there last year with my mom and Nancy to look for her 12th grade prom dress. The store was pretty small and all the fat women inside had to keep saying "Excuse me" and "Pardon me" as they passed each other between the racks. Most of the women were old, even older than my mom.

"There's nothing in here," Nancy said.

"Well, you've hardly looked, Nancy," my mom said. She was holding up a purple dress that was as big as a tablecloth. "This is nice. Why don't you try it on?"

Nancy said she didn't like it. She didn't like anything in the store.

"Everything in here is so ugly."

I started going through the racks because I knew that if I looked hard enough, I'd find the perfect dress for Nancy. A couple of the women gave me funny looks, but I didn't care.

"What about this one?" I asked, holding up a black dress with sequins. I thought it was very dramatic.

Nancy shook her head.

"What about this one?" I showed her a blue dress.

"Perfect if I was Mother of the Bride," Nancy said.

"Why are you being so difficult, Nancy?" my mom asked. "You're not even trying. Surely there's got to be something in here that you like."

"Can I help you?" A saleswoman came up to us. She was chubby and wearing too much perfume. I started gagging.

"We're here looking for my daughter's prom dress," my mom smiled.

"Oh, how exciting!" the saleswoman said. She clapped her hands together and I noticed she had silver rings on every one of her chubby fingers. "A young woman's most important night! We just got some new styles in the other day! Hold on for one minute!" Then she went to the back of the store. I was glad to see her go because I could breathe again.

"I want to leave," Nancy said.

"Don't be silly," my mom said. "You heard the lady. They just got some new styles in. Maybe something you'll like."

She was trying to sound cheerful. Nancy looked like she was going to puke.

"Please," she said. "Let's just go, okay?"

She started walking toward the door but then the saleswoman came back with an armful of dresses in plastic bags.

"Miss!" she called out in a loud voice, so that all the other women in the store turned to look. "There's one here that I'm sure you're going to love! What size are you? Sixteen? Eighteen?"

Nancy practically ran out of the store.

"I don't know what's gotten into you lately," my mom said while we were driving home. "I mean, honestly, Nancy. That was terribly embarrassing, leaving your brother and I just standing there."

"You're right," Nancy said, looking out the window, "I'm just so incredibly insensitive."

Nancy didn't end up going to her prom, even though my mom said she'd regret it. Instead, she and André went for dinner at the all-you-can-eat Chinese buffet on Confederation Road.

Nancy's boyfriend is fat, too, so they have that in common. They met through her job at Dunkin Donuts. He wears Orange Tab Levi's and drives the ugliest, loudest car I've ever seen or heard. He's not very friendly, either, and always has a wad of pink bubble gum rolling around in his mouth. I don't know what Nancy sees in him, but they got engaged last Christmas. They haven't set a wedding date yet. Nancy says it'll be soon. I'm not sure why, because lately all they seem to do is fight.

"You might want to hold off on things for a while, Nancy," my mom said once. "You know, until André manages to find a job and all that other trivial stuff."

Neither of my parents likes André very much. Nancy says the only reason they don't like him is because he's French.

"That's not true!" my mom gasped. "How can you say something like that when I've been friends with Mrs. LaFlamme next door for years?"

"You watch *Another World* together and drink Pepsi," Nancy said. "If she didn't have air-conditioning, you wouldn't give her the time of day."

"I don't know where you come up with this nonsense!"

I think the real reason my parents don't like André is because he's poor. He lives on the south end of town, right outside Chemical Valley. I was over at his house once and the living room had wood paneling on the walls. That's a sure sign of poverty. Plus, the house smelled like cigarette smoke and mildew and I'm almost positive I saw mouse poop on the floor next to the sofa.

Nancy always tells my parents that André has things lined up. "It's just a matter of time. He's not just going to rush into anything. We're talking about his *life* here."

"What does André want to do?" my dad asked once. "Does he have an interest in anything?"

"He can draw amazing unicorns," Nancy said.

"Well, in that case," my mom said, "let the wedding plans begin."

• •

Christine is refusing to go to the Conch Shell for my mom's birthday.

"Can anyone think of me for once?" she asked the living room wall. "If it's not too much to ask, that is."

"Where else do you want to go?" my dad asked.

"I don't know," Christine said, like she was insulted he asked the question. "How about a place where they don't slaughter living creatures so that pathetic humans can stuff their faces?"

Christine is a vegetarian. She used to eat meat all the time. In fact, she was the fattest of all three of us. But that was before the Junior Band walk-athon two years ago. The school was trying to raise money for new instruments. Christine played the oboe. On the day of the walk, Christine called home. She was crying and said her thighs were rubbing together and that a boy walking behind her kept saying he smelled something burning. So my mom had to go and pick her up. When they got home, my mom made Christine put a bag of frozen peas between her legs.

"Don't you worry about those corduroys," she said. "I can patch those holes good as new."

That night, Christine locked herself in the bedroom with her oboe. She played "Send in the Clowns" over and over until my mom said she either had to stop it or she would call the fire department to break down the door.

When Christine finally did come out, she said, "I'm a vegetarian."

"That was the beginning of the end," my mom always says.

"Fish isn't meat, Christine," my dad sighed.

"It's meat, Dad."

"Why do you always have to be such a pain?" That came from Nancy, who was sitting on the sofa. She stuck her tongue right into the cream hole of her Ding Dong.

"I'm sorry if having convictions makes me a 'pain,'" Christine said. "But someone's got to have some in this family."

Christine thinks she's better than Nancy and me just because she's thin and has opinions and works at Peoples Jewelers. When she got called for the job interview, you'd have thought she won the lottery or something.

"This just proves it!" she said as she put the receiver down.

"Proves what?" my mom asked.

"That I'm adopted," Christine said. She turned to my dad. "I'll need a suit for the interview."

"You're not adopted, Christine," my dad said. "We've been over this a million times. And you're not getting any more new clothes, either. You've got a whole closetful that are just fine."

"No they're not!" Christine cried. "Everything I own is too casual. I don't have any business attire at all."

"Business attire?" my mom shrieked. "You're applying for a part-time job at the mall!"

"In case I didn't make this clear, Mother, I'm interviewing with Peoples Jewelers. They sell diamonds."

My parents refused to buy Christine a new suit. Instead, she borrowed a pink jacket and white skirt from Mrs. LaFlamme. The day of her interview, she had so much lip gloss on, her mouth kept sliding all over the place.

"Let me get the camera," my mom said as she ran off down the hall.

"I don't have time," Christine said, grabbing her purse. "My interview is in an hour."

"It only takes ten minutes to get to the mall," my mom called back.

"I need to get there early so I can go over my notes."

"Oh my god," Nancy said. She had just gotten home from her shift at Dunkin' Donuts and was tearing open a bag of day-olds. "Don't tell me you're serious."

"You tell me the difference between a ruby and a garnet, Nancy. Then we'll talk."

Christine's been working at Peoples for six months now. She buys all of her own business attire, even though my parents tell her she should save her money. And none of us can visit her while she's working.

"No family members," she said with a smile. "It's a Peoples policy."

• •

Christine got outvoted on the Conch Shell, so the day of my mom's birthday, we all piled into the Granada, except for Nancy and André, who were meeting us there.

"Well isn't this a nice surprise," my mom said when we told her. It sounded like she already knew. "Whose idea was this?"

"Peter mentioned it," my dad said.

"Of course," my mom turned to smile at me in the back seat, "always so thoughtful."

Christine gave me a jab in the ribs. She was still pretty upset about going and said the only thing she'd eat was a dinner roll, swear to god.

We stopped to pick up Uncle Ed. My dad had to honk three times before Uncle Ed came to the door and waved to us. Then he went back inside.

"Honestly!" my mother said. She leaned over and gave the car horn another honk. "No one to think about except for himself. It's my birthday dinner, after all."

Uncle Ed is always late for everything. He says it's not his fault and that everyone else is just early. My mother honked again and Uncle Ed came out wearing a purple Hawaiian shirt. Everyone watched as he waddled over to the car.

"Another fine purchase straight out of the 'Look at Me' catalogue," Christine said.

"What's in the news?" Uncle Ed said when he opened up the back door. He was wearing too much Hai Karate aftershave. "Better shimmy over, Peter, and give me some room."

I heard Christine say "Oh god" under her breath as

I slid over and squished against her. Uncle Ed backed himself in through the door. By the time he closed it, Christine's hand was pressed up against the window and she said she was having trouble breathing.

"I think I cracked a rib."

"Hold on," my mom said. "We'll be there in a few minutes."

Christine shot me a dirty look. She *was* turning a little blue, but what could I do about it? It was Uncle Ed's fault, not mine. He read every sign we passed out loud.

"Jimmy's Char Grill… Gene's Furniture Emporium… Road Slippery When Wet."

Nancy and André were supposed to meet us at the restaurant, but when we got inside, Nancy was sitting by herself in a peach dress, gnawing on a breadstick.

"Where's loverboy?" Christine asked. Nancy made a face. She looked like she'd been crying so maybe she and André got into a fight.

"Did something happen?" my mom asked. Then she looked around. "This is so fancy!"

Halfway through dinner, I looked up and saw a woman at another table staring at us. Then she leaned over to her husband to say something and the two of them laughed. I couldn't figure out what was so funny until I looked around the table and saw what she saw. Except for Christine and my dad, we were a table of fat people. I took a sip of the vanilla shake I'd ordered with my fish and chips. My face felt hot and I just wanted to go.

"Mom made us all fat." That's what Christine told me once after she'd lost all her weight. "Think about it. How many moms do you know start their children's day off with Tang and Cocoa Puffs? How sick is that?"

I thought Christine was wrong. My mom always buys us chips and makes cookies and there's always dessert after supper. But she doesn't force us to eat anything. I mean, I could always ask for a grapefruit for breakfast.

But I wondered if Christine was right. It's an awful thing to say, because I don't think my mom wants us to be fat. But she never told us to stop eating, either.

"This has been a wonderful dinner," my mom said as our waitress took our plates away. "I can't tell you how much I appreciate this." Then she got up and went to the bathroom.

My dad looked pretty relieved. Nancy was flipping a pack of Sugar Twin between her fingers. Christine looked bored. Uncle Ed was picking at his nails with a fork and talking to no one in particular. I was just happy to know we'd be out of there soon.

"Anyone for dessert?" my dad asked. "Nancy?"

"Why are you asking me?" Nancy said.

My dad shrugged. "Just asking," he said.

"Wouldn't mind some rice pudding, if they have some," Uncle Ed said, just as my mother was coming back to the table.

"Oh, Ed! How can you possibly have room for…"

Then my mom disappeared and there was this "thud" sound. Everyone turned to look. The waitresses, the other tables, the couple who'd been laughing at us before. The whole restaurant got very quiet. My mom had missed the chair and was sitting on the floor with this awful expression on her face, like when Natalie on *Facts of Life* found out her dad was having an affair on her mom. We all just sat there.

I looked at my mom, sitting there on the floor. And I said to myself, "You should get up and help her," but I didn't. I just sat there, thinking about how I'd had to tie Brian Cinder's shoelaces three times that day. Then, just as my dad was getting up from his chair, one of the busboys came over and helped my mom stand up.

"You been nipping into the sauce again?" Uncle Ed chuckled.

My mom sat down in her chair and held up the dessert menu in front of her face.

"Are you all right?" my dad asked.

"Fine," she said, but when her cherry cheesecake arrived, the tears had started. She didn't say a word for the rest of the night and by the time my dad paid the bill, my mom looked like a pudgy raccoon. She didn't even open her presents until the next morning.

I hope she doesn't cry on her fiftieth birthday.

three

Six days a week, I deliver the *Bluewater Observer*. It doesn't come out on Sundays, so that's my day off. You have to be ten years old before you can work for the *Observer*. It's a pretty important job and I have to get the paper to my customers on time. If I don't, they get all bent out of shape. It's like the end of the world for them or something.

I'll be celebrating my third anniversary of working for the *Observer* this November. It seems like only yesterday that I noticed the Help Wanted ad in the classified section.

"Are you a responsible young adult?" the ad read. "Do you live in or around one of the following areas? Are you looking to make your own money and have fun all at the same time? If the answer to both these questions is yes, the *Bluewater Observer* is looking for YOU!"

I felt like writing to the *Observer* to point out that they had asked three questions, not two. But when I saw that one of the neighborhoods on the list was mine, I called them up right away. The very next week, I had my own canvas *Observer* bag and thirty-two people who relied on me to bring them the world every night.

The person I replaced was John Geddes. He lives on Elm Street. I think John is a bit retarded. He wears thick glasses and slippers instead of shoes and buttons his shirts up to the top, even in the summer. He's older, too. Not old like my dad, but too old to be a paperboy.

"He's fuckin' thirty-five," Daniela told me once. John Geddes lives behind her, so she spies on him all the time.

"How do you know that?" I asked her.

"Because his mom told me. He was having a birthday party in the backyard. Just him and his mom and that fuckin' little poodle they got. They were wearing these stupid birthday hats and playing pin the tail on the fuckin' donkey."

"Are you sure that's how old he is?" I asked. "What kind of thirty-five-year-old plays birthday games with his mom?"

"A retarded thirty-five-year-old," Daniela said. "I'm telling you the truth. I heard it from his own fuckin' mom's mouth. You know what, though? I heard Mr. and Mrs. Geddes were brother and sister. That's why John wears slippers instead of shoes."

I asked my mom if that was true, but she said Daniela was pulling my leg.

"That's terrible!" she said. "She shouldn't go around telling lies like that."

Then my mom said that the real reason John was "off" was because Mrs. Geddes went on the Scrambler at a county fair while she was pregnant.

"You shouldn't do those things when you're pregnant," my mom said. "All that jerking around. It's no wonder he didn't turn out right."

Anyways, one day John was caught rolling around in

the field at Clarkedale with Linda Eckerman. Linda is retarded, too, and lives at the end of Birch Street with her mom and two brothers.

"He was sucking on Linda's tits like there was no tomorrow," Daniela said, even though she wasn't there. But she did see the police car pull up in front of the Geddes' house.

I guess someone called the *Observer* to report what John had done. Maybe it was Mrs. Eckerman. She was probably scared that John and Linda were going to do It and then Linda would have a retarded baby.

So John got fired and that's how I got the job as an *Observer* paperboy.

There are lots of kids out there dying to make the cash I do. After my collecting is done, I make close to twenty dollars a week, sometimes more, depending on the tips. Most kids my age just get an allowance, and you can't work at a regular job until you're fifteen. Then you make minimum wage at McDonald's.

I know Daniela wants my job, but she doesn't come out and say it. That's because she's too proud, but I'm not really sure what Daniela has to be proud about.

Daniela and I are kind of friends, but it's weird to think that, because we have nothing in common. She's not very stylish and wears tank tops that show off the stubble in her armpits. Plus, Daniela is Catholic and goes to St. Michael's. She says that the two big differences between public school and Catholic school are that you have to take religion classes and that you have nuns for teachers.

"Do they look like the nuns on TV?" I asked her.

"No," Daniela said. "The nuns on TV are young and pretty. At St. Mike's, they're all bitches and have B.O."

Daniela told me the nuns beat students if they talk in class. She said that one time, her cousin Teresa got locked in a broom closet just because she sneezed during religion class.

"They forgot about her being in there and the janitor found her the next morning. She'd been in that closet for the whole fuckin' night. To this day, if you show Teresa a broom, she goes ballistic. That's how fucked up she is."

Daniela is chunky and her nose is always plugged up, so when she talks, it sounds like she has a cold. She has curly black hair that hangs down to the middle of her back, too. One day, she told me that her hair was her best feature, but I said she had split ends.

"You should give yourself a hot oil treatment," I said.

The next day, Daniela chased me down the street with a baseball bat. She had poured hot olive oil on her head and burned her scalp.

Daniela's parents don't speak English very well, even though they moved to America before Daniela was born. They subscribe to the *Observer*, but I don't get that, because if you can't speak English, you can't read it. Maybe they're just trying to fit into the neighborhood. There aren't many other ethnic people on my paper route besides Mrs. Guutweister. She's a German lady who makes apple head dolls. She's married, but I've never seen her husband. I know he's alive, though, because every time I go collecting, I can hear him coughing. Maybe he's on his death bed and Mrs. Guutweister has to make apple head dolls to help pay for doctor bills. Either that, or Mr. Guutweister is very mean and keeps Mrs. Guutweister a prisoner in her own home. Sometimes, when I take her money, I check to see if anything is written on her dollar bill, like "Call the police!" or "Help me, Peter!" But so far, there's been nothing.

Mr. Bertoli is short and fat and has a blind eye that creeps me out. I never know who or what he's looking at. He owns the Papa Bertoli restaurant in the Westown Plaza. I have to be very quick when I walk by the window on my way to the Shop 'N' Bag or else Mr. Bertoli will yell at me to come inside. At least, that's what I think he's yelling. Like I said, Mr. Bertoli doesn't speak English too well. But I've figured out a system. If I think he's *asking* me something, I'll answer "Yes" because that's safer than "No." If I think he's *telling* me something, I'll nod my head and say "Hmm…" and hope for the best.

Mrs. Bertoli is tall and thin and missing a few teeth. She always wears a Orioles cap on her head, even in the summer. For the longest time, I thought she was bald. But when I asked Daniela, she got mad at me and said her mom wears the Orioles cap because she gets bad headaches and what was I, fuckin' stupid or something?

Gianni, Daniela's older brother, is a bit of a rebel. He's seventeen and works at Burger King. He hardly ever shaves and drives a powder blue Camaro that Daniela says is a piece of shit. I don't think I've ever said one word to Gianni. He scares me because he's kind of a Banger.

I know that Daniela wants my job because she watches for the *Observer* van to drop off my bundle of papers at the corner. If I'm late picking them up, she carries them to my house.

"You better get these fuckin' delivered," she'll say when I open the door. "People are waiting."

Daniela says the f-word more than anyone else I know. I think someone played a trick on her once and told her that the f-word was part of normal English language. She sticks it between any two words she feels like.

"Here's Peter's fuckin' papers," she said to my mom one day last winter.

I never saw my mom's face turn green before.

I know Daniela will never get my job, because you can't go around saying things like "Good f'n afternoon, Mr. Philips" or "You f'n owe me a dollar f'n eighty-five this week, Mrs. White" without them calling to complain about you. It's not very professional. Besides, I think Daniela is a little stupid.

For starters, she failed 6th grade. She said it was because her nun-teacher was jealous of her naturally curly hair, but I don't think that's true. And besides, Daniela is stupid in other ways because she still wets the bed.

I know this because I've been over to her house a couple of times. I think the Bertolis are poor, because they don't have carpeting. Their furniture is pretty old, too, and there's not much of it. The only expensive thing they have is a life-size statue of the Virgin Mary that stands in a corner of the living room. Daniela says it's a "loaner" from St. Mike's.

"Everyone gets to borrow her for sixty days," she told me. "We've got fifteen days left, thank god. From here, we pack her up and send it to my Aunt Francesca's apartment."

When I asked Daniela why her family has a life-size Virgin Mary statue in the first place, she said, "It's a Catholic thing. You wouldn't understand. I'll tell you one thing, though. I'll be happy as a fuckin' clam when she's gone. Every time I get up in the middle of the night to take a whiz, she scares the crap out of me."

In their kitchen, the Bertolis have a small table in the corner and not much else. They do most of their cooking in the basement. They're the only people on my paper route that have a stove, a sink, and a refrigerator in the basement.

"Why do you have two kitchens?" I asked Daniela once.

"Because we're Italian, that's why," Daniela said, which didn't explain anything.

Anyways, I know that Daniela wets the bed because her room smells like Lysol. It's so strong that it's hard to breathe and I can taste the Lysol in my mouth. But I know why the smell is so heavy, because underneath the Lysol, I can smell pee. A normal person might not be able to detect it, but I'm not normal. I have super-strong smelling powers, or as I call them, the SSP. People are amazed by what I can smell. Like one night last summer, Christine and I were outside on the back porch and I could smell corndogs. So I said to her, "Somewhere in this city, right now, a wiener is being battered and deep-fried." Christine said, "How do you know that?" I put the tip of my finger on my nose and whispered, "The SSP."

Christine said that I was a retard and went back into the house. But later that night, my parents and I drove by the Sears parking lot and sure enough, there was a mini-carnival set up with a Tilt-a-Whirl and Skee-Ball. And as plain as the nose on my face, there was a booth selling corndogs. I made my dad pull over and I ran out to buy one. It was the best-tasting corndog I ever ate.

• •

Another reason why Daniela wants my job is because she doesn't get paid for any of her jobs. She waitresses at her dad's restaurant during the week, and on Saturday nights she works at the Basilico Club, the Italian club in Bluewater. Most people have their wedding receptions at the Basilico Club whether they're Italian or not. That's because the only other decent place to have a reception in Bluewater is the Golf Club, and three years ago, someone almost got a concussion when a golf ball crashed through the window.

Daniela works as a banquet server. Her boss doesn't give her any money, but she gets a free meal at the end of the night.

"Sometimes chicken, sometimes roast beef," she told me. "Depends on how much money the bride's parents cough up."

Daniela says that the banquet servers are very competitive.

"It's fuckin' hell," she said. "Every bitch wants to serve the head table."

Serving the bridal party is the highest honour and only girls who have worked at the Basilico Club for a long time get to do it. It's like getting a badge of bravery in the Italian military. I guess that's because if you spill any food on the bride's dress, you could get sued.

Daniela says that her manager doesn't let her serve the head table, even though she's worked at the Basilico Club for three years.

"I haven't spilled one drop of minestrone since I started working there. But the asshole says I make him nervous so he gives it to Maria Punta and she's only worked there six months. You know why Maria gets to serve the head table? Her tits are so big, she could rest a fuckin' platter on them."

I don't understand why Daniela would work and not get paid, but then, there are lots of things I don't understand about Daniela and her family. For example, why do they leave their Christmas lights up all year? And why doesn't Mrs. Bertoli take an aspirin to cure her head-aches?

Anyways, the other day while I was delivering papers, I saw Daniela in her garage. She was bent over, laying out rows of tomatoes on paper to ripen. The Bertolis make their own sauce every year.

"Why do they go through all that trouble when there's Ragú?" my mother always asks.

Daniela didn't see me coming up the driveway and when I called her name, she practically jumped ten feet in the air.

"Don't fuckin' do that!" she yelled, dropping a tomato. "What are you, a jerk or something?"

"I wasn't trying to scare you," I said. "What's your problem?"

"Nothing, I just got a lot on my mind, okay?" She picked up the tomato, spit on it, then wiped it off on her apron. "Fuckin' bruised."

She turned to look at me and sighed.

"Listen, I didn't mean to snap at you or anything, okay?" She sat down on an empty milk crate. "I've just been under a lot of pressure lately. I'm talking large fuckin' pressure. The kind that builds and builds until one day, you go psycho and start killing everyone with a bread knife."

Daniela can be very dramatic when she wants to be and she's always talking about murdering someone. A few weeks before, she was planning to kill her mom because Mrs. Bertoli had let Gianni go out instead of cleaning the garage. She made Daniela do it.

"She lets that lazy son of a bitch get away with everything," Daniela had said. "She thinks he shits gold nuggets. One of these days, I'm going to sneak up on the fuckin' old toad and strangle the life right out of her."

"Why are you under pressure?" I asked.

"I went and signed up for the Miss Basilico contest," Daniela sighed. "I'm gonna be in a fuckin' beauty pageant."

Every September, the Basilico Club puts on the St. Marco Festival. I asked Daniela once what St. Marco did to get a festival named after him and she told me that he drove the mange-cakes out of Italy. The St. Marco Festival is like the carnival in the Sears parking lot, only it's for Italian people. I guess white people could go, but everyone's afraid of the Bluewater Mafia.

Every year, a young Italian virgin is crowned "Miss Basilico" on the last night of the St. Marco Festival. There are many duties she has to fulfill as a beauty queen. For example, she has to be nice to people all the time and pose for pictures. She also has to dress as an elf at Christmas and hand out candy canes to children at the mall. Most important, Miss Basilico has to set an example for Italian girls everywhere and show them that no matter what your dreams are, they can come true if you really believe in yourself.

"I'm looking forward to winning the food basket," Daniela said, picking a scab off her knee. "Nutella for days."

She sounded pretty impressed, but I wasn't. Beauty pageant winners are supposed to win money, not groceries. Besides, I was getting a bad feeling about this beauty contest. What was going through Daniela's head? She wouldn't look good in a bathing suit and what kind of beauty queen has armpit stubble? The bottom line was that Daniela wasn't pretty enough to enter the Miss Basilico contest. I know it wasn't a very nice thing to think, but it was the truth. And I didn't want Daniela to find out the hard way.

"Are you sure about this?" I asked her. I could almost hear the audience and judges laughing when she stepped across the stage. "Beauty pageants are kind of sexist, you know."

"Who the fuck cares? This is my big chance! I'm gonna get that crown on my head if it's the last fuckin' thing I do. Then they're all gonna be sorry when they see my picture on the front cover of the paper."

Each year, Miss Basilico gets her picture in the *Observer*, which I guess is a pretty big deal for someone who failed 6th grade. I had my picture in the *Observer* when I was nine. My parents and I were at a home show at the Bluewater arena when some guy came up to me and asked me if I'd lie down on this waterbed. I thought he was a pervert at first. But then I noticed his camera and the *Observer* badge on his shirt. He must've thought I had star quality. Anyways, the picture came out a few days later and my fly was down. I was so embarrassed. Everyone at school teased me. My mom bought a bunch of papers and sent them to all my relatives, even though I asked her not to.

I knew that I wouldn't be able to change Daniela's mind, at least not without telling her the truth, and even though Daniela bugs me sometimes, I just couldn't do it. So instead, I smiled my best fake smile and said, "If you need any help deciding what to wear, feel free to ask me."

• •

There are lots of rules a young Italian girl must follow if she wants to enter the Miss Basilico contest. For starters, she must be pure Italian, which means that neither of her parents can be white, because then she's a half-breed.

She must be between fourteen and eighteen. She must also say a speech in Italian. But the most important thing of all is that the young Italian girl must have a talent.

"That's where it all comes down," Daniela said. "That's when the winner gets separated from the losers."

We were sitting in Daniela's garage. The pageant was only a week away and Daniela said she was "sweating buckets," that's how nervous she was. I asked her what she planned to do for the talent competition.

"Are you going to serve tables at the pageant?"

I wasn't trying to be mean, but Daniela got pretty angry.

"What, you think that's the only thing I'm good at doing?"

"Well, what are you good at? Can you sing?"

Daniela thought for a bit. "No," she said, shaking her split ends. "I sang 'Ti Amo' once at my cousin Angela's wedding, but everyone booed me. Gimme a break. I was only eight."

"Can you dance?"

"How the fuck should I know?" Daniela said. "You think anyone ever asks me?"

Daniela said that she *could* play the accordion, though. "Is that a talent?"

"Are you any good at it?" I asked.

"It's an accordion," she said. "They all sound the same."

Daniela said the two songs she knew off by heart were "Ti Amo" and "I Will Survive."

"Well, maybe you should stay away from 'Ti Amo,'" I said. "Do the other one. It's a very powerful song."

"You think so?" Daniela asked me.

"Yes. It's about a woman who falls in love with an alien. One day, he comes back from outer space and she tells him to leave his key on the table, get back on the spaceship, and never come back. It's very dramatic. People will relate to the message."

Daniela spat on a tomato and rubbed it on her pant leg. "Dramatic," she said. "That's a good thing, right?"

• •

Every day when I delivered the papers, I'd see Daniela in her garage, standing in the middle of the tomatoes, practising on her accordion. When she hit a wrong note, she would yell "FUCK!" and smack the accordion. She was driving my mom nuts.

"When is that pageant again, Peter?" She was pacing in front of the living room window with her hands on her hips.

"Saturday night," I said.

On Wednesday night, Mr. and Mrs. Bertoli took Daniela to pick up her dress at La Mirage, Bluewater's fanciest dress store. It's where all the girls get their prom dresses. Daniela came home with a red poofy dress and a big white tent with hula hoops. She told me it was a "crinoline."

"My parents paid two hundred bucks," she said the next day when she unzipped the bag to show me. "Two hundred bucks. That's real fuckin' taffeta, too." Then she whistled through her teeth.

"How are you going to do your hair?" I asked her. I was eyeing her split ends.

"Lots of baby's breath," Daniela said. "I saw it in a magazine. My aunt works in the hair salon over on Huron Street. I'm going to see her and she'll fuckin' fix me up and then I'm going to the Merle Norman to get my face painted on."

I watched Daniela as she zipped up her dress bag and took it back into the house. I just knew I'd have to stop her from going into that pageant and embarrassing herself, but I couldn't figure out how to do it without hurting her feelings. Maybe I could write the Basilico Club a sinister note with letters cut out from magazines.

"Danger!" it would read. "Death to all beauty queens! Cancel the pageant or else!"

Or what if I could convince the judges that Mr. and Mrs. Bertoli weren't really Daniela's parents, that Daniela was born white and had been thrown into a dumpster behind Mr. Bertoli's restaurant by her white low-class mom and the Bertolis had found her and raised her as the Italian daughter they never had? Then Daniela wouldn't be allowed to compete because she wouldn't be a true Italian. She'd be an impostor.

Just then, Mr. and Mrs. Bertoli pulled into the driveway.

"Uh-oh," Mr. Bertoli said to me as he got out of the car. "Ow are you tomorrow, boss?"

At least, that's what I think he said.

"Isa time for collection?" Mrs. Bertoli asked. One look at the Orioles cap on her head told me that no one was going to believe that the Bertolis were anything *but* Daniela's real parents.

"No, not tonight," I said. "I just came by because Daniela wanted to show me her dress."

"It'sa nice, okay?" Mrs. Bertoli said.

"Yes, it's a very nice dress."

"You know, I tell Daniela, I say 'Why you wanna be

Miss Basilico? It'sa too much work. You gotta smile alla
time. You gotta wave alla time.' But Daniela she say, 'Dis
isa someting I gotta do for me. You understand?'"

Mrs. Bertoli sighed.

"I say to Daniela, 'No I'ma never understand.'"

"Uh-oh," Mr. Bertoli said. "Ow are you tomorrow,
boss?"

I smiled and said "Yes."

• •

The rest of the week, I think I was more nervous about
the Miss Basilico pageant than Daniela. I just couldn't figure out why Daniela was entering the contest in the first
place. I kept thinking back to what Mrs. Bertoli had said,
about Daniela saying how she had to do it for her. What
did she mean by that and did she really think she'd win?
Part of me felt guilty, like I was watching her walk into a
room full of tigers. Another part of me felt angry at her
for wanting to walk in the room in the first place. Daniela
couldn't be *that* stupid, could she?

When Saturday night came, I sat on my front porch
to watch Daniela leave for the pageant. She had some
problems getting through the front door in her red dress
and accordion, so Gianni had to push her from behind
while Mrs. Bertoli pulled on her arm.

"Careful!" Daniela yelled. "You're gonna fuckin' rip it!"

Her hair was piled up and looked like a big black bee-
hive. She had clumps of white stuff stuck in it, which I
guess was the baby's breath, but looked more like cob-
webs to me. Mr. Bertoli had on a tie and a green shirt that

was too tight. Mrs. Bertoli was wearing a dress that matched her hat.

Gianni was wearing his Burger King uniform.

"Good luck," he said and got into his Camaro. "You fuckin' cow!"

Daniela started yelling back at him, but I couldn't hear what she was saying because Gianni backed his car out of the driveway, squealed his tires, and roared off down the street.

Then Mr. Bertoli made Daniela stand on the front lawn while he took pictures of her. "Hurry up," she said. "My back is fuckin' killing me. This accordion weighs a ton."

Just before Daniela's parents squeezed her into the car, she looked across the street and saw me sitting on the porch.

"What do you think?" she yelled and twirled around. "Pretty fuckin' hot, eh?"

I nodded and gave her the thumbs up.

"I lost two fake fingernails pulling up my pantyhose and I got so much make-up on, I think I'm going to fuckin' tip over."

I just hoped Daniela wouldn't use the f-word in her speech.

Once Daniela's parents had her stuffed into the back seat, the Bertolis took off for the Basilico Club. A black cloud of smoke followed them all the way down our street.

As I watched their car disappear, I started to wonder. What if Daniela actually won? What if she didn't swear in her speech? What if she hit all the right notes on her accordion? What if the judges thought she'd make the perfect Christmas elf? What if she really *did* set an example for Italian girls everywhere by showing them that dreams *can* come true if you believe in yourself?

I went inside the house, grabbed a box of Wheat Thins and a bottle of pop, went to my room, and locked it with the chair.

"Bravo!" the people called. I turned my desk lamp so that it was staring me right in the eye. I squinted and smiled.

"Bravo!"

Lifting my hand to my side, I cupped it and slowly twisted my wrist, waving to them all. I brought my other arm against my chest, holding my bouquet of red roses. I mouthed the words, "Thank you."

"Do you want any popcorn?"

It was my mom at the door. I quickly turned the desk lamp down.

"I thought about making some, if you want it. What are you doing in there, anyway?"

"Homework," I said. "And no, I don't want any popcorn."

I wouldn't be surprised if my mom put hidden cameras in my room.

• •

I didn't see Daniela at all the next day, but when I picked up my papers on Monday after school, I looked through a copy before delivering them. On the first page of the "Local News" section, there was a photo of the new Miss Basilico 1984. It wasn't Daniela.

When I went up to the Bertolis' house to drop off the

paper, Daniela was sitting in the garage, cleaning off her tomatoes with a rag. She was sitting on a small stool, wearing a pair of ripped jogging pants and a white T-shirt. She still had white bits in her hair. I thought about pretending not to see her, because I didn't know what to say. What if she started to cry? Or what if she was angry at me for not stopping her? I headed up the driveway and kept my eyes on the paper in my hand, like I was really interested in one of the stories.

"What the fuck?" Daniela said. She wasn't talking to me but said it loud enough for me to hear. "All these fuckin' tomatoes have bugs in them."

"Oh, hi, Daniela," I said, walking over to her. "You scared the crap out of me. I didn't see you sitting there. What's new?"

"Not much," Daniela said. She squished a small black bug between her fingers.

"How did the pageant go?" I asked, trying to sound as casual as possible.

"Fuckin' stupid," Daniela said and spit on a tomato. "The whole thing was fixed. Gina Marzapona won and only because she wore a dress that showed off her tits. Even *my* parents were cheering for her. What kind of fuckin' loyalty is that? She sucked in the talent part, too. I mean, I only missed two notes on my song. Her, she put on a pair of rubber boots and sang 'Singin' in the Rain.' It was like listening to a cow trying to yodel. I think I went deaf in one ear. Who cares, anyway? It's just a stupid con- test. There's no way you'd catch me dressing up as a fuckin' elf at Christmas. I got too much self-respect for that."

Even though she was acting tough, I knew Daniela
was upset. She had practiced so hard and her parents had
spent two hundred dollars on a dress and she believed in
herself and it didn't get her anywhere. She was still in her
garage, cleaning off tomatoes.

"Maybe you can enter again next year," I said.

"Hey, you only get this once," Daniela said, pointing
at herself. "If they can't realize what a good Miss Basilico
I would've made, fuck them. Just because I have more
class than to show my tits to the world."

I watched Daniela wipe off another tomato and had
an idea. I ripped the page with Gina Marzapona's picture
from the newspaper and poked it through a nail on the
far wall of the garage.

"What are you doing?" Daniela asked.

"You know what you need to do, Daniela," I said and
pointed to the tomato she had in her hand. She looked
down at it, back at me, and turned to the picture of Gina.
Then I saw her eyes light up.

"You're fuckin' evil," she said and brought her arm back.
"But I like that. Take *that*, bitch!" she yelled at Gina just as
the tomato left her hand and smashed like a bomb into the
wall. She missed the picture, so she took more time with
the next tomato. It hit Gina right on her smiling face.

"Fuckin' great," Daniela said and bent down to grab
another tomato. She whipped it at the wall, but it hit too
low and splattered on the lawnmower.

"Maybe you better stop," I said. "You might break
something and then your mom would have a fit. Besides,
you already hit her."

"Yeah, okay," Daniela said and wiped her forehead. She was breathing heavy. "That felt pretty fuckin' good, though."

She sat back down on her stool. I had one more idea.

"I'm going away out west next summer," I told her, "and I might need someone to cover my paper route for a couple of weeks. Do you think you'd want to do it?"

Daniela squinted. "How much cash you pull in?"

"Usually about twenty dollars a week," I said. "Sometimes, I make more with tips, but you have to be really nice to people."

"I could do that," Daniela said. "I'm pretty fuckin' nice when I want to be."

I bit my bottom lip and tried to smile. I told Daniela we'd talk about it later.

"Forgive me, Mr. Hanlan," I whispered and went on to deliver the rest of my papers.

BEDTIME MOVIE #2

I'm a contestant in a beauty pageant. My hair is blonde and curly and hangs down to the middle of my back. My name is Vanessa.

I know that I'm going to win the pageant. That's what everyone tells me.

"You're the prettiest," Mr. Hanlan tells me. He's one of the judges. "It's a no-brainer."

I laugh and toss my hair back and tell Mr. Hanlan that he shouldn't pick the winner before the competition has even started.

"It's not fair to the other girls," I say. Then I look over at the other contestants and see Daniela standing off to the side. She's got her accordion strapped to her chest. She pretends like she's practising her song, but really, she's watching me out of the corner of her eye. Daniela is wearing her red La Mirage dress. She looks like a giant tomato.

I tell Mr. Hanlan to get back to the judge's table before someone notices.

"It's illegal for us to be talking like this," I say.

"Can I visit you in your dressing room after the show?" Mr. Hanlan asks me.

"We'll see," I say. "I don't have time to discuss this now. I have to practise my song."

I have the most beautiful voice and for the talent competition, I've chosen "Ave Maria."

"It's written by one of my favorite Italian composers," I tell the audience before the lights go down and the orchestra starts up. I can hear the people gasp as I begin to sing. My voice fills the auditorium. No one has ever heard anything more beautiful. I can't see the audience but I know that most of them are crying by the time the song ends. That's how my voice touches people. I get a standing ovation.

When it comes time to pick the winner, all of the contestants are standing together and holding hands. We're pretending to be best friends.

"I hope you win," I whisper to Daniela. She's beside me and her hand is hot and clammy.

"Fat chance," Daniela says.

When the announcer calls out "Vanessa!" I put my

hand against my large breasts and pretend to look surprised. I even start to fake-cry.

Mr. Hanlan comes onstage and puts a tiara and sash on me. Then he hands me a big bouquet of long-stemmed roses.

"Tonight you're mine," he says, which makes me nervous. He's very determined.

I walk down the runway, cradling the roses in my arm and waving. Everyone is on their feet, cheering. A reporter from the *Observer* takes my picture.

"You're front page tomorrow!" he yells.

When I turn around and walk back to the stage, I see Daniela standing there with her accordion. I feel very bad for her, because even though she's acting tough, I know the real Daniela better than that.

"I know what I need to do," I whisper to myself and take the microphone from the announcer.

"I'm very touched by your kindness," I tell everyone. "Your love means the world to me. But unfortunately, I cannot accept this crown."

I can hear people in the audience say things like, "What?" and "Did I hear that right?" Mr. Hanlan looks confused. The room gets very quiet.

"Although I'm very flattered by your decision, there's someone here tonight who deserves this crown more." I pause, leaving everyone on the edge of their seats. "That person doesn't have it easy. She failed 6th grade. She wets the bed. Her mom makes her do all the housework and her dad has a blind eye. But she had the courage to enter this pageant, even though there was no way she'd ever win. Ladies and gentlemen, I give you Daniela Bertoli."

I walk over to Daniela, place the crown on her head, and hand her the roses. Her whole body is shaking, she's so nervous.

"Go on," I say. "Go meet your public."

And then it's Daniela's turn to walk down the runway. I stand back with the other contestants and applaud with everyone else, watching her wave to the crowd. I'm a little sad, but I'm glad that I was able to give Daniela this.

"It's more important for her to win this pageant than it is for me," I think to myself. Besides, I already have too many crowns at home.

Suddenly, a hand slips around my waist. "Your Christianity makes me want you even more," Mr. Hanlan whispers behind me. His body is pressing against me. A chill runs down my spine. He won't let me escape. There's no choice but to give him what he wants. I sigh and turn around to face him.

Then I fall asleep.

four

It's October now and cool enough to wear my jacket. But I can't wear my jacket indoors or else I'll look suspicious. The Scotch tape doesn't work anymore. I tape my nipples down in the morning and by recess, the tape would be peeling off. So after school last week, I went to the Shop 'N' Bag and bought a big roll of masking tape.

"It's for a school project," I told Mr. Bernard, even though he didn't ask me.

Now, I wrap the tape around my chest three times every day before I go to school. It holds much better than the Scotch tape, but it's hard to breathe, and when I pull the masking tape off at night, it hurts.

My nipples are sticky and sore and now look like maraschino cherries. In some ways, I feel bad that I'm not taking better care of them. I keep taping them down when all they want to do is grow. It's not their fault. They're angry at me.

"Maybe if you were normal, *we'd* be normal, too," they say. "Did you ever stop to think about that?"

"You're cruel!" I tell them. "I'm perfectly normal."

"Who are you kidding? You can't even go out and find a boy friend."

"You're terrible! Don't say another word or I'm going to get the ice cubes. I mean it!"

The truth is, my nipples are right. I do need to get myself a boy friend. My mom's been on my back about that lately.

"Surely there must be someone for you to pal around with," she said once. My dad was in the room. I was so embarrassed. "Isn't there *anyone* in your class, Peter?"

My parents have always wanted me to be normal, although they don't come right out and say it. But I know I don't always make the choices they want me to make. My mom tried to get me to sign up for hockey last year. Instead, I signed up for a calligraphy class.

"Don't you want to get out there and get all rumble tumble with the other boys?" she asked. She put the Bluewater Hockey form on my desk.

"Not really," I said. I was practising my W, a very tricky letter to do in calligraphy. "And watch that you don't knock over my jar of ink."

And I know that my dad would've liked me to dress up like a soldier or a pirate for Halloween in 4th grade. Instead, I borrowed a blonde wig from Mrs. LaFlamme, one of Nancy's dresses, and an old pair of high heels from Christine, and went trick-or-treating as Marilyn Monroe. My dad wore his baseball cap, kept his head down the whole time we were out, and stood in the middle of the road while I went up to the houses.

"That you, Henry?" Mr. Blake called out when he looked past my shoulder. He lives three doors down from us.

"What's that?" my dad asked, even though he heard Mr. Blake. His voice sounded deeper, too, like he was doing an impersonation of someone else.

"Thought you only had two daughters!" Mr. Blake yelled and tossed a bag of chips into my pillow case.

I thought Mr. Blake was complimenting me. My dad started coughing. He seemed pretty relieved when I broke a heel and had to call it a night.

The truth is that I feel bad about not being normal, but I just can't help it. I've tried to make my parents happy, but it just never works out. For example, I signed up for shop class this year instead of home ec. We had to take a half year of each in 7th grade. But in 8th grade, you can choose one or the other for the full year. Even though I really wanted to learn how to make pants and lemon meringue pies, I knew I had to do the right thing and sign up for shop like all the other boys. I wasn't looking forward to it and the shop teacher, Mr. Gilvary, is very annoying. He has the biggest butt I've ever seen on a man. When I took shop with him last year, he was always saying things like, "Watch yourselves, students. One slip and suddenly, you're missing an arm" or "Keep your goggles on at all times. Had a student in '76 who didn't listen. Now, he's got a marble for an eye."

I tried to get myself excited as I handed in my form on the last day of 7th grade. It had taken me a good ten minutes to make a red circle around the word "Shop."

"Peter, this is your chance to be normal," I told myself. "Who knows? Maybe you'll even make a boy friend. You can do it!"

But during the first week of class this year, something bad happened. We were going to make plastic key chains, Mr. Gilvary told us. He brought in large sheets of colored plastic that had to be snapped into smaller pieces to make our key chains.

"Put your goggles and gloves on before you do this," he said. "Then secure the plastic sheet good and tight in the vise. Now grip the top and give it a sharp pull toward you."

When Mr. Gilvary snapped the sheet, the sound was so loud, I screamed and ducked behind one of the wood-working tables.

Everyone turned to look down at me and started laughing. Brian Cinder sniffed loudly.

"I think he crapped himself."

No one came within ten feet of me for the rest of the day. That night, I sat my parents down and told them the school had made a terrible mistake.

"They overbooked the shop class," I sighed. "Now some of us have to go into home ec. No one volunteered, so they made us draw straws. And guess what?"

I tried to do my best disappointed look, but inside, my stomach was doing flip-flops. There was just no way I could spend the rest of the year in shop class.

"What do you mean, they overbooked it?" my mother asked.

"I don't know," I said, "that's just what they said." I hoped she wasn't going to ask any more questions.

"Why should *you* have to switch classes?"

"I told you. I drew one of the shortest straws."

"How many other students had to switch?"

"Um, I don't know. Three or four, maybe." It felt like my armpits were raining. "Look, it's not that big of a deal. I mean, I'm kind of upset, but what can I do?"

"Well, we can call the school for one thing," my mother said. "Why should you have to suffer for a mistake that they made on their end?"

This wasn't going well at all. My parents couldn't call the school or else Mr. Mitchell would tell them that I said *they* were the ones who wanted *me* out of shop class and into home ec.

"My mother isn't a very good cook," I'd told him and shrugged.

"You can't call the school," I said, "or else everyone will say I'm a whiny baby. I pulled the shortest straw, Mom. Fair is fair."

"But I don't see why…"

My dad, who hadn't said a word, held out his hand.

"Give me the form," he said to me.

"But Henry! We can't just…"

"Peter, give me the form." He didn't sound angry, just very tired. I gave him the form along with a pen.

"I was really looking forward to making a birdhouse this year," I said as he signed the sheet.

He made a strange noise in his throat and handed me back the form.

"Thanks for being good sports about this," I said as I walked out. Even though it's not very Christian to lie to your parents, I couldn't let them find out the truth. Especially my dad. The last thing he needs is to find out just how un-normal I really am.

Now, I'm just finishing up my first sewing project. It's a pillow shaped like a hot dog. It even has yellow and red felt for mustard and ketchup. Next month, I'll start working on my first piece of clothing. I think I'll make a sweatshirt for my dad.

The home ec teacher, Mrs. Williams, thinks I'm very talented.

"You certainly have a knack for the art of domesticities," she said to me. "But I do wish you'd keep your fingers out of the cookie dough, Peter."

• •

I used to be more normal when I was younger. I'd always get invitations to birthday parties or sleepovers. Sometimes, I'd go roller-skating with Todd Moffat at Skate City, but that was before I broke my arm at his eighth birthday party. I never learned how to use the rubber stoppers on my skates, so I'd grab onto the railing to slow myself down before getting off the rink. But that day, I missed the railing and went flying into the lobby. Everybody was screaming and jumping out of the way. I was going that fast. I ended up running into the vending machine. I bounced back, landed on my butt, and broke my right arm. Mr. Moffat had to drive me home. He kept asking me if I was all right and I said, "Yep, I'm okay," but as soon as I walked through my front door, I started bawling. I had to go to the emergency room and get a cast.

I didn't get invited to Todd's ninth birthday party.

I even used to be friends with Craig Brown, which is really weird when I think about it, since he's the leader of the Athlete Group at Clarkedale. In 6th grade, my parents took Craig and I to the Parkview Fair. It happens in a small town of the same name every Thanksgiving. There's a midway and cotton candy stands and cows with runny noses and competitions to see who grew the biggest gourd.

Craig and I went on the Tilt-a-Whirl and the Scrambler and the giant swings. Later, he bought a chocolate sucker shaped like a boob and I bought a bag of beer nuts, which Craig said were made with real beer. We had a great time, even though I stepped in horse crap on the way out and my mom made us drive home with the windows open.

That was two years ago. Now, Craig acts like he doesn't know me.

I guess things started to change in 7th grade. The year started out the same, with everyone hanging around each other. But then, halfway through, we started taking sex ed and by the time June came around, everyone was divided off into groups.

Every group at Clarkedale has a leader. Craig is the leader of the Athlete Group, the most popular group. All of the Athlete Group boys play on the school sports teams. The Athlete Group call each other by their last names and yell things like:

"Thompson! Over here!" and

"You're a doofus, Wilkie," and

"Shake it off, Lewis. Don't let him get to you."

All of them are thin, even though they're always eating. Sometimes, I think they eat more than me, which makes me angry because that's not fair. But most of the boys in the Athlete Group are dumb and don't get good grades. They're not very good dressers, either. I try to stay clear of them at all times, especially Craig. I'm afraid of their touchdowns and last names and loud voices.

Eddy Vanderberg is the leader of the Short Group. The Short Group is made up of boys who haven't reached puberty. Most of them are smaller than the girls in my class. The Short Group plays horse at recess. Eddy Vanderberg always yells out the rules to everyone, as if no one's ever played the game before.

"No spiking! No dribbling!"

I think it makes Eddy feel taller to yell.

Most of the Short Group members are dumb, like the Athlete Group boys. Eddy gets pretty good grades, but he doesn't want anyone to know. I think he thinks he wouldn't be the cool leader anymore if people found out he was really a nerd. The truth is, everyone knows that Eddy *is* a nerd, so he's not fooling anyone.

Sean Dilworth is the leader of the Geek Group. The members of the Geek Group are good at math and science. They stand around at recess, in the far corner of the school yard, talking about science fiction movies and passing around *Fangoria* magazines.

"Check out this one!" they say, pointing to pictures of zombies or people with knives sticking out of their heads. "That's totally putrid!"

Margaret Stone is the leader of the Goody-Goody Group. That group is kind of like a girl Geek Group, even though you'd never catch them looking at *Fangoria* magazines. Instead, the Goody-Goody girls go to Girl Scout meetings in church basements and trade stickers that they keep in photo albums.

"Mmm, smell this one," I'll hear them say. "Peach."

"This one's fuzzy. Touch it."

The Goody-Goody Group also make friendship pins which are little safety pins with beads. They pin them to their shoelaces. Sometimes, they make friendship pins, using letter beads, so the pins spell things like "love" and "pal" and "classy."

Eric Bird is the leader of the Indian Group, the toughest group at Clarkedale Middle School. You don't talk to the Indian Group unless you're an Indian yourself. Every morning the yellow school bus drops them off. They come in from the reserve, which is outside Chemical Valley.

I don't think the Indian Group likes Clarkedale, even though we do Indian crafts sometimes. I heard Eric say that everyone at Clarkedale is a "bejoggin head." I don't know what "bejoggin" means, but something tells me it doesn't mean "super nice."

Michelle Appleby is the leader of the Slut Group. The Slut Group is made up of girls on the wrong side of the tracks. They wear dangly earrings and lip gloss and dark blue eye shadow. There's always some story going around about them, like so-and-so put a thermometer up her vagina to see what the temperature was, or so-and-so gave a boy a BJ in the path behind the school.

Whenever the Slut Group hears one of these stories, they yell "THAT'S A LIE!" like they're angry. But then they start to giggle. Except for one time, when people were saying that Lisa Miller put peanut butter on her vagina so that her dog would lick it. She started crying and had to be sent home that day.

The Banger Group leader is Brian Cinder. Banger Group boys date Slut Group girls. Most of them are poor and live in the South End, where the low-rentals are in Bluewater. The Banger Group listens to Def Leppard and AC/DC and wear black-and-white concert T-shirts and bang their heads against the brick walls of the school for fun. That's how they got their name.

The Banger Group picks on everyone except for the Indian Group. Each thinks they're the toughest group at Clarkedale and there's always some kind of fight going on. On Monday, it was between Darryl Lascelles and Ronnie Doucette. It started because Darryl said he fingered Ronnie's girlfriend, Andrea, after school one day. Everyone was very excited about the fight, even me. I was just glad I wasn't involved, because I'm sure that either one of them could've pounded the crap out of me.

At the end of the day, everyone gathered in a circle behind the gym while Darryl and Ronnie went at it. All the Indian kids were yelling "Kill him!" and all the members from the Banger and Slut Groups were yelling, "Punch him out!"

I felt sick to my stomach because I could hear the punches hitting body parts and Darryl's nose was bleeding and it was very disturbing. The fight didn't last for too long, because the principal came running out and everyone scattered. Darryl and Ronnie were suspended for three days.

Then there are people that don't fit into any group. Like Jackie Myner, who as well as being the ugliest girl at Clarkedale is poor and stutters and doesn't dress very well.

Sometimes, I'll see Jackie trying to talk to Arlene Marple. Arlene doesn't belong to any group. That's because she has dandruff and B.O. and wears sweatshirts with kittens on them. But even Arlene doesn't like to be seen with Jackie. That's how bad it is for Jackie.

I guess I don't belong to any group either, but I'm not like Jackie or Arlene. Even though I'm overweight and have deformed nipples, I never stutter. And there's no way I'd be caught dead wearing a kitten sweatshirt.

Back in September, I started hanging out with the Goody-Goody girls, but that was only because most of them were in my home ec class and Margaret goes to my church. Then, Brian Cinder noticed me trading stickers with a couple of the girls at recess.

"Look at Peter Paddington," he said in a high voice, "he's just one of the girls."

Since then, I haven't said two words to a Goody-Goody girl and I signed up to be a Clarkedale library assistant. I don't mind working every recess, even though Mrs. Kraft said she only expects me to come in three times a week.

"Your friends will think you don't want to be around them anymore," she said. I just smiled and told her that I have a very strong work ethic.

"I've been delivering papers for three years," I said. "Hard work is in my blood."

The truth is, I'd rather be in the boring old library, putting books away and making ditto copies for the teachers than outside with everyone else. It's safer.

Mrs. Kraft is very nice to me. She's divorced and wears

sandals with pantyhose and always has a Kleenex stuffed up her sleeve, even though I've never seen her blow her nose. She's best friends with Ms. Robillard, the 6th grade teacher. They hang out together at recess, talking over the ditto copier and sipping coffee. They don't say too much when I'm around, though. I guess they don't want me to hear. Maybe they talk about what students they hate the most. Or what teacher is having an affair with another.

But one time, I overheard Mrs. Kraft say, "I forgot my watch today, and I just feel so naked without it. So completely naked."

I felt pretty weird when she said that, because all I could think about was Mrs. Kraft wearing nothing except for her pantyhose and sandals. I bet Ms. Robillard was thinking the same thing, too. A lot of students think Ms. Robillard is secretly a man. That's because she's not married and has hairy knuckles and when she wears high heels, she slides all over the floor, like she's on ice. Maybe Ms. Robillard is a secret agent, assigned to investigate our school.

"Nothin' to report today," the secret agent would tell his boss over the phone, pulling off his high heels and wig. "Just a bunch of smart-ass kids. 'Cept for that library assistant. He's been on to me since Day One. Maybe we should offer him a job on the force."

At lunch, I walk home. My mom will usually have a bowl of Alphagetti or two grilled cheese sandwiches waiting for me, or if she's in a really good mood, she'll make sloppy joes with French fries.

"How was your morning, dear?" she always asks me.

"Fine."

"Did you learn anything new?"

"Not really."

After that, I'll eat a row of Oreos or a couple of Pinwheels with a glass of chocolate milk. Then I'll go downstairs to watch *I Love Lucy*. As soon as the end credits roll and the announcer says "*I Love Lucy* is a Desilu production," I leave to go back. I get there just as the bell is ringing. I've got things timed pretty well.

• •

It doesn't really bother me that I don't have a boy friend. But I think it bothers everyone else, especially my parents. Sometimes, while we're watching *Love Boat* on Saturday nights, I'll catch my mother looking over at me, like she's trying to figure out a crossword puzzle. That makes me uncomfortable. Or Uncle Ed will say something stupid like "You planning to play ball this summer, Peter?" right in front of my dad and I'll want to yell, "No! And stop asking me! I'm not planning to play football or soccer or hockey or any other stupid sport, okay?"

But I never do. Instead, I'll always say, "Maybe," and hope that my dad forgets about it.

But the other day, I overheard Margaret Stone and Julie Tilson talking after school about becoming locker partners for 9th grade.

"I don't want to share a locker with Lisa," Margaret said. "And I just know she's going to ask me. So why don't we agree to be locker partners and then when Lisa asks me, I can say, 'Oh, sorry. Julie already asked me.'"

"Okay," Julie said. "I guess that's not really lying, is it?"

I never even thought about having a locker partner for 9th grade! Later, as I was delivering the paper, I couldn't stop worrying about how I was going to find someone in time. September wasn't that far away.

And here I thought I'd figured everything out. I knew that things would be different for me by the time high school started. I planned to start my life over as a whole new Peter Paddington. I'd be thin and wear all the right clothes and I'd be very popular. When I walked down the halls, everyone would say "Hi Peter!" but I'd pretend like I didn't hear them. I'd head straight for the cafeteria to eat my lunch with my new friends. I wouldn't have to go home for lunch anymore and I wouldn't have seen an episode of *I Love Lucy* in I don't know how long.

The thing is, I never thought about sharing my locker with anyone. But after hearing Margaret and Julie, I realized how stupid I was. But I can't just go up and ask a boy in my class to be my locker partner next year. You have to be friends first before you ask personal questions like that. But what boy would I ask? Who could I pick to be my boy friend?

My biggest problem is that I don't know how to make boy friends. I never know what to say around other boys and I'm afraid that if I *do* say something, I'll sound stupid. I guess I've always felt weird around other boys. It's like all the other boys are normal, except for me. Sometimes, I'll spy on everyone at recess from behind the library curtains. I'll watch Eddy and his Short Group members playing horse from the library window. Or I'll watch Craig Brown and his friends playing touch football in the field. Or Brian Cinder and his goons leaning up against the side of the school. And I'll think to myself, "They don't have Bedtime Movies. They're not fat. They don't have taped-up nipples." It's like being a boy is the easiest thing in the world for them.

But enough is enough. I have to swallow my fears and find myself a boy friend on the double. There's no time to lose.

I sat down at my desk and wrote out the names of all the boys in my class. Then I pretended having conversations with them.

"Hi Brown. Would you like to teach me how to play football?"

"Hi Sean. Want to look at pictures of mutilated people this weekend?"

"Hey Eric. Got a light?"

But instead of each one saying "Sure" or "Let's meet up after school," all I could hear was Brian Cinder's voice.

"Peter Paddington is just one of the girls."

Then I came to Andrew Sinclair's name. He's the most attractive boy in 8th grade. He has long eyelashes, blue eyes, and really thick brown hair. I wonder if he conditions it. I put Miracle Whip in my hair once, because I read that mayonnaise is a good conditioner. But I guess I left it in too long. My hair was greasy for days and I smelled like an egg salad sandwich gone bad.

Andrew is also very fashionable. He wears button-down shirts and khaki pants and penny loafers. But instead of pennies, he puts dimes in them. He's that kind of guy. Andrew is rich, too, so he can afford to buy designer clothes I see in magazines.

When Andrew came to our school, all the girls had crushes on him. I think it was because he was new. Most of the time, people move *away* from Bluewater, not *to*. Margaret Stone liked him the most. She bought him little gifts, like rabbit's foot keychains and chocolate-scented stickers, and left them in his desk for him to find.

Margaret never said she was the one leaving the gifts, but everyone knew it was her. She even made a friend-ship pin for herself with Andrew's initials on it, although I heard her tell Eddy Vanderberg that "A.S." stood for "Absolutely Smart." She made all of her Goody-Goody friends write Andrew notes in class. Margaret would never look over at Andrew while he read the notes. Instead, she'd pretend to be doing her work or arranging her scented stickers into smell categories.

Sometimes, Andrew wrote back to the Goody-Goody girl who had sent him the note, sometimes not. Depend-ing on his mood. I saw one of his notes back once. It fell out of Margaret's coat pocket one afternoon and I picked it up before anyone saw me.

"Dear Andrew," it read. "How R U? Someone in this class likes you VERY MUCH!! Do you know who it is? If you do, write her initials on the back of this paper and send it back."

I flipped the note over to read what Andrew had written.

"I am fine. But U are bugging me! If it's who I think it is, then her initials are P.U.!"

I felt bad for Margaret after that, but I don't think

what Andrew said was wrong. She *had* been bugging him a lot. You have to be careful around boys, because if you get on their nerves, they'll treat you like dirt. Instead, it's better to be vague and pretend like you don't care about them at all. That drives them crazy. Or so I read.

I watched Margaret very closely after that. I wasn't sure how upset she'd be. Maybe she'd try to kill herself by sticking her friendship pins into her wrists. But then I heard Margaret asking the Goody-Goody girls to send notes to Eddy Vanderberg. Maybe she thought she had more of a chance with a midget.

Andrew doesn't play sports. That's another thing we have in common. He doesn't collect stickers, and I'm pretty sure that he doesn't listen to heavy metal. He spends most of his recess time hanging out with Sean Dilworth. I don't know what Andrew sees in him. I think the truth is that Andrew doesn't want to be friends with Sean, but he doesn't have anyone else to talk to. Maybe Andrew secretly wants to be my boy friend, too.

I'm not sure about that, though. He's a bit of a mystery. Sometimes Andrew comes into the library at recess. I'm always afraid I'm going to have a heart attack or do something stupid while he's in there. The last time he came in was October 12th. I hid behind a trolley of books and watched as he signed out a book on the Loch Ness monster. He didn't notice me, which was fine with me because I had a big zit on my chin and even though I take my job seriously, being a professional library helper isn't the coolest thing in the world.

Andrew's mom married John DeLouza after they

moved to Bluewater. I saw the wedding picture in the *Observer*. Some people say that he's in the Mafia. I didn't know if that was true or not, but thought I'd better find out. Otherwise, when Andrew and I are boy friends, he might try to get me to rob old ladies or something. This afternoon, while I was delivering my papers, I saw Daniela sitting in her parent's car, listening to the radio full blast. She does that a lot and says it's the only place she can get privacy.

I knocked on the window and yelled, "Is there a Mafia in Bluewater?"

"What?"

"Is there a Mafia in Bluewater?"

"What?"

"Turn off the radio and roll the window down!" When she had, I asked again. "Is there a Mafia in Bluewater?"

Daniela gasped and her eyes popped out of her head.

"What are you, crazy?" she whispered, hopping out of the car and pulling me into her garage. "Don't go fuckin' saying those things in public. They have spies everywhere."

Daniela told me there's a Mafia that rules every city in the state. She said her Uncle Tony is part of the Bluewater gang.

"They meet at the Basilico Club the first Wednesday of every month," she said. "I eavesdropped on them once. There was a group of them, maybe ten or so, sitting around this small table in one of the rooms. They were smoking these big fuckin' cigars and playing cards. The whole time, they talked about killing a bricklayer named

Silvio who had screwed one of the guys' wives. They said they were going to kill him and fuckin' chop him up and stick him in the deep freezer at the club."

"Did they do it?" I asked.

"How the hell should I know? You think I'm stupid enough to go looking in that deep freezer? Let's just say that some serious shit goes down. Business deals, murders, all that stuff. They got the Bluewater police chief by the balls. He doesn't do anything without fuckin' clearing it with them first."

Daniela started to give me the creeps. She was grabbing onto my arm like there was no tomorrow and her eyes looked like golf balls. I told her I had to go.

"Don't breathe a word of what I said to you," she said before I left. "They're probably watching us right now. Holy fuck, I'm a dead woman!"

Then she ran back into the car, locked the door, and turned the radio up. I stood there in her garage for a few minutes, looking around to see if I spotted any hidden cameras or noticed anything moving behind the boxes. I started to freak myself out and hurried down the driveway. When I passed Daniela in the car, she didn't even look at me. Instead, she stared straight ahead, mouthing the words to "Gloria," which was playing on the radio.

While I delivered the rest of my papers, I kept wondering if I should believe Daniela. She can be a bit of a liar sometimes. But even if it's true that Andrew's stepfather *is* in the Mafia, I don't care. It means that having Andrew as my boy friend will be dangerous. I'll just have to be careful, that's all.

• •

During recess, I signed out the same Loch Ness monster book as Andrew and another one called *Crimes of the Century*. I figure I'll read them and then Andrew and I will have things to discuss.

"Someday, they'll find Nessie. That's my dream, anyway."

"Why can't people understand that being in the Mafia isn't just about killing people? It's about families sticking together."

I decided to ask Andrew to the movies and figured it would be the best thing to do on our first friend meeting. Maybe after the movie, Andrew would ask me to go for an ice cream float somewhere. Then we'll talk all night long about what we want out of life.

I knew I'd be too nervous to ask Andrew to the movies in person. So I took the phone book from the telephone table in the kitchen and went to my room. I found his number and memorized it. I wrote out what I was going to say, then sat in front of my mirror, practising.

"Hi Andrew. It's Peter. Peter Paddington. How are you doing? You were just about to call me? Well, how about that! Listen, I was wondering if sometime, you maybe want to go to the movies. Great! How's Saturday night? My dad can drive."

When I went to pick up the phone and dial, I froze. What if Andrew said no? What if he laughed at me or told Sean Dilworth? I couldn't set myself up for something like that. I put the receiver back down.

I watched Andrew out of the corner of my eye the next day. He was wearing a blue and white striped shirt, stonewashed jeans, and his brown penny loafers.

"Would you do that to me, Andrew?" I asked him through a mental telepathy message during geography. "Would you hurt me like that?"

"No," he replied. "I'm not like the other guys. I'm different. You know that. Trust me, Peter."

"I wish I could," I said. "I wish I could."

Michelle Appleby turned and gave me a look. Was she able to hear our mental telepathy messages? Or did I say something out loud? Either way, I bent my head down and concentrated on coloring South America with my yellow pencil.

By the time spelling rolled around in the afternoon, I made up my mind that I wasn't going to call Andrew. I couldn't. It wasn't worth the risk and when I saw that one of our words in the lesson plan was "destiny," I could only sigh and nod.

"What would ours have been?" I wrote in the margin of my workbook. I would never know.

When I got home from delivering papers, I went to my room with two Pinwheels and a glass of milk and stuck my desk chair under the doorknob. Then I pulled off my sweatshirt and my T-shirt and carefully pulled off the masking tape around my chest. I usually try to change the tape twice a day to keep it fresh, like a Band-Aid. Then I crumpled the tape into a ball, pulled out my bed, lifted out the floor vent grate beneath, and placed the tape inside the metal tube. This could be dangerous if I was a stupid person, because the tape ball could go rolling down to the furnace and cause a fire. Good thing I'm smart and make sure to stick the end piece onto the metal so it stays put. Even better that I'm a genius and take the tape balls out every other day and put them in my coat pocket and drop them into the garbage can outside of the Shop 'N' Bag. Otherwise, the balls would get all clumped together and stop the heat from getting into my room. In some weird kind of way, I guess it's lucky that someone like me would have deformed nipples. If it had happened to someone stupid like Brian Cinder, I doubt he'd still be alive to tell about it.

Anyways, just as I was about to wrap some new tape around myself, my nipples stopped me.

"You're really starting to bug us," they said. "If you don't pick that phone up and make yourself a boy friend, we're going to tell your parents about how you tape us up every morning. We're going to tell everyone your secret!"

"You're evil!" I said and shook my fists at them. But I knew they were right. Calling Andrew was the only way my nipples—and the rest of me—would ever become normal. I had to do it. I finished taping my nipples up, put my T-shirt and sweatshirt back on, and sat down on the floor.

"I hope I remember his number," I said to myself as I put the phone down beside me. Then I unwrapped one of the Pinwheels, ate it, and rehearsed the lines again. My heart was beating a mile a minute, but somehow I managed to pick up the phone and dial. It rang once. Then again. And again.

"No one's home," I thought and just as I was about to put the receiver down, an older man's voice said, "Hello?"

I gasped. It was John DeLouza! I hadn't even thought about someone other than Andrew answering the phone.

"Hello?" he said again.

I was about to say, "Oh, hello. Would Andrew be available?" when someone started knocking on my door.

"Peter! Supper's ready!" It was my mom. "You get out here right now before it gets cold!"

Then I heard John DeLouza say, "Who is this?"

And my mom yelled, "What are you doing in there?"

And John DeLouza said, "What did you say?"

And my mom said, "I mean it!"

I was almost crying, I was so confused. Should I yell at my mom to be quiet or should I pretend there wasn't a maniac pounding down my door and just ask for Andrew?

"Is this some kind of prank?"

"Peter!"

"Who?"

"Why aren't you answering me?"

I did the only thing I could do and slammed the receiver back down. My face was burning and I was shaking. Did John DeLouza hear my mom call my name? What if he went to Andrew and asked, "Do you know someone by the name of Peter?" and Andrew would say, "Yeah, he's this big loser in my class. Why are you asking?" and John would say, "Well, you're not going to believe this, but…" Or even worse, what if John sent the Bluewater Mafia after me for thinking I was an obscene phone caller?

I was so angry at my mom for ruining everything, especially when she was the one who wanted me to find a boy friend in the first place.

"I'll be out in a minute!" I screamed back at her. I must've scared her pretty good, because she was quiet for a couple of seconds. Then she said, "Okay, dear. No rush."

I hardly ate any of her casserole that night.

I wanted to fake being sick the next day so I wouldn't have to go to school and see Andrew. But that meant having to spend the whole day with my evil mom. I kept my fingers crossed the whole time I was walking to Clarkedale.

When I got to the school yard, Andrew and Sean were leaning against the side wall, looking through a magazine. I had to walk past them, so I took a deep breath and told myself I was too busy thinking about a very serious problem (like my mom dying) to notice them. It'd be like they weren't even there.

"Wicked," I heard Sean say as I passed them.

"How do they get the bone to look so real?" Andrew asked.

"My mom has six months left to live," I thought as I walked by.

I breathed a sigh of relief when I made it into the school. But I knew I'd have to be vague around Andrew for the rest of the day. Otherwise, he'd catch on that I was the mystery caller.

During math and history, I made sure to keep my eyes on my desk. At recess, I hurried off to the library before Andrew had the chance to corner me. At lunch, Andrew walked across the field to his house. I went the opposite way. My mom had sloppy joes waiting for me. During afternoon recess, I watched Andrew and Sean from the library window. They were talking and laughing. While I was walking home at the end of the day, I realized I didn't have to be vague. I didn't have to be anything at all. Andrew didn't say anything to me. Andrew didn't look at me. It was just like any other day of the week. I grabbed my bundle of papers at the corner but it seemed heavier than usual and I had to stop three times to switch arms before I made it home.

BEDTIME MOVIE #3

It's a dark and stormy night. I'm home alone. My parents and sisters have gone away on a very long vacation. I'm a little nervous, because lightning is flashing in the sky and the thunder makes the dishes in my mom's china cabinet shake.

"Everything is fine," I tell myself as I look out the living room window. "You're just on edge, that's all."

Suddenly, there's a knock at the back door. I freeze. Who could it be at this time of the night? There's another knock, this one louder. I grab a knife and crouch over to the door.

"Who's there?" I call out. "I've got a knife."

It's Andrew Sinclair. I'm shocked. What's he doing here?

"Please let me in," Andrew says. He sounds very upset.

I open up the door and let Andrew in. He's soaking wet.

"What's wrong?" I ask him.

"Before I say anything, do you have any dry clothes I could change into?" he asks. I shrug and say sure but when I go to my room, the only thing I can find in my dresser drawer is a red Speedo.

"Isn't that the strangest thing?" I whisper to myself. It's not even mine.

"It's the strangest thing," I say to Andrew. "But this is all I have."

I turn around to give Andrew some privacy while he changes. At any second, I could turn around and see Andrew naked. But I don't. We're friends.

After Andrew puts on the shorts, I offer him a drink. Andrew says sure, so I make him my specialty—an orange pop float with Neapolitan ice cream.

"This is really tasty," Andrew says. "You must be the top student in your home ec class. I guess there are a lot of things I don't know about you."

I tell Andrew it's nothing, really. "I'm not as complicated as you might think," I say.

Then Andrew tells me the reason he came to see me. His stepfather came home from a Mafia meeting and shot his mom and sister. Andrew ran out of the house before his stepfather had a chance to get him, too.

"You were the first person I thought to run to," Andrew says. Even though he's upset, I can tell he's happy that I was home.

I know that Andrew needs me to help him. He wants me to be the Voice of Reason.

"We have to call the police," I tell him. "We have to report your stepfather."

"No!" Andrew says. "You don't know how powerful my stepfather is. He has the police force by the balls. If we call them, we're dead men."

"Well, what do you think we should do?"

Andrew stares at me for a good, long time. "We have to run away," he says. "Pack your bags. We're catching the first train to the city. We can find jobs and get an apartment and go shopping together and stay up all night, talking about our dreams."

"I can't up and leave," I tell Andrew. "Too many people here depend on me. I've got papers to deliver tomorrow."

Andrew nods slowly. We both know what the other must do, even though it's tearing us apart.

"Crime doesn't pay, Peter," Andrew says softly. He wipes his eyes.

"Hey there," I say, "don't let them beat you."

I go over to the phone. "I'll book your ticket and pay for it," I tell him.

"No, please don't," Andrew says, "you've already done so much."

"It's something I want to do," I tell him. "We're friends, remember?"

"Best friends," Andrew says. Then he looks down. I can tell he's embarrassed and wants to say something else.

"What is it?" I ask him.

"Before I go, could I have a hug? I mean, I can understand if you don't want to, but it's just that whenever I'm around you, I feel protected and safe."

"Of course you can," I smile. Andrew starts walking over to me. I can hear his heart beating loudly and I notice the tiny blond hairs on his chest. All of a sudden, there's a big flash of lightning that cuts the power in the house. The lights go out and then Andrew and I are standing in the dark.

Although I can't see him, Andrew is so close to me that I can smell the orange pop on his breath. I want to ask him, "Do you condition your hair?" but I can't. The words get frozen in my mouth. The rain gets louder.

Then I fall asleep.

five

I'll never be able to leave the house again, thanks to Uncle Ed.

Michelle Appleby's older sister, Janice, works at the Donut Delite on Huron Street. Michelle told me that Janice told her that Uncle Ed came in there last week. He ordered two dozen donuts and a Diet Coke.

When Uncle Ed found out where Janice went to school, he pulled a picture of me out of his wallet and asked her if she recognized me. When I first heard the story, I wasn't thinking about Uncle Ed. I was too excited by the fact that Janice recognized me. She was very popular, mainly because she let guys finger her at recess. I never said two words to her, but she must've thought highly of me.

"What did Janice say?" I asked Michelle. Maybe Janice had a secret crush on me.

"She said she kind of remembered you, that you were in my grade and fat, right?"

"Oh."

"So your uncle said, 'Yep, that's the one all right. He's my sister's kid.' Janice says he comes in there every Tuesday and orders a couple dozen donuts. She said he always makes up some story that they're not all for him, but everyone knows he's full of shit."

I was so embarrassed and angry. Now everyone in Bluewater would know that I was related to Uncle Ed.

"Why did you give him a picture?" I asked my mom. "I asked you not to. I knew he'd do this."

"Well, he asked me for a picture and what was I supposed to say?" my mom asked. "He's proud of you, that's all."

"That's not true," I said. "He's just trying to embarrass me. He's going around to everyone in Bluewater, telling them things about me. Private things."

My mom crossed her arms against her chest. "Now what would Uncle Ed possibly know about you that would be so private?"

"Plenty," I said, even though I couldn't really think of anything. But that wasn't the point. Just knowing that Uncle Ed had my stupid 8th grade picture crammed in his wallet was enough to freak me out. I told my mom to tell him to take it out.

"He's highly sensitive at this age," I heard her say to him on the phone. "Remember how you were at thirteen, Ed?"

I don't think Uncle Ed could remember that far back. He told my mom he wouldn't show my picture anymore, but didn't understand why he had to keep me a secret. Uncle Ed doesn't realize that *I'm* the one trying to keep *him* a secret.

• •

As if people finding out that I'm related to Uncle Ed wasn't bad enough, my dad told me that he'd made an appointment for me to see Dr. Luka.

"Why?" I asked. I felt my nipples twitch beneath my sweatshirt.

"Because you haven't gone in a long time," he said, "and it's important for you to have a checkup."

I don't like Dr. Luka very much, even though he's never been mean to me or anything. He's just very, very old—old enough to be in the Guinness Book of World Records as the World's Oldest Living Doctor. He has cold hands, too. I think he's German because he can't pronounce w's. He says them like v's. So does his wife, Mrs. Luka. She's old, too. She's the receptionist and sits at a desk in the living room. When she's not on the phone yakking to one of her friends, she makes sock monkeys. I don't know if she sells them or gives them away to poor kids or what. All I know is that whenever I come to an appointment, there are monkey arms and monkey legs and monkey heads all over the place. I think she's almost blind because she holds everything really close to her face. The few times I noticed, I thought she was sniffing the monkeys, which disturbed me a bit. Then I realized she couldn't see where she was sticking the needle. I'd be careful if I were her.

There was no way I was going to see Dr. Luka. For sure he'd discover my deformed nipples and tell my parents and he'd probably even call some photographers to take pictures to include in one of those "Freaks of the 20th Century" books.

"The nurse at Clarkedale does physical exams on all the students," I told my dad. "She's pretty good and even checks for lice using toothpicks. So I don't think I need to see Dr. Luka."

"Well that may be, but I still think it's important for you to see a regular doctor."

My mother walked into the living room. "A doctor? Is something the matter?"

"No, Beth," my dad sighed. "I was just telling Peter I made an appointment for a checkup. But he doesn't seem to want to go."

"Is there a reason you don't want to go?" my mother frowned.

I felt like a bug about to be squashed. Both of my parents were looking at me. I knew that if they started to get suspicious, they'd tell Dr. Luka to examine me extra carefully.

"Cover every square inch," my dad would say.

"He's hiding something!" my mother would whisper/scream to Mrs. Luka in the waiting room. "We'll find out what it is soon enough!"

"No, I don't mind going," I said and tried to smile. "I just have a lot of tests coming up that I need to study for. Maybe I can go see Dr. Luka in a couple of months. Or next year, even."

"I've made the appointment for next Tuesday," my dad said.

"Oh."

• •

The next day was Sunday, which meant Uncle Ed was coming for dinner.

When he opened the back door, he yelled, "What's in the news?" Then he threw a garbage bag full of dirty laundry down the stairs. "Look out below!"

My mom washes his towels, shirts, and pants. She never washes his underwear, though.

"He says he washes them on his own," she said once. "But all he has is mother's old wringer-washer and I'd be surprised if he knew how to work it. More than likely, he washes his shorts in the sink and I don't know how hygienic that is. Of course, he never *was* the cleanest person."

She never washes his bed sheets, either. The last time she did was in 1976. She said they went into the washing machine gray and came out white. "I haven't seen them since and that was eight years ago. Lord only knows what color they are now."

I heard my mom say, "Hello Ed," in a voice that was between angry and tired. "Did you remember to pick up the rolls?"

"Beth, you know I don't drive."

"Don't be smart," my mom said. "You know what kind of rolls I'm talking about. You forgot to get them, didn't you?"

"Guilty," Uncle Ed said.

"Oh for god's sake, Ed. I ask you to pick up one thing for me. Well, we just won't have rolls tonight. And if anyone asks why, I'll look at you and you can do the explaining."

"I'll take the heat," Uncle Ed said. "Fair enough."

"But you better start tying a string around your finger or something, Ed. I mean it."

"Where are the kids?"

Nancy and I were sitting in the living room. "Oh god," she whispered.

"In the living room, watching TV."

"What's in the news?" Uncle Ed asked when he walked in. He was wearing a Detroit Red Wings baseball cap and a red Hawaiian shirt.

"Not much," Nancy said.

"Not much," I said.

"Where's Christine?" Uncle Ed plopped down in the brown velour chair with a grunt.

"In her room."

"Where's your dad?"

"Downstairs."

"What are you watching?"

"Some movie."

"Wonder what that football score is now."

"Do you want to check?"

"Maybe just for a minute."

It's the same every Sunday. Uncle Ed always manages to get the television turned to whatever sports game is on that afternoon. And it never is "just a minute" because a half hour will go by and then my mother will call "Supper!" and he'll look up, kind of surprised, and say, "Is it dinnertime already?" But no one really minds if he gets the TV because it means he talks less.

I was a bit nervous that he was going to bring up

Janice Appleby, but he didn't say anything to me. Sometimes, I feel bad about being embarrassed by Uncle Ed. I mean, it's not his fault he's the way he is.

"You can't get a leopard to change his spots," my mom said once. We were all waiting for Uncle Ed to show up for dinner. He was forty-five minutes late and the chicken in the oven had shrunk to the size of a chickadee. "If only Ed wasn't Ed, things might have turned out all right for him."

She always says that if Uncle Ed lost weight, he could find someone else to do his laundry.

"Not just cooking and cleaning and things like that," she said. "But someone to take care of him, too. Emotionally, I mean. Someone to say 'Ed, you put down that fork,' or 'Ed, are you having sugar with your coffee or coffee with your sugar?' God knows I'm tired of doing it. And I shouldn't have to do it in the first place."

"Why didn't Uncle Ed ever get married?" I asked her once.

"Mother smothered him," she sighed. "The sun just rose and set on Eddy, there was no doubt about that. Now look how he's turned out. Can't cook for himself. Can't clean. Can't even wash a towel. And not a wife in sight for miles. And then, of course, there's the other thing."

"What other thing?"

My mom looked at me hard. "Nothing," she said. "I'm just talking nonsense. But just promise me you'll never let yourself become like him, Peter. I mean it."

• •

I kept trying to think of ways to get out of my appointment with Dr. Luka, but it was a dead end. There was no way of getting out of it unless I died and I didn't really see that happening anytime soon.

The night before my appointment, I decided I had no choice but to go with untaped nipples and keep my fingers crossed. Considering Dr. Luka was so old, it might not be too hard to confuse him, anyway.

"Take my sweatshirt off? Dr. Luka, I just put it back on!"

My appointment was at 4:30 p.m. so I had just enough time to come home, peel off the masking tape, and rub some of my mother's skin lotion on my nipples.

"You can't shut us up this easily," they said.

"Take a hike," I said.

My mother ended up coming with us because she wanted to go to K-Mart. You can only get to K-Mart by making a left-hand turn, so she doesn't get there too often.

"I have to get a dozen glass ashtrays," she said. "We're making candle holders at the next UMW meeting. I don't know how you get a candle holder out of an ashtray, let alone twelve of them. However."

Having her with us made me more nervous, but she promised she wasn't going to interfere.

"You won't even know I'm there," she said.

Mrs. Luka was on the telephone when we arrived. She waved a monkey arm at us and mouthed "Come in!"

The office was hot and smelled like old people. It wouldn't kill either of the Lukas to crack open a window once in a while.

"Vell, how are you today?" Mrs. Luka said when she

hung up the phone. "Little Peter, I have not seen you in a very long time. Vhat grade are you in now? Five?"

"Eight," I said.

"Oh yes. Vhy don't I go and tell the doctor you are here?"

When Dr. Luka came out to get me, I thought about a movie I saw once about an Egyptian mummy who comes back from the dead.

"Valk this vay, young man," Dr. Luka said. He turned to my parents. "You can vait out here. There are some magazines on the table if you like."

Once I got into Dr. Luka's office and sat down on the examining table, I started to get a little nervous. What if he asked me to take off my jacket?

"Now Peter, vhy don't you take off your sweatshirt and your pants and lie back on the table?"

I froze. Dr. Luka was shuffling around, looking for his stethoscope. "Why?" I asked. It was a stupid question, I know, but it was the only thing I could think of.

Dr. Luka turned around to look at me. "So that I can examine you," he said.

"Oh. Can I keep my T-shirt on? I mean, it's just a bit cold in here."

"Sure, sure," Dr. Luka said. "Vhatever makes you happy."

I pulled off my sweatshirt, stepped out of my rugby pants, and laid back, resting my hands over my nipples.

After tapping me on the knee a few times with his hammer and listening to my heartbeat, Dr. Luka told me to step onto his scales.

"Pardon?" I asked. I was so worried about my nipples that I didn't even think that Dr. Luka might want to weigh me. I couldn't remember the last time I stepped on a scale, especially while there was another person in the room.

"It vill only take a moment," Dr. Luka said.

I kept my eyes closed the whole time I was on.

"Okay, Peter. Vhy don't you put your clothes back on? I'm going to bring your parents in here for a minute."

When my mom and dad were sitting down in the room, Dr. Luka pulled out my file. "Peter is thirteen years old. And he veighs two hundred and four pounds. If you don't change his eating habits, I guarantee you there vill be health problems in the future."

My mother laughed her fake laugh. "Dr. Luka, Peter is a teenager," she said. "And you know how teenagers eat. I can't monitor him at all hours of the day. Besides, it's natural. Every other teenager I know eats French fries and fast food and hot dogs. Why should Peter be denied that? I don't think it's very fair to ask a teenage boy to live off yogurt and celery sticks, do you?"

The more she went on, the higher her voice got. My dad sat there and said nothing. I wanted to disappear. Dr. Luka just kept looking at his papers.

"Fatness runs on my side of the family," my mom said. Her voice was hurting my ears. "Come to our family reunion, Dr. Luka! You'll see!"

Things got worse on the car ride home.

"Why is everything my fault?" my mom asked my dad.

"No one said it was anyone's fault, Beth."

"The doctor didn't have to. I could see it in his eyes. Blame the mother! Blame the mother! Why not? Everyone else always does. Look at how Nancy treats me now."

My mom said that because something's different about Nancy. She broke up with André a few weeks after my mom's birthday dinner at the Conch Shell and bought a Jane Fonda record. I watched the other day as she poured a packet of Sugar Twin into her tea.

"Those chemicals aren't good for you," my mother had said.

"Neither is obesity," Nancy said and went back to her room.

"It's not my fault he doesn't play sports," my mom said to my dad. "You should take him golfing more often, Henry. That's what a father does with his son."

I almost died when she said that. She turned to me in the back seat.

"You just need to exercise more, dear," she said. "That's all. Less time in front of the TV and more time out playing with your friends."

"I'd have a boy friend right now if it wasn't for you," I felt like saying. But I didn't want her to know about Andrew. She'd be on my case all the time, asking me if I called him. So I bit my tongue.

"Beth, I don't think the solution to this is golf," my dad said.

"Well what *is* the solution, Henry? Assuming there is some kind of problem to begin with. Personally, I don't think there's anything wrong with Peter. He's my little angel."

"There you go again," my dad said as we pulled into the driveway.

"What do you mean?"

"Smothering him. Making excuses for him. Setting him up just like you know who."

"Who?" my mother asked. "Who?" She sounded like an owl.

My father didn't say anything. He just got out and left the two of us sitting in the car.

"Don't pay any attention to him, Peter," my mother said, "he's just grouchy from shift work. It happens. Oh no! I forgot about getting the ashtrays!"

She ran into the house to get my father. I got out and went straight to my room, shut the door, and stuck my desk chair under the knob. I should've been happy that Dr. Luka didn't discover my nipples, but I wasn't. All I kept thinking about was what Dr. Luka had said when he stopped adjusting the scale.

"Vow."

Two hundred and four pounds. I reached between my mattresses and pulled out a list I had made when I turned thirteen last year. I had written down all the things I needed to change in order to become a new and improved Peter Paddington.

1) Lose weight.
2) Buy more clothes.
3) Learn how to play sports.
4) Try to look Mr. Hanlan in the eye.
5) Get a boy friend.
6) Smile more.

7) Be vague.

8) Get tanned.

9) Act confident.

10) Lose weight.

And here I was, almost a year later and I hadn't managed to do one thing on the list. In fact, the list only got bigger. I grabbed a pen.

11) Get normal nipples.

"You think getting rid of us is going to turn you into the 'new' Peter Paddington?" my nipples asked.

"It'd be a start."

"Give us a break," my nipples said. "You made us this way in the first place."

"I did not!" I said. "I'm innocent."

"That's a bunch of baloney. Let's see. Who was it checking out the men's underwear section in the Sears catalogue last night?"

"I need new underwear," I said. "How do I know what kind to get unless I see what the latest styles are?"

"Face it," my nipples said. "We're going to be together for a long, long time. You might as well get used to us."

I got out the masking tape and shut them up. I was so angry at my evil nipples. Who did they think they were, anyway?

I needed to do something to take my mind off things so I decided to play the Mirror Game. The Mirror Game is kind of creepy, so I only do it when there's someone else home. I never do it late at night, either. To play the Mirror Game, I turn off all the lights and close my curtains and light the candle I keep in the right-hand drawer of my desk. I sit in front of my mirror and put the candle beside me. The trick is to keep staring at yourself without blinking. Once you blink, you lose your concentration and have to start all over again.

After a while, everything will start to get cloudy. Then I'll see other people's faces. Sometimes, I see the face of an old woman. Sometimes, an old man. There's a guy with a dark beard that shows up sometimes, too. One time, I think I saw the Devil, which creeped me out pretty good.

Once, I told Christine about the Mirror Game. She said that the faces I saw were proof of reincarnation.

"Your soul goes into another person that's being born at the same time and you live your life as someone else," she said. "Anyone with half a brain knows it's true."

"Can a man come back as a woman?" I asked.

"You could come back as anything—a tree, an eagle, even a fly. You just never know."

I don't know if I'd like to come back if I had to be a boring old tree. Or if I had to be a fly and eat dog poop all day. If I had a choice, I'd like to come back as a fashion model or an Athlete Group boy.

Christine told me that in a past life, she was Joan of Arc.

"Why do you think I'm so petrified of fire?" she asked.

Maybe Christine is right and the Mirror Game shows me all the people I once was. Or maybe they're the people I'm going to be. I was thinking about that while I sat staring at my reflection, wondering if I was anyone famous, too. Then, I started to see someone in the mirror. It was a face worse than the Devil. And before the

Hawaiian shirt got any clearer, I blinked really hard to break the spell and blew out the candle. I stayed in my room for the rest of the night and didn't come out once, not even when my mom knocked on my door to tell me she had made peanut butter cookies.

"Your favorite, Peter."

I said thanks and told her I'd be out in a little while.

"What are you doing in there?" she asked in this fake-happy voice.

"Nothing," I said and waited for her to walk away. She didn't. I could hear her breathing on the other side of the door. I sat there, quiet as I could, staring at the door knob. I knew that if I saw it start to turn, I would lose it on her. I'd scream at her to stop going through my drawers and stop calling me her "angel" and stop LISTENING AT MY DOOR WHEN ALL I WANT IS PRIVACY!

But the doorknob didn't turn. After a couple of minutes, I heard the floor creak as she walked back down the hall.

From now on, when I need to take my mind off things, I'm using my Ouija board.

six

There are only three weeks left before Clarkedale's annual Christmas pageant and Mrs. Forbisher, the music teacher, has already had two breakdowns. Twice a week, the class has been practising our big show-stopper, "One Tin Soldier." It's the saddest song I've ever heard and when we get to the part where the valley people turn over the stone only to have it say "Peace on Earth," I get goosebumps.

We've been rehearsing since the beginning of November, so you think we'd have it perfect by now. But a lot of students can't remember the words, even though Mrs. Forbisher gave us ditto copies. And Mrs. Forbisher can't get any of the boys to sing. She's tried being nice, telling them that some of the world's most admired singers are men and did you know that Santa doesn't visit children who won't sing? But none of the boys are buying it. Instead, they either laugh or whisper to each other or keep their lips pressed shut. I guess it's been getting on Mrs. Forbisher's nerves. I feel bad for her, smiling that phony smile and blowing into her round harmonica to get everyone on the same note. But the bottom line is that the boys never sing, no matter how nice Mrs. Forbisher acts.

They'll scream and shout to Banger music, but they can't sing a normal song. I don't know why. That's just the way it is. Secretly, I like singing and I think I have a very nice voice. But I'd never let anyone find that out.

Anyways, there we were this afternoon, halfway through the third chorus. I was standing in the back row between Greg Walsh and Tony Marlot. They both belong to the Athlete Group and were fighting over who got to stand next to me.

"I want to," Greg said to Tony through a mental telepathy message. "You got to stand beside him last time."

"Well, he likes me better than he likes you!" Tony yelled back to Greg.

I was afraid they were going to come to blows. And what message of peace would that send out to the audience?

"Gentlemen, please," I said. "For the record, there are two sides of me. Someone pick the left and someone pick the right and let's call it a day."

Mrs. Forbisher was standing in front of us, mouthing the words like she always does and swooping her arms like a pterodactyl. Just when we got to the part where the valley people turn the stone over, Mrs. Forbisher blew into her harmonica so hard it flew out of her hand like a flying saucer and almost beaned Carrie Linely in the head.

"Why aren't you singing?" Mrs. Forbisher yelled. Everyone looked at each other to figure out who she was talking to.

"Can someone please explain to me why the *hell* you aren't singing?"

I heard someone gasp and Eric Bird say, "Wicked." No other teacher in the history of Clarkedale has ever said the "h" word before.

"Can someone please tell me what's so damn difficult about singing a song?"

Another gasp. Tony leaned over to Greg and circled his finger around his temple.

"Why am I even here?" Mrs. Forbisher was walking in a circle. "Can someone tell me that?" she asked the floor. "Why am I here? Is this it? Is this what it all comes down to? This is it, isn't it?"

Angie Mayer, one of the Goody-Goody girls, started crying. Hearing Mrs. Forbisher use the "h" and "d" words like that must've scared her. Then again, Angie cries when the eraser breaks off her pencil, so you never know. Margaret Stone slipped out of the gym and it wasn't long before she came back with Mr. Gray. He called Mrs. Forbisher "Hilary," took her by the arm and led her outside. Then Mr. Mitchell came to take us back to class. No one saw Mrs. Forbisher for the rest of the day, although I heard Eddy Vanderberg say that he saw her getting into a white van wearing a straitjacket. I wouldn't be surprised if Mrs. Forbisher ends up in a mental hospital. Music teachers can be very emotional people. I think it's because when they were young, they thought they'd be Broadway stars someday. Instead, they end up teaching songs to a bunch of kids who don't want to sing in the first place. It must be very depressing.

The next day, Mr. Mitchell told us that Mrs. Forbisher was on vacation for a couple of weeks and that he'd be taking over our music lessons. He didn't look very comfortable with the idea.

"What was the song you were rehearsing?" he asked.

"'One Tin Soldier,'" Margaret said.

"Hmm," Mr. Mitchell put his finger to his lip, "doesn't exactly seem the most fitting song to celebrate the birth of Christ, does it?"

Now we have to sing "Away in a Manger" complete with all the hand motions. It's very embarrassing and this will be the most humiliating Christmas pageant ever. The only person who gets out of doing it is Alexander Allesio. He's a Jehovah's Witness and has to stand outside in the hall when we say the Lord's Prayer. So he got excused from singing at the Christmas pageant and sits in the library while we rehearse.

I thought about telling Mr. Mitchell that my religion forbids me to sing Christmas songs, too, but something tells me that wouldn't work. I'm Methodist, which means I'm not very religious. Methodist people aren't afraid of God like Catholics and they don't come knocking on your door like Jehovahs and you never see a Methodist minister healing crippled people on TV. When I think of the Methodist Church, I think of Goldilocks and the porridge that wasn't too hot or too cold.

I've been going to St. Paul's all my life. It's right around the corner from where I live, so it's very convenient. Down the street from St. Paul's Methodist is our rival, St. Michael's Catholic Church. Well, maybe I shouldn't say "rival" because that's not really true. The congregations don't shoot spitballs at each other when church gets out.

But there are some big differences between Catholics and Methodist.

For starters, Catholics are much more religious. They go to church all the time, even on Saturday nights. That upsets my mom because the Catholics park their cars along our street.

"What is it with them? Those people just come out in droves. And what if we were having company over, hmm? Where would our guests park?"

"Well, we're not having company over, Beth."

"That's not the point, Henry. It's the principle of the matter. You'd think those Catholics would take over the whole city if they could."

I think my mom gets upset because she'll see families coming out of the cars. Christine and Nancy don't go to church anymore. Christine stopped going because she said she had too much self-respect. Nancy stopped going because she said church was boring. When my mom brought up the topic of Christmas Eve service last weekend, I knew there was going to be trouble. Even before she finished asking Nancy and Christine the question, she was already misting up. It was Sunday and Uncle Ed had bought Kentucky Fried Chicken for us. I was on my second chicken breast. My mom blew her nose into her napkin.

"It would be nice for all of us to go. That is, if you don't think you girls would burst into flames the second you stepped inside the church."

Christine said she would think about it.

"It's still a month away," she said, picking at a piece of

relish in her macaroni salad. "Do we need to make reservations?"

Nancy said that she might go over to Bubbles' house for Christmas Eve. Bubbles is her new best friend. I don't know Bubbles' real name, only that she got her nickname because she chews bubble gum all day.

"Plus I'm perky," I heard her tell Christine. "You know, how when you blow bubbles, it makes you feel kind of warm and gushy inside? I'm like that."

"You don't say," Christine said.

Nancy and Bubbles became best friends just after Nancy dumped André. She said she didn't have anything in common with him anymore. I don't think it was nice of Nancy to break up with André even if he was a loser, and I don't like Bubbles and lately, I'm not so sure I like Nancy herself. She's gotten really annoying and walks around with a calorie counter booklet all the time.

"Can anyone guess how many calories are in one glazed donut? Hmm? Anyone?"

Nancy says she's lost twelve pounds, thanks to her calorie counter booklet and Bubbles. But she looks the same to me.

"Well, is Bubbles' family going to church?" my mom asked. She reached for another napkin.

"I don't know," Nancy said.

"What religion are they?"

"How should I know? Catholic. Born Again. Jehovahs, probably."

"Oh Nancy!" my mom whisper/screamed. "Don't joke about something like that!"

"They're not Jehovahs, Mom," Nancy said, "calm down."

"Bubbles can worship the Tooth Fairy for all I care," my mom said. "I'm just sorry that you'd rather spend time with someone else's family instead of your own. I guess I was expecting too much from you girls this year. I should have known better."

Then my mom pushed her chair back and went to her bedroom.

Christine and Nancy rolled their eyes. My dad put his head in his hands. Uncle Ed asked me to pass him the drumstick on my mom's plate.

• •

The Sears Christmas flyer came in the mail the other day. After I looked through the men's underwear section to check out the latest styles, I flipped to the clothing section to see what new styles of sweatshirts were in. I stopped on a page that showed two male models laughing like they were best friends. I bit my lip and thought about Andrew Sinclair.

"That could've been us," I whispered. "Is it too late to try again, Andrew?"

There are only ten months left until freshman year and I still haven't made a boy friend. Or cured my nipples. Or lost weight. In fact, I think I've gained more weight. When I did my knuckle test the other day, it went halfway between my second and third knuckle, so that means I've put on a half-knuckle's worth of weight since September. I know I have to go on a diet soon if I'm going to be thin by next September. But in order for your diet to work, you have to focus all your concentration and lately, I've got too many things on the go, like writing down the things Andrew and I can do when we're best friends.

To cheer myself up, I decided to go down to the Shop 'N' Bag to say hi to Mr. Bernard and maybe get a Butterfinger. When I passed the Papa Bertoli restaurant, Daniela was just finishing her shift.

"What the fuck was that all about?" she said, pulling out her ponytail. "That was the busiest lunch ever. My hair smells like veal parmigiana. Come here and sniff it."

I almost gagged when she said that. I couldn't imagine putting her split ends that close to my face. "That's okay," I said, "I'll take your word for it."

"You going to the Shop 'N' Bag? I'll come with you. I gotta buy the new issue of *Cosmo*. My cousin Teresa says there's a sex survey in it that tells you if you're any good in bed."

"Why do you need to know something like that?"

"Hey, just because I stink like veal parmigiana doesn't mean I couldn't fuckin' get some action if I really wanted to!" Daniela said. "I could name a lot of guys who would kill to go around the way with me."

"I think you mean go '*all* the way,'" I said, rolling my eyes.

"Yeah, yeah, whatever. The point is that *Cosmo* tells you everything you need to know about screwing. You name it: blowjobs, diddling yourself, Chinese positions. It's in there."

"What's the big deal about that?" I tried to sound

casual, but my dink went kind of hard when Daniela said "blowjob" and I heard Mr. Hanlan asking me if I wanted big or small marshmallows in my hot chocolate. I pulled my bomber jacket down as far as I could.

"I'm just doing my homework, that's all," Daniela said with her hand on the Shop 'N' Bag door handle. "I'm teaching myself the stuff I'll need to know when I get laid for the first time. Besides, I'm fourteen. I'm practically a woman. I should know these things."

Mr. Bernard had a big smile on his face when Daniela and I walked into his store.

"Here comes my favorite couple!" he said. He thinks Daniela and I are girlfriend and boyfriend, which grosses me out. If I had a girlfriend, she wouldn't be anything like Daniela. She'd be sweet and condition her hair and read magazines that teach you how to apply mascara, not how to "diddle yourself."

Mr. Bernard was out of the latest issue of *Cosmo*, so Daniela just bought a Hershey bar and a Chunky. I bought a bag of sour cream and onion chips and a Butterfinger.

"You two stay out of trouble, now," Mr. Bernard said and winked. Daniela looked at him like he was an alien.

"That old fucker is gonna go out of business soon if he doesn't catch up with the times," Daniela said as we made our way home. "You've got seventeen dusty packages of clothing dye and you don't have a single fuckin' copy of *Cosmo*? Gimme a break."

As we were walking past St. Michael's Church, Daniela stopped me and said she had to run inside for a minute.

"I almost forgot. I'm supposed to light a candle for my cousin Rosa today."

"Why? Is it her birthday?"

"No! What are you, stupid? She's dead! Today is the third anniversary of her death."

"What did she die from?"

"No one really knows," Daniela said. "Some people, they say kidney stones. Some people, they say heart attack. Me, I say it was *malocchio*."

"What's that?" I asked.

"The Evil Eye." Daniela's eyes popped out of her head. "It's a curse that someone puts on you because you've done something to piss them off."

"What did your cousin do?"

Daniela checked over her shoulder and then leaned in close to me.

"Rosa borrowed a pasta maker from old Mrs. Travatti, her next-door neighbour," she whispered. "And she never returned it."

I stopped and waited for Daniela to finish the rest of the story. But instead, she blew her nose into her mitten.

"That's it?" I asked. "Someone killed your cousin over a pasta maker?"

"Hey!" Daniela pointed her snotty mitten at me. "Don't fuck with wops. If you borrow something, you better fuckin' return it."

I sighed. I <u>never</u> know when Daniela is telling the truth or when she's lying. Maybe she doesn't even know herself.

"Isn't the church closed?" I asked, looking at my watch. It was only two o'clock.

But Daniela said St. Michael's is open all the time, like the 7-Eleven. That way, people can go in and light candles or ask forgiveness any day of the week.

I told Daniela that I'd wait for her, but to hurry up because it was freezing.

"Why don't you just come with me?" she asked.

"I'm Methodist," I said.

"So? You can still come inside. Just don't touch anything. And be fuckin' respectful."

I didn't think Daniela had any business telling me to be respectful when she's the one that swears like a hooligan, but I didn't say anything.

I'd never been inside St. Michael's before, so I was a bit nervous. When Daniela told me I had to cross myself with holy water before stepping inside, I got all confused and mixed up the order.

"Just remember: Forehead, chest, tit, tit," Daniela whispered. "It's easy to remember that way."

"Does it matter which tit I touch first?" I asked. My nipples might be jealous if I picked one before the other.

"Don't be stupid," Daniela said and started walking down the centre aisle. I followed right behind her, figuring that so long as I stayed close to her, no one would discover that I was a Mehodist spy.

The church was empty, except for a couple of old ladies who were kneeling in the pews. I thought one of them was dead because her lips weren't moving and her head was tilted off to her shoulder. Pretty soon, the priests would start to smell something funny and the terrible discovery would be made.

Then the old lady snorted and her head flopped to the other side.

St. Michael's was very beautiful inside, just like God would want. Along the walls, there were stained-glass windows of important Jesus scenes: a dead Jesus on the cross, a baby Jesus in the manger, and a sad Jesus with his heart on the outside of his robe. They were very dramatic.

At the front of the church, a huge crucifix hung down from the ceiling with an actual Jesus on it. At St. Paul's, there's only a plain wooden cross at the front that looks like someone made it in shop class. It jiggles when the ceiling fans are on, so I'm always nervous it's going to fall and kill Mr. Archill, the organist.

"I bet Christine and Nancy wouldn't have any problem going to *this* church," I thought.

Daniela led me over to a red glass lantern that was hanging from the ceiling.

"When the candle is lit, it means that God is here," she whispered and crossed herself.

"Who lights it?" I asked her and crossed myself.

"No one," she said. "It just goes on by itself. That's the miracle of God."

"The miracle of God," I whispered.

Then Daniela pointed to three sets of wooden doors.

"That's where it all comes down," she said.

People made confessions on the other side of the doors. They told the priests all the bad things they'd done and the priests gave them punishments. Daniela told me that she has to go to confession at least once a week.

"What do you tell the priest?" I asked her.

"Everything," she said. "If you don't, God will get you when you die."

I wondered if Daniela told the priest that she wets the bed, but I'm not sure if that's a sin, really. If I had to confess, I know I'd be in there with the priest for a long time. I'd have to tell him about hanging up on John DeLouza and how I discovered I can make sperm using the showerhead and how I think about Mr. Hanlan in a red Speedo, even though I know I shouldn't.

"And you wonder why your nipples look like the tops of badminton birdies?" the priest would ask. "Please."

"Does the priest ever get angry at you or tell your parents?" I asked Daniela.

"Don't be stupid," Daniela said. "He's there to forgive you. It's his job. Whatever you tell him is a secret between you and him."

That made me feel a little better.

Daniela went to light her candle. There were three rows of candles in small glass holders. Some of them were already lit. Daniela put fifty cents in a small tin box. I guess it was like a vending machine. While Daniela was lighting Rosa's candle, I looked up and saw a Virgin Mary statue, staring down at me. She was standing behind the rows of candles. I don't know why I hadn't noticed her before. Mary was wearing a white dress with a blue robe and matching veil. Her hair was brown and the expression on her face was sad. Maybe she felt sorry for all the lit candles. I was standing there, looking up at her when I felt something inside of me. I can't really explain it, but it was almost like the Virgin wanted to tell me something. A secret that she wanted to share only with me and no one else. I looked closely at her mouth and eyes to see if they moved at all.

"What is it?" I asked through a mental telepathy message. "You can tell me."

"C'mon," Daniela said and grabbed my arm, "let's get out of here."

I didn't want to go. I wanted to stay there, in the church, until Mary told me what she wanted to say. But Daniela was yanking on my sleeve, saying she had to get home or else her mom was going to kill her, so I mouthed the words "sorry" to Mary.

"You're very lucky to be Catholic," I said to Daniela as we walked home. I was still thinking about the beautiful stained-glass windows and the red lantern and the sad face of the Virgin Mary. "Being Methodist is very boring."

"If that's what you think," Daniela said.

Just before we turned onto our street, Daniela told me that her mom once went to Ripley because the Virgin Mary had been spotted there.

"Where?" I asked her. "Like at the grocery store or something?"

"No, stupid," she said. "The Virgin appeared in a field outside of the city. As soon as my Aunt Francesca told my ma about it, she packed up her rosary beads and was out the door like a fuckin' bullet."

"Did she see her?"

"No," Daniela said. "She sat in the field for six hours. She said a bird flew by and shit on her hand, but that was about it."

Daniela said that the Virgin can appear anywhere, at

any time. Sometimes, her face can appear in a window or a rock. Daniela told me that her grandmother even saw the Virgin in a pot of tomato sauce.

"Staring right at her, right in the sauce," Daniela said. "My Nona could see her eyes and nose and ears and everything. Just goes to show you. The Virgin is one tricky lady. You never know when or where she's gonna show up next. So be on your fuckin' guard at all times."

I went home and didn't think too much about it after that. Like I said, it's hard to know when Daniela is telling the truth. But all that changed at 7:02 p.m.

I know the exact time because I had just looked at the clock. I was sitting on my bed, trying to figure out some stupid math problem that Mr. Mitchell has assigned that day.

"The students who answer the question correctly will receive their very own scripture pocket book!" Mr. Mitchell said, like it was a million-dollar prize. "You can take this scripture book with you wherever you go. Read it while you're walking to school. Or on family trips. Or how about before you go to bed at night?"

Arlene Marple put up her hand. "Aren't you going to get in trouble handing those out? You got in trouble when you gave us those Bible bookmarks."

"Arlene, I'm sorry that *some* parents don't see the relevance of God in their child's life. But what do you want me to do? Fiddle while Rome burns to the ground?"

Arlene was twirling a pen inside her ear. She shrugged.

"Does everyone else understand that?" Mr. Mitchell asked, looking around at all of us. No one said anything.

I was surprised that Mr. Mitchell knew how to play the fiddle. Then Jackie Myner put up her hand. I could tell that Mr. Mitchell wanted to pretend like he didn't see her, but there was no way out.

"You had something brief to add, Jackie?"

"Mr. M-M-M-Mitchell, c-c-c-can you tell me if g-g-g-guinea p-p-p-pigs go to h-heaven?"

Mr. Mitchell looked up at the ceiling, as if he were checking.

"Why yes, Jackie. I'm sure guinea pigs go to heaven. If they've been good, that is."

"M-m-m-my g-g-g-guinea p-pig died. One time, he ch-ch-chewed through the phone c-c-c-cord so that we c-c-c-couldn't use it anymore. D-d-d-does this mean he was b-bad?"

Jackie once brought her guinea pig to school for Show and Tell. She named him Adrian after Adrian Zmed. It was the ugliest guinea pig I'd ever seen. Jackie told us she had given Adrian a haircut the night before, but she didn't do a very good job. Adrian was bald in some spots. Now Jackie was sitting on the edge of her seat, waiting for Mr. Mitchell to tell her whether her guinea pig was in hell or not. She must've been very close to Adrian.

"Well, Jackie, forgiveness is very important," Mr. Mitchell said. "Did you forgive your guinea pig for chewing through the phone cord?"

Jackie nodded. "But m-m-my mom got p-p-p-p-pretty mad. She said I h-h-had to give Adrian away. But I didn't. I k-k-k-ept him in a T-T-T-Tupperware c-c-container under my b-b-bed. That's how he d-died."

"Oh dear," Mr. Mitchell said. He looked very uncomfortable. "Well, I would say yes, Jackie. Your guinea pig is just fine and is running around heaven as we speak."

"E-even if my m-m-m-m-..."

"Yes, Jackie. Even if your mom never forgave him for chewing through the phone cord. Now, why doesn't everyone pull out their spelling workbooks and we can start on today's lesson?"

Jackie looked pretty relieved after that. I kept wondering what she did with Adrian. I mean, if she was keeping him in a Tupperware container under her bed, maybe he was still there. In a little while, Adrian would start to smell pretty bad. Maybe there would be maggots crawling all over his body. What if Jackie's mom found the container one day while she was cleaning? She'd be so angry she'd put Jackie in a Tupperware container, too.

Anyways, there I was at 7:02 p.m., trying to figure out this math problem, even though I didn't want a scripture pocket book. All of a sudden, I stopped and looked up at my closet door. I don't know why I did it. I just did. It was almost like a voice said "Look at the door, Peter," but I don't remember hearing a voice.

And there, in the wood, was the image of the Virgin Mary. I could see her head and eyes and the outline of her robe, which I think would be blue, but since my closet door is painted beige, I couldn't really tell.

I rubbed my eyes and opened them again, because I thought I was seeing things. But after staring at my door for a few seconds, she appeared again, right in the grain of the wood. I couldn't believe that I'd lived here all my life and never noticed her before.

"Ave Maria," I whispered and made the sign of the cross. I think I screwed up the order, but I didn't care. I was too excited. I thought about calling the *Observer*. They'd send a reporter and a photographer out right away.

"Tell me all about it, kid," the reporter would say. "Jeez, this is the story of the year!"

He'd write down everything I had to say on a small pad of paper, shake his head, and whisper "incredible" over and over again.

"BOY DISCOVERS VIRGIN IN CLOSET DOOR," the headline would read the next day. There would be a picture of me looking very serious and pointing to the closet. Or maybe they'd prefer if I was on my knees, praying to the door. Or maybe they'd just want to photograph me alone because they thought I had star quality.

But before I called the *Observer*, I knew I needed to talk to Daniela first. I ran out of my room and put my winter coat and boots on.

"Where do you think you're going?" my mom asked me.

"I'll be back in two seconds."

When Mrs. Bertoli opened the door, she was wearing a pink jogging suit and her Orioles cap. The smell of Lysol hit me like a wall.

"Isa time for collection?" she asked.

"No, not today," I said. I bet Mrs. Bertoli would be very jealous if she found out the Virgin had come to my closet door and not hers. "Is Daniela home?"

"DANIELA!" Mrs. Bertoli screamed. Then she asked me if I wanted something to eat. I shook my head.

"What do you want?" Daniela said when she came to the door.

"Listen," I said. "You know how you were telling me about the Virgin Mary showing up in Ripley? If she appears, like say in a field or maybe a door, for example, what does she want?"

"What are you talking about?"

"The Virgin Mary. Why did she appear in the field in Ripley? Was she trying to tell someone something?"

Daniela chewed the inside of her cheek and thought for a moment.

"Well, usually, she's trying to give people a message. Y'know, like they shouldn't fight or they should pray to Jesus or else they'll burn in hell. But sometimes, she heals people, too. Like my Nona. She said that before she saw the Virgin Mary in the sauce, she had really bad gas. So bad that she couldn't even fuckin' go to Kmart without cutting it right there in the ladies department. After the Virgin appeared in the sauce, she didn't have the problem no more."

I was getting so dizzy that I felt like I was on a Tilt-a-Whirl. If what Daniela said was true, then maybe the Virgin had come to heal my nipples.

"But you have to build a shrine to her before she'll do anything," Daniela said. "The Virgin doesn't like giving up anything for free. She's not gonna just hand miracles over. You gotta earn them. Now fuck off. It's freezing."

Then Daniela shut the door.

I couldn't get to sleep that night. Every couple of minutes, I'd turn my nightlight on to look at the Virgin.

It was kind of weird having someone else in the room with me. I knew I couldn't tell anyone about the Virgin in my closet door. No one would believe me. After all, no one believed the women who said that Jesus wasn't in the tomb anymore. And even if I showed them the door and pointed her out, they still may not see.

"Blind are the eyes of the unfaithful," I whispered. I surprised myself with that one. It just came out of my mouth. Maybe the Virgin was using me to spread the Bible's word. I got out of bed, turned on my lamp, and wrote the line down in my school notebook.

Before I left for school the next morning, I kneeled and crossed myself in front of the closet to pay my respects to Mary and to ask her for guidance.

"May I continue to be thy tool, Virgin," I said.

That morning, Mr. Mitchell started off the day by reading us a story from his *Christian Tales for Modern Youth* book. I listened very carefully to a story about a teenage girl who stays at a sock hop past her curfew and makes her mother cry. When he finished, Mr. Mitchell asked what the moral of the story was. My hand shot up like a bullet.

"Yes, Peter?" Mr. Mitchell looked pretty shocked. I don't put my hand up very often.

"Blind are the eyes of the unfaithful, Mr. Mitchell."

Someone behind me snickered. It was probably Brian Cinder, but I didn't care. I had the Virgin on my side now. "Devil worshipper," I said to him through a mental telepathy message.

"That's a very valid point," Mr. Mitchell said. "I'm not

sure if it's exactly the moral of *this* particular story, but in general, yes, that's very true. Um, anyone else?"

I worried all day about what Daniela had said; that I had to build a shrine to the Virgin to make her happy. Then she'd cure my nipples. Maybe she'd even help me lose weight and get a boy friend! But what kind of shrine should I make? Like Daniela said, the Virgin was pretty tricky and something told me she had very high expectations.

Later that night, the answer hit me over the head like a hammer. I was looking through the *Observer* and saw an ad for a do-it-yourself nativity scene. The kit included life-size illustrations of Mary, Joseph, and the baby Jesus. All you had to do was glue the figures onto a sheet of plywood and cut them out along the dotted line.

"So simple to do," the ad said. "Makes a lovely addition to any yard. And just in time for the Holiday Season! What a perfect way to remind your neighbours that Jesus is the Reason for the Season!"

I told my parents about the ad and asked if we could order it.

"I think it's a perfect way to remind our neighbours that Jesus is the Reason for the Season," I said.

"You're being a little strange about this," my mom said. "What's going on?"

"I don't see why not," my dad said. "How much is it?"

Every night before I went to bed, I crossed myself in front of the Virgin and told her to be patient.

"Have faith in me, Mary," I whispered to her. "Your shrine should be arriving in the mail any day now."

A week later, a big cardboard tube showed up at our

door and my dad and I went downstairs to get started. I could tell he was excited because we had to use his power tools. He was probably happy that we were finally doing something that fathers and sons are supposed to do. I was happy, too.

"This is like our very own shop class," I thought to myself.

My dad even went upstairs to make himself a coffee, which he doesn't usually drink, and came back down with a plate of Cinnamon Swirl cookies and a hot chocolate for me. It was good to be around him and actually have something to talk about.

"Now take a damp cloth, Peter," he said. "And wipe down where you've glued so you don't get bubbles. That's it. Gently ease into the wood with the saw. Peter, pay attention. Peter, look at what you're doing. For god's sake, Peter! Follow the dotted line! You're as blind as your mother!"

We finished everything that afternoon. I think I did a very good job, because even though some of the lines around the manger were a little jagged (I was trying to make the straw look more realistic) everything else looked very professional. Joseph was wearing a brown robe with a yellow rope tied around his waist. Jesus had a face that seemed a bit too old for someone just born, but he always looks that way in Christmas paintings. Mary was the best, though. She was wearing a white dress with a blue veil that covered her brown hair. She was looking up at the sky and her hands were pressed together in prayer. She didn't really look like the Virgin in my closet, but I knew which one was the real deal.

My dad attached poles to the backs of the figures and we took them outside. We arranged them beneath the living room window and then hammered the poles into the ground. Then my dad said we should put a spotlight on the nativity scene so that people could see it at night. So we went to Swenson's. While we were there, I saw Craig Brown with his dad. They were looking at hockey sticks. Craig's dad was old, even older than my dad, and he was wearing a baseball hat and a big ugly parka with fur trim around the hood.

"You and your dad go buy your stupid hockey stuff, Craig," I said through a mental telepathy message. "My dad and I are doing something much more important. Something religious. You wait until my picture is on the front page of the *Observer*. Then you'll really regret not talking to me anymore." I hurried off before he spotted me.

"The Virgin will be pleased," I thought when my dad plugged the spotlight in.

"Oh my," my mom said when she came out to look at it. "I can't wait for the Catholics to see *this*."

• •

Once my shrine was set up, it was time to take care of the other stuff. I signed out a book on the Catholic religion from the school library and made a list of all the tools I would need to make the Virgin happy.

I cornered Daniela the next day. She was out shovelling her driveway.

"I don't know if I'd be bothering to do that if I were

you," I said. "It's supposed to snow again tonight. You'll just have to do it all over again."

"Yeah, well. What else is fuckin' new?" Daniela said. She was huffing pretty hard and there were clumps of snow in her black hair, reminding me of her Miss Basilico baby's breath.

"You're doing a great job," I said. I knew I had to be extra nice to her.

Daniela looked at me like I was retarded. "You think so, do you?"

"Yes," I said. "But then again, you always do a great job. You're a pro, Daniela. A world-class pro."

"What the fuck are you talking about? And what the fuck is that in your front yard?" She pointed to my Virgin shrine.

"None of your business," I said, crossing my arms.

"What do you mean, 'none of my business?' It's in your fuckin' front yard!"

"So?"

"You put a fuckin' spotlight on it!"

"Deaf are the ears of the ignorant," I whispered. Another message from the Virgin! I'd have to remember to write that one down in my notebook.

"What did you say?"

"Exactly," I said. "Look, I need you to help me out on something. Remember when we went to St. Michael's to light the candle for your cousin?"

"Yeah."

"Well, remember those necklaces that the old ladies were holding in their hands while they were praying?"

"The rosaries?"

"Yeah. Listen, where do I get one? A rosary. Is there like a Catholic store in Bluewater?"

Daniela threw her shovel down into a snowbank. "Why the fuck do you want a rosary?"

I wondered if I should tell Daniela about my religious experience, because when I stopped to think about it, she was the one who introduced me to the Virgin in the first place. If she hadn't taken me to St. Michael's that day, or told me about her mom going to Ripley, I might never have noticed the Virgin in my closet. But I knew I couldn't say anything until my plan was complete. I didn't want to take the chance of betraying the Virgin. Then she might never heal me. Besides, Daniela would probably tell her mom and I'd have every Italian woman in Bluewater knocking at my door.

"Well," I said, slowly. "I'm thinking about becoming Catholic and like any good Catholic, I need to get some supplies before I devote myself to God."

That was partly true. If the Virgin *did* heal my nipples, the least I could do was turn Catholic. I knew my mom would have a fit, but she'd understand once I showed her my closet.

"Ah, jeez," Daniela said. "You just can't go into Kmart and buy a fuckin' rosary, y'know. And you can't wake up one day and decide to be a Catholic, either. You have to be born into it. It's part of your heritage."

I promised Daniela I was being serious.

"Look, I can't talk about this, but let's just say that I'm on to something very, very big. Something that would make your mom want to be my best friend and then I could tell her not to make you shovel the driveway or clean the garage because she'd do anything I said."

"What are you talking about?" Daniela narrowed her eyes and rubbed her coat sleeve under her nose.

"I told you," I said, "I'm forbidden to speak. You can try all you want, but I won't say anything. But believe me—I'm talking about major stuff, Daniela. I'm talking about the fate of the world and saving starving babies and front-page headlines."

"God, you're bugging me," Daniela said. "I'll see what I can do. But this will cost you some large cash. Rosaries don't come cheap, y'know. Ten bucks. Take it or leave it."

"Eight."

"Ten."

"Nine."

"Ten."

"Nine-fifty."

"Ten."

"Nine-seventy-five?" I asked. But the look on Daniela's face gave me the answer.

"Ten," I said. "But I need the rosary by tomorrow. There's no time to lose."

After school the next day, I went to St. Michael's instead of going home. The place was empty, so I was in luck. The first thing I did was go over to the Virgin Mary statue and make the sign of the cross.

"I now know what it was you were trying to tell me," I whispered to her.

Then I deposited fifty cents in the tin box and lit a can-

dle for the world. On my way out, I took the turkey baster
that my mom keeps in her dresser drawer and squeezed up
some of the holy water from the dish by the entrance.

I hurried home. I had to be very careful and hold the
turkey baster like a candle, so none of the holy water
would leak out. When I got home, I tiptoed to my room
and squeezed the water into an empty Imperial margarine
container. Then I hid it on the top shelf of my closet.

"It will only be a matter of time now," I said to my
nipples as I slowly peeled off the masking tape. "Only a
matter of time."

• •

The next day, while I was carrying my bundle of papers
home, a firm hand grabbed me from behind.

"Don't turn around," a husky voice whispered. "I got
something for you. Meet me in my garage tonight at
seven. Tell anyone and you're fuckin' dead."

When I opened the Bertolis' garage door that night,
Daniela was pacing back and forth. She was wearing a
black beret and a pair of sunglasses.

"You got something for me?" she said, walking over to
close the garage door.

"Yeah," I said. I turned up the collar of my jacket and
sat down on the bumper of the Bertoli's car. "You got
something for me?"

"First the money," she said.

"One five now," I said. "The other five when you
hand it over."

Daniela sighed and put out her hand and I gave her

the money. Then she pulled a Ziploc bag out of her coat pocket.

"I went through a lot of trouble to get you this," she said. "I hope you fuckin' know that."

I grabbed the bag and handed her the other five dollars.

"You do good work," I said. "I might hire your services again. Do you shovel driveways?"

"Get out of here before I bash your fuckin' head in."

That night, I had to lie awake until everyone else had gone to bed. It wasn't hard, though. I was too excited. I waited until I could hear my mom snoring and I crept out of my bed and tiptoed over to my closet to get the Imperial margarine container. I took the rosary out from my sock drawer and grabbed my Mirror Game candle.

I lit the candle and put it on the floor on top of my math book. Then I got on my knees in front of the closet door and took my shirt and tape off.

I dipped my fingers into the holy water and sprinkled a bit on each breast. My nipples crinkled up as soon as the water touched them. I gasped. Had the Virgin healed me that quickly? But then I remembered that whenever my nipples get cold or wet, they always shrivel up. So I wasn't sure.

Then I recited the prayer that I'd written and memorized.

Oh Virgin, the mother of Jesus,
Thou are good and very giving.
At this moment, I pray to you,
To shrink my nipples back to normality,

So that I may stop having to put masking tape on them.
And while I pray to you at this moment, Mary,
I also ask you to make me thin by September,
and that you command Andrew Sinclair to call me.
In exchange for thine kindness, I promise
That I shall say twenty Hail Marys every night,
And turn into a Catholic.
Bless you, Virgin Mary. Bless you for all eternity.

I made the sign of the cross, making sure I did the right order. Then I squeezed my eyes shut and waited for the Virgin to perform her miracle. I must've stayed there on my knees for about five minutes or so. It felt like forever. But nothing was happening. I snuck a peek down at my nipples to see if anything had changed, but they were still there, big and puffy as dumplings.

My parents' bedroom door opened. It was my mom, getting up for her nightly pee. I was afraid that she would see the candlelight coming from under my door and start screaming "Fire!" so I blew the candle out and waited until the toilet flushed and I heard her go back to bed. Then I put the Imperial margarine container back in the closet and the rosary beads back in the Ziploc bag.

I put my T-shirt back on and lay there in bed, staring at my closet door. I was pretty disappointed, but I also knew that the Virgin works in mysterious ways. She's one tricky lady, just like Daniela said. She was testing me to see if I really deserved to be cured or not.

"I won't let you down, Virgin," I whispered. "You'll see how good I am."

My nipples twitched underneath my shirt.

I decided right then and there that I couldn't have any more Bedtime Movies. They were evil. Devil films, as Mr. Mitchell might say.

When my car breaks down in front of Mr. Hanlan's house and he comes out in his red Speedo to help, I yell, "Stop!" really loudly in my head. "Go back into the house! I can walk to my photo shoot!"

Mr. Hanlan looks kind of hurt. I hope he understands how important this is for me. "It's not you!" I call out to him. "It's me!"

But I don't know if he hears me. He's already gone back inside.

seven

Christmas isn't much fun anymore. I'm too old for toys and too young to get anything expensive, like a car. Not that my parents have the money to buy me a car, but you never know. When I get my licence in a couple of years, we could be a lot richer than we are now.

This year, my Christmas list is pretty short. I'm asking for a Stephen King book, a new pair of slippers, a new bathrobe, an Italian cookbook, a new sweatshirt (Sears catalogue, page 135, Item 331 786 29YA, size large, color ash gray, although black is okay), and an inflatable chair. I don't really have the space in my bedroom for an inflatable chair, but I figure I'll deal with that if I get it.

The week before Christmas, the holiday tips from my paper route customers came rolling in. All in all, I made seventy-six dollars this year, which is up from sixty-eight in Christmas '83. I also got six boxes of chocolates, thirteen Christmas cards, three McDonald's gift certificate books, and an apple head doll from Mrs. Guutweister. I almost died when Mr. Hanlan gave me a ten-dollar bill and told me to have a Merry Christmas.

"Dan, you shouldn't have," I wanted to say. But all I could manage was a stupid "Thanks."

I was about to turn away when Mr. Hanlan said, "Do you have any special plans for the holidays?"

I couldn't believe it! Mr. Hanlan was trying to make conversation!

"Um, not really," I said. "You know, the usual. Church. And turkey. And maybe some movies. That's about it."

I took a deep breath and squeezed the ten-dollar bill in my fist. "Do. You. Have. Any. Special. Plans?"

"Nothing out of the ordinary," Mr. Hanlan said. "Probably about the same as you. Although I can't say I like turkey."

I was just about to lie and say, "Me, too!" when evil Mrs. Hanlan poked her head from behind Mr. Hanlan's shoulder.

"Hi Peter," she said in this really fake voice. "Happy holidays."

"Same to you," I said. Why did she always have to ruin everything?

"Dan, did you tell Peter about us going away?"

"No, I hadn't mentioned it."

"We're going away in January," Mrs. Hanlan said to me, "so we'll be stopping the paper for a week."

"Going to a troubled marriage camp?" I wanted to ask. "It'll never work."

"Okay," I said.

"We'll be gone from the 10th to the 17th. Just so you know."

"Okay," I said. "Not a problem."

"I hope you have a great Christmas, Peter," she said.

"You don't even know the real meaning of Christmas,"

I said through a mental telepathy message.

"Excuse me?" Mrs. Hanlan was smiling, but in a weird way. I froze. Did I say something out loud or was Mrs. Hanlan able to read my thoughts? I wouldn't be surprised if she'd been able to all this time. I started feeling sick to my stomach.

"I said I hope you experience the real meaning of Christmas."

"Oh. Okay. Well, thanks," Mrs. Hanlan said.

I raced back down the driveway and told myself I'd have to be extra careful around her from now on.

Once I added up my tips, it was time to head to the mall to do my shopping. I had to buy presents for my parents, my sisters, and Uncle Ed. I figured seventy-six bucks would cover everything, plus maybe a little something special for myself.

"Are you sure you're going to be all right?" my mom asked me when we pulled up in front of Kmart. "Why don't I just come with you?"

"Because then you'll see what I get for you."

"I won't look, I promise. Besides, I can help you pick out something for the girls and your dad. And how will you know what to get for Uncle Ed?"

I knew my mom didn't really want to help me. She just gets all weird whenever I go anywhere by myself. She thinks something bad is going to happen to me, like a pervert is going to come up to me and ask if I want candy. I'll be reluctant at first, but he'll put the pressure on.

"C'mon," he'll say. "You know you want some."

Then he'll tell me to follow him out to his van.

"That's where the candy is," he'll say.

I'll be a bit nervous, but I'll go along. "He looks harmless enough," I'll say to myself.

But when we get to the van, the handsome stranger will push me inside and say "Game's over, kid." He'll tie me up and gag me and then take me back to his house and do perverted things to me. Things I can't even bear to think about—that's how perverted they are. After he's had his way with me, he'll drop me back off at the mall.

"If you tell anyone about this, kid, I'm gonna have to come back and do it to you again," he'll say.

"You can't scare me with your threats," I'll say.

"Oh yeah?" the handsome pervert will laugh. "Well, just watch your every move, kid, because I'll be back when you least suspect it."

"I'll be fine," I said to my mom. "If I need anything, Christine's at work. Just meet me back in front of Kmart at two o'clock."

"Do you have your whistle?"

My mom makes me wear a whistle around my neck when I go out in public alone. I tuck it under my clothes so no one can see it. I'm supposed to blow it if anyone takes my wallet or starts to follow me.

"Just drop everything and blow this whistle," my mom said when she first gave it to me. "For god's sake, Peter, blow it for all you're worth."

"Yes, I have my whistle," I said. "Meet me back here at two." I jumped out just as she was asking me if I had dimes for the payphone.

Once I got inside the doors at Kmart, I dug in my

pocket for the Christmas list I'd made out earlier that day.
I had to get a tie for my dad (because that's what I get him
every year), a pair of silver clip-on earrings for my mom, a
red and blue scarf for Nancy, a ten-dollar gift certificate for
Uncle Ed from Sam the Record Man, and a pair of black
leather gloves for Christine.

Kmart was pretty busy with holiday shoppers, but I
managed to squeeze my way through the crowds. First
off, I went to the jewellery department to find my mom's
earrings. They didn't have much of a selection and none
of the earrings were on sale, so I bought her a necklace
that was 50% off. At regular price, it was more expensive
than the earrings, so I was sure she'd like it.

Then I headed off to the ladieswear department to
find Nancy's scarf and Christine's gloves. I couldn't find
any red and blue scarves, even though Nancy wanted
something to match her new red jacket.

"I got this at Suzy Shier!" she screamed when she
brought it home.

I picked out a purple scarf because it was on sale.
Besides, red and purple go together, too. I'd have to
remind Nancy of that when I gave her the gift.

As I passed through the bra section on my way to the
glove section, I heard a woman and her daughter talking
in front of one of the displays.

"If I don't start now, they won't grow properly," the girl
was saying. She looked my age, maybe a year younger.

"Well, I don't think it's a life-or-death thing," her
mom said. "But let's get a training bra and you can try
that out and see how you like it."

I just about died! A training bra? I glanced over at the girl's chest. She was pretty flat—flatter than me, anyway. If she needed a bra, did I need one, too? And what did she mean when she said they wouldn't "grow properly"? I saw my nipples pointing in different directions, like Mr. Bertoli and his glass eye. Then I'd really be in a pickle.

I was so worried about my nipples that I just grabbed the first pair of gloves I saw for Christine, put them in my basket, and headed for the men's department on the other side of the store. I found a tie in a sale bin that I was sure my dad would like. Well, not that he'd really know the difference between a nice tie and an ugly one.

While I was in the men's department, I looked around to see if I could find anything for myself. But most of the clothes at Kmart aren't the same kind of quality that you get at Sears. Then I started wondering what I would buy for Mr. Hanlan for Christmas.

"What would Dan like from his favorite paperboy?" I asked myself. Before I knew it, I was standing right in the middle of the underwear section.

"I bet Dan would like these," I thought as I picked up a pair of red bikini underwear. They were very sexy. I knew Dan would appreciate them.

"Thanks," he'd say. "Maybe I should try them on to see if they fit. Can I count on you to tell me if they look okay?"

"I guess," I'd say and shrug, "if you really need a second opinion."

I started to feel pretty warm and dizzy so I put the red

bikinis back down. Then I checked my watch and realized I'd better get to the cash register.

All in all, I spent $42.64, which I thought was pretty
good. I still had to get Uncle Ed's gift certificate so I
headed into the mall.

As I passed Peoples, I glanced in to see if I could see
Christine, but she wasn't behind the counter. Maybe she
was on her break. Or maybe she was in back of the store,
polishing diamonds or whatever she does. Even if family
members *were* allowed to say "hi," I wouldn't have gone
in. I had too many important things to do.

After I picked up Uncle Ed's gift certificate, I decided
I was hungry. I checked my watch and saw that I still had
a half hour left before I had to meet my mom. Even
though I don't usually eat in public, I figured I'd just have
a small salad and be on my way before anyone noticed
me. Besides, I deserved to treat myself, seeing as how I got
everyone such great deals on their Christmas gifts.

When I got to the food court, my super-strong smelling
powers went into overdrive. I could smell french fries and
hamburgers and donuts and pizza. I changed my mind
about getting a small salad and ended up ordering a
cheeseburger, medium fries, and a medium Diet Coke
from the Burger Depot. I found a table in the far corner
of the food court and set my tray down. I was a bit
uncomfortable about sitting by myself, but then I figured
it made me seem mysterious. People started to notice me.

"Who's that?" they whispered to each other. "I've
never seen him before."

I sighed and popped a french fry in my mouth.

"I can't believe someone as good-looking as him would be eating alone. What's he all about?"

I pretended to be too interested in reading the Burger Depot tray liner to hear.

"Hey look! It's Peter Fattington."

Someone else said that. That voice didn't come from inside my head. Out of the corner of my eye, I could see a pair of blue jeans standing beside me.

"Having the pig trough special?" the voice asked. It was Brian Cinder. I heard someone else laugh. I didn't look up. I couldn't. I was too scared. The table jiggled as he sat down across from me.

"I'm doing you a favor," he said as he grabbed my fries. "The last thing you need is to gain more weight."

He was with Paul Roxbury, another member of the Banger Group. Paul grabbed my pop out of my hand. "This better be diet," he said.

My burger flip-flopped in my stomach and my heart was beating so fast I thought it was going to explode. And then I would die, right there in the Bluewater Mall food court, just a few days before Christmas, all because of Brian Cinder.

They finished off all of my food. Then Brian said it was time to hit the arcade. "You got any money?" he asked. I looked up at him and shook my head.

"You sure about that? Because if you're fuckin' lying to me, fat boy, I'll have to pound the shit out of you."

I gulped. I had shopping money left over in my wallet, but there was no way I was going to let him know that.

"I don't have any," I said.

"What was that?" Brian leaned across the table.

"I said I don't have any."

"I don't believe you. I'm gonna check your pockets, lardass. And if I find out you're lying to me, you're fuckin' dead."

I remembered the whistle around my neck. I felt it underneath my sweatshirt.

"C'mon," Paul said to Brian. "We don't have time. We were supposed to meet Michelle a half hour ago."

Brian sat there looking at me for a couple of seconds. He was chewing on his bottom lip. "All right," he said, getting up from the table. "Let's go. This pig's making me sick, anyway."

I watched them walk away. Just when I thought I was safe, Brian turned around and came back. "My lace is undone," he said.

There was no way I was going to bend down and tie his boot lace in the middle of the food court. There were too many people around. I didn't move. Brian stood there, looking at me.

"I said my lace is undone."

I kept my eyes on my tray. "Just blow the whistle," I thought. "Someone will come to help."

"Tie it."

Just blow the whistle. That's what it's for.

"Tie it!"

I slid from my chair and got down on one knee. My hands were shaking, so it was hard to tie the laces. It took me three times.

"Fuckin' fat pig," Brian said. Then he and Paul walked away.

I counted to sixty before I dared to look up from the tray liner. I scanned the food court, but they were gone. But where? They could still be in the mall. I had to make it back to Kmart to meet my mom. Could I do it without running into Brian? What if he beat me up in the middle of the mall? Getting up from that table was the hardest thing I've ever had to do, but I didn't have a choice. I started walking toward Kmart, quickly checking for Brian as I passed each store.

Brian Cinder was a loser, plain and simple. And he was poor—so poor he probably didn't have money to buy his own french fries. And he was ugly. And one day, one day...

Brian was in Pantorama! I started walking faster, my bags swinging along my sides. Then I remembered Christine. She was working. If Brian came after me, I could run into Peoples and tell Christine to call the police and I would be safe.

I checked over my shoulder and Brian was coming out of the store with Paul and Michelle Appleby. They were laughing so they must've seen me. They'd catch up to me any second and I didn't know what they'd do to me then.

"Christine," I said to myself and just as I reached the entrance of Peoples, I saw her. She was standing behind the counter, smiling and talking to an older woman. When she noticed me, her whole expression changed. It was like she was scared of me—almost as if I was going to come into the store and do something bad to her. I knew that family members weren't allowed in the store, but this was different. This was an emergency. Brian was heading straight toward me. Christine's boss would understand.

Christine mouthed two words to me.

"Go away."

I stood there for a second. Maybe Christine didn't understand the situation. Maybe she didn't realize.

"Go away." This time she looked angry.

I felt something fall inside me, like I had swallowed a cold stone. Brian and Paul and Michelle were still heading in my direction. So I turned and walked as fast as I could. I walked so fast that my ribs started to hurt and I thought I would faint. I walked so fast that my inner thighs started to burn. I walked so fast that for a second, I thought maybe I could disappear into the air. I made it past the bra section and the men's department, past the jewellery and finally out the doors. My mom wasn't there yet. I stood behind a phone booth and waited, trying to catch my breath.

"Did you get all your shopping done?" she asked me when she pulled up a few minutes later. "Did you talk to Christine? Did you see any friends from school?"

I clicked my seatbelt into the lock. "I didn't see anyone," I said.

• •

For New Year's Eve, my parents and I went to the Archers. Mr. Archer works with my dad in Chemical Valley. I don't think my dad and him are best friends or anything, but Mr. Archer and his wife were having people over.

"It beats sitting at home watching Dick Clark," my mom said.

"Might as well watch it at someone else's house," my dad said.

I'd only met the Archers a couple of times before. Mr. Archer is short and fat and old. He's always out of breath, so you think he's about to have a heart attack or something. Mrs. Archer is fat, too. She's younger than Mr. Archer, but I'm not sure by how much. Her name is Nadia and every time I see her, she's wearing a muumuu, like Mrs. Roper on *Three's Company*.

The Archers have two children—Kate and Billy. Both of them are adopted. My mom told me once that Kate and Billy are "behavioural" kids and that Mr. and Mrs. Archer are foster parents.

"I don't know how they do it," my mom said. "Opening their doors to all that chaos and such. Those kids come from such damaged homes."

I'd met Kate and Billy last year at the Chemical Valley Kid's Christmas party. It takes place every year in an old movie theater. They have musicians and a magician and a guy dressed like Santa comes in at the end to hand out crappy presents. This year's C.V.K.C. party was supposed to happen on December 15th, but there was some chemical spill in the Bluewater River that day, so the party was cancelled. But I wouldn't have gone anyway, because I'm too old to go to kid's parties now.

Kate Archer doesn't think she's too old to go to kid's parties, because when I saw her at last year's C.V.K.C., she looked the same age as Christine. She was fat, like

Mrs. Archer, so you'd think they're related, even though they're not. She had a pageboy haircut that didn't suit her and thick black glasses that made her eyes look humongous. Kate was pretty quiet and sat in a back corner all night long, sucking on candy canes. Billy, who's a year older than me, didn't look anything like her. I guess that makes sense, since they didn't come from the same parents. He was thin and had a gap between his front teeth and long, greasy hair. He kept running around the theater, tearing down the red and green streamers, yelling, "This sucks! This sucks!" over and over again.

Mrs. Archer kept trying to catch up to him. She was holding a pill in one hand and a glass of punch in the other.

"Now Billy," she kept saying. "Don't be like this. Take your pill. Now Billy."

Finally, one of the dads at the party grabbed Billy and put him in a headlock.

"I got the little punk now," he said. "You just try and get away from me, you little nut. I played for the Chicago Bears."

"There's no reason to be rough," Mrs. Archer said to the Bears man. "He's just a child, you know."

Billy kept trying to squeeze his way out from under the Bears man's arm.

"Lemme go," he was saying. "Lemme go, you big asshole."

Mrs. Archer managed to get the pill into Billy's mouth while he was in the headlock. She told the Bears man to let him go.

"He'll be fine in a couple of minutes," she said. By the time Santa came to deliver presents, Billy was sitting in the back corner beside Kate. He didn't do anything for the rest of the night except pick his nose and wipe the boogers under his seat.

• •

When my parents said that we'd been invited over to the Archers for New Year's Eve, I told them I didn't want to go.

"Can't I just stay home?" I said. "I'm feeling sick to my stomach."

That was partly true. Ever since Brian Cinder came up to me in the mall, I felt like my stomach was twisted up like a pretzel. Everywhere I went, I kept checking over my shoulder to make sure he wasn't behind me. I was so glad that school was out for the holidays, but I didn't know what I'd do when it was time to go back.

Besides, Billy Archer was a Banger. What if he knew Brian?

"Peter, you're too young to be home alone on New Year's Eve," my mom said. "If the girls were here with you, it would be different. But they're both going out."

"But Billy makes me nervous," I said.

"If he gives you any trouble, just tell us," my dad said.

"I'm sure they sedate him when company comes over," my mom said. "He'll probably be in his own world all night long."

I kept my fingers crossed that Billy wouldn't be home. Maybe he'd go out with some of his Banger friends and it would just be me and pageboy Kate. As we drove over, I almost convinced myself that everything *would* be okay and that I had nothing to worry about. Then we pulled into the Archers' driveway.

"What's that?" my mom shrieked. She was pointing toward the Archers' bushes.

Someone was in the front yard, crouched by the bushes, unscrewing the Christmas lights.

"Henry, do you think we should call the police?" my mom whispered as the last red bulb went out. Then Mrs. Archer came running out the front door, wearing a red and green striped muumuu and carrying a glass in her hand.

"Billy! Where are you?" she yelled. "Momma's got something for you!"

"I think we can hold off," my dad said.

Then the dark figure in the bushes took off down the street. Mrs. Archer didn't see because she had spotted our car in the driveway. She waved her arm at us.

"I was just stepping out for a breath of fresh air," she said as we came up the front steps. "Come in, come in! Let me take your coats for you."

Mrs. Archer looked over her shoulder before she shut the front door. "Awfully chilly out there tonight, isn't it?"

Mr. Archer was sitting in the living room. "Well, here comes trouble," he said and started to get up.

"Alfred, don't you dare get out of that chair!" Mrs. Archer said. "You know what the doctor said. And remember—no cocktail wieners for you. I mean it, Alfred. Honestly Beth, aren't men a handful? Now listen, you all have a seat and let me grab some drinks. Peter, is Pepsi okay for you?"

The Archers' house smelled like mothballs and Pepto Bismol. Mr. Archer was sitting in an orange chair with electrical tape on the arms. The couch was covered in plastic, so that when we sat down, we all made a crinkling sound. Even the cushions and lampshades were covered in plastic.

A deformed Christmas tree sat in the corner of the living room and the windows were divided into squares with electrician's tape and sprayed with fake snow. But whoever did it sprayed the opposite corners of the squares, so in one pane, the fake snow was in the bottom right corner and in another, the bottom left-hand corner. It looked like the Archers' living room had been hit by a blizzard from the inside.

"I guess we're the first ones here!" my mom said and laughed her fake laugh.

"Well, actually, you're the party," Mr. Archer said and burped into his fist. "Turns out everyone else we invited couldn't make it tonight. Too many other things going on this evening, I guess."

"Oh," my mom said.

"I hope you brought your appetites with you!" Mrs. Archer said, coming back into the room with a tray. "Because we certainly have enough food to feed an army!" She laughed a fake laugh, too. "Beth, try some of my shrimp ring. I made the cocktail sauce myself. I got the recipe from *TV Guide*, so I hope it tastes all right."

"Holy Christ, Peter," Mr. Archer said, "you're getting to be a big fella, aren't you? You got him signed up for football yet, Henry?"

"Well, maybe one day," my dad said.

"Stand up for a second, Peter," Mr. Archer said. "Jesus. Thighs on you the size of redwoods."

I tried to smile because I figured that Mr. Archer was only trying to be nice, but most people don't take the Lord's name in vain when complimenting people. He shook his head.

"Like a brick house," he said and whistled. I sat back down.

"Now Alfred, you leave him alone," Mrs. Archer said. "Peter, why don't you go downstairs to the rec room? Just go through the kitchen and take the stairs. There's some chips on the coffee table and Kate is down there, watching TV. I'm sure Billy will be joining you in a bit. He had to run to the store to get me something."

I didn't move off the couch.

"Go on, Peter," my mom said and gave me a nudge, "don't be shy."

"This may be the last time you see me alive," I said to my parents through a mental telepathy message. My feet felt as heavy as bricks as I made my way past everyone and into the kitchen. I made a pit stop at the table. There were bowls of pretzels and chips, a cheese ball, a plate of cocktail wieners with toothpicks sticking out of them like little flagpoles, a crock pot of meatballs, a platter of Fig Newtons, chocolate haystacks, shortbread cookies with bits of green maraschino cherries on top, and a plate of celery and carrot sticks with dip. I helped myself to a couple of Fig Newtons, making sure that I rearranged the platter so it didn't look like anything was missing.

Then I went downstairs.

Kate was sitting on the couch with a big bowl of chips in her lap. She was wearing one of her mom's muumuus. Unfortunately, she still had that pageboy.

"Hi," I said. I felt kind of awkward.

"Hi," Kate said. She didn't even take her eyes off the TV.

The Archers' basement was even tackier than their living room. There wasn't any carpeting, just a cement floor with wood paneling on the walls, an ugly brown couch and chair, an old television, a ping-pong table, and a stereo inside a milk crate.

"What are you watching?" I asked, sitting down on the other side of the couch.

"Television," she said. "You ever heard of it?"

"Um, yes. We have two. But one is black-and-white."

"Chips are in the cupboard in the laundry room. Go crazy."

"You keep chips in the laundry room?" I asked. "Isn't that a little strange?"

Kate turned to me. "Have you met my mother?"

I grabbed three bags and came back.

"There are more chips in that cupboard than at the 7-Eleven," I said and sat down on the opposite end of the couch. I cracked open a bag of BBQ chips. I started to feel more comfortable. "Sour cream and onion is my favorite flavor, although BBQ comes in at a close second. What's your favorite?"

"Do I look like I discriminate?" Kate asked and smashed more chips into her mouth.

We sat there, crunching away for a couple of minutes.

I tried to think about topics to talk about.

"Do you have any New Year's resolutions?"

"Yeah," Kate said, "I'm aiming for a bigger ass."

I could see this wasn't going anywhere. I thought about asking her if she was always this perky when a loud crash came from upstairs. I heard Mrs. Archer saying, "You clean that up, young man! Do you hear me? Here, take this pill first."

Then something came roaring down the stairs and the next thing I knew, Billy was standing in the basement doorway. He looked the same as the last time I saw him, but his hair was even longer and greasier. Billy looked at Kate and then at me, then back to Kate and back to me.

"Who's your new boyfriend?" he asked and started to laugh.

"Screw off, asshole," Kate said. "Can you act civilized for once? We have company over. This is…"

"Peter."

"Right. This is Peter. His favorite chip flavor is sour cream and onion. And Peter, this vision before you is the antichrist."

Billy really *did* look like the antichrist. He was wearing a black and white Def Leppard concert T-shirt, tight red parachute pants with black triangles, and a red bandanna tied around his wrist. I also noticed he was wearing a gold chain with a shark tooth pendant. I wondered why all Bangers wear shark tooth pendants.

"Hi," I said. "I think I met you once last year. At the Chemical Valley Christmas party?"

"That party sucked," Billy said. He went over to the

stereo and began to pull record albums out. "Where's my Def Leppard album? Where is it? Did you take it, buttface?"

Kate didn't say anything. She just kept eating her chips and staring at the TV. I didn't know what to do, so I stared at the TV, too. I thought that maybe if we ignored Billy, he'd go away.

"All he wants is attention," my mom had said to me on the car ride over. "He's hyperactive, like a Mexican jumping bean. But if you ignore him, he'll leave you alone."

But Billy wasn't going anywhere. He put a record on and turned it up full blast. I think it was Foreigner. Nancy has the same album at home. Billy started jumping up and down on the armchair, pretending to play the guitar.

"Rock it!" he kept yelling. "Rock it all night long!"

"You are such a moron!" Kate yelled. "Turn off the stereo! I mean it!"

But Billy didn't do anything except scream "Rock it!"

"You are such a little shit! Turn it off! We have fucking company!"

Billy kept jumping. I stared at the television.

"You're an asshole!" Kate screamed. Her face was purple. "A motherfucking asshole!"

She got up off the couch and stormed out, taking her big bowl of chips with her. That meant I was alone with Billy, who by that time was doing jumping jacks in the middle of the room.

I thought I'd make a break for it, but Billy shut the rec room door.

"Thank god," he yelled over the music. "She bugs me."

He sat down where Kate had been.

"You like my pants?" he asked.

I thought they were tacky, but I didn't want Billy to beat me up.

"Yes," I said as loudly as I could without yelling, "they're very nice."

"They're my rocker pants," Billy said and hopped up again, playing his fake guitar.

"Rock it! Rock it!"

I kept wondering how I was going to get out of there. If Billy went to my school, he'd be best friends with Brian Cinder. I thought about that day a few weeks ago when Brian made me tie his shoelace in the food court. Now, there I was in the basement with someone who could be the president of Banger Groups everywhere. It was a very scary situation. My palms were sweating buckets.

"You listen to Def Leppard?" Billy asked.

"Yeah," I lied, "all the time."

"What's your favorite Leppard song?"

"Uh, the first one," I said. "The first one on the album."

"Yeah, that one rocks!"

Billy went over to the stereo and turned it off.

"I'm bored," he said.

"Do you want to watch something on TV?" I asked. I looked at the clock above the television. It was only 10:00 p.m. I was stuck at the Archers for another two hours at least. I wondered where Kate had gone. Was she sitting upstairs in the living room with the adults? If so, why didn't my parents come and rescue me from psycho Billy or at least call down to see if I was okay?

Or what if Kate had gone straight to her room and no one upstairs noticed?

Or what if the Archers were *all* crazy, just like Billy? What if other people *had* shown up for the party and the Archers had poisoned them and stuffed their bodies into the deep freezer? I sent my parents a mental telepathy message.

"Don't eat the shrimp cocktail!" I screamed as loudly as I could in my head.

"TV sucks," Billy said, sitting down beside me on the couch.

"You don't watch TV?" I asked him.

I checked the clock. It was 10:01 p.m.

"TV's boring," he said. He picked up a couple of pencils that were on the coffee table. "I'd rather rock." He started rapping the pencils on the coffee table like they were drumsticks. I was getting a headache.

Billy was very annoying, but at the same time, he was sitting very close to me. I started to feel a little sexy and snuck a couple of peeks at Billy's pants, even though they were ugly.

I decided I should get out of there before Billy caught me looking at his pants or before he started spazzing out again.

"I think I'll go upstairs," I said. "My parents probably want to check up on me."

Billy stopped playing the coffee table and looked at me.

"You drink?" he asked.

"I've got a Pepsi already, thanks."

"No, stupid. Like beer and shit. I can make a couple of Jungle Juices. Stay there."

Then he took off. I thought I should make a run for it while he was gone. I didn't know what a Jungle Juice was. But I stayed there on the couch, because part of me was getting excited. It was just the way that Billy said, "Stay there." It was almost like he liked me.

"Maybe Billy could be my new boy friend," I thought. We could go to the mall together and to the movies. We'd eat in the food court and if anyone ever made fun of me, he'd walk right over and pound the crap out of them. And he'd always take his pill whenever I was around. In fact, he wouldn't take it from anyone else but me.

Billy came back downstairs with two glasses. "Try it," he said, handing me one, "it's really good."

I took a sniff and almost barfed. "What's in here?" I asked him.

"Everything," Billy said and sat down next to me again. "Rum, some vodka, some orange juice, and some white wine. Squeeze your nose before you take a drink. That way, you can drink more and get drunk faster."

I watched Billy pinch his nostrils and take a big gulp. I did the same. I almost gagged, but by the time I went for my second drink, it was a bit better. Besides, I didn't want to disappoint Billy. He made the drink for me, after all.

After a few more drinks, I started thinking in a weird way. I felt like picking up the phone and calling Andrew Sinclair and saying, "I don't need you anymore. I have a new boy friend."

"Do you have a phone book down here?" I asked Billy.

"No," he said. "Why do you want one? Man, I am soo bombed!"

"Yeah," I said. "Me, too." I think I really was bombed. I took another drink and snuck a peek at Billy's pants. They were very tight.

"You got a girlfriend?" Billy asked.

"No," I said. "Not right now, anyway. There's a couple of girls in my class that like me, but, you know how it is."

I'm not sure if Billy believed me or not. He just belched and nodded.

"You ever make out with a girl?" he asked.

"Um, not really," I said. "I mean, not… y'know… really."

"You ever suck on a girl's tits?"

"Um, well, I mean, I think you'd have to kiss a girl before she… um… let you suck on her… um… tits and all, right?"

"Not necessarily," Billy said. "Man, I'm bombed. I'm gonna pass out."

Billy fell back on the couch so that his foot was touching my thigh and closed his eyes. I just sat there, looking at his foot. I'd never been this close to another boy before, not even the time I took mouth-to-mouth resuscitation in Cubs. Even then, you couldn't practise on an actual person. We had to use a dummy named Sam, who tasted like plastic and rubbing alcohol.

I couldn't move. Everything in the house got really quiet. I couldn't even hear the TV anymore, only the sound of my heart. It was beating so loudly, I thought it would break through my ribs. My nipples started vibrating. I knew I should get up and go, that this might be my only chance at freedom. But I was still feeling dizzy. I was afraid of falling and cracking my head open on the coffee table or something. And I didn't want to wake Billy up or make it so that we weren't touching anymore. I just wanted to sit there on the couch all night long.

"Put your hand on his leg," my nipples whispered from beneath the tape.

"No," I said. "That's wrong."

"He touched you first," they said.

"No," I said again. My nipples were evil. "It's wrong."

But my nipples took control of my hand and the next thing I knew, it was on Billy's ankle.

"Stop it!" I whisper/screamed to my nipples. "He's going to wake up at any second!"

It didn't do any good. My nipples had a mind of their own. I watched as my hand moved further and further up Billy's red pant leg and past the black triangles. And then, my hand stopped over Billy's dink. I couldn't catch my breath and I was afraid I'd start coughing and then Billy would wake up and give me a knuckle sandwich.

"Take my hand away," I told my nipples.

"But then he might wake up," they said.

My nipples had a point. It was better just to leave it there.

"That's my new boy friend's dink," I thought as I stepped out of the car. I don't have time to stop and talk, Billy. I have a photo shoot to get to! But what choice do I have with a broken-down car? I run my fingers through my hair and lift the hot chocolate to my lips. Who put marshmallows in here? I said I wanted small ones! Why doesn't anyone listen to me?

I couldn't pinch my nose with one hand on Billy's dink and the other one around my glass, so I just closed my eyes. But as soon as I took a drink, my tongue swelled up like a balloon and I felt something like a sneeze coming on, only it wasn't a sneeze. I jumped up from the couch, yanked the rec room door open and made it to the laundry room sink just in time to puke my guts out. I could see bits and pieces of Fig Newton's and chips.

"Oh Mr. Hanlan," I whispered through my coughs. "Poison. How could you poison me?"

"I wanted you all to myself."

"You didn't have to kill me." My stomach felt like an accordion. "I'm going to tell Andrew and he'll get the Mafia after you."

I thought I was going to die. But somehow, I managed to turn on the faucet and wash most of my puke down the drain. I stayed there for a few minutes, hunched over the sink. I'd never felt so awful in my life.

"Have to get back to Billy," I said. "He needs to take his medication."

I stumbled back into the rec room. Billy was gone. The couch was empty. I looked around the room to see if he was hiding somewhere, but he was nowhere.

"Kidnapped?" I wondered. I lifted the couch cushions, looking for a ransom note. Why would Mr. Hanlan do something like that?

"If I can't have you, no one can."

"Stop it! Billy is innocent! He's my boy friend. You're going to have to set me free, Dan."

I slowly walked up the stairs to the kitchen and ate a haystack to try to get rid of the puke taste in my mouth. Then I went into the living room.

When my mom saw me, she said, "Oh my Lord, Peter," and came running over. "What happened?"

"I think I have an idea," Mrs. Archer said, waving her hand in front of her nose.

"I think we'd better take you home, young man," my dad said. "We can talk about this tomorrow."

"But I have to tell you what Dan did."

"What?"

"He kidnapped him. We've got to find him."

"He's talking nonsense," I heard Mr. Archer say.

Mrs. Archer went to the bedroom to get our coats. "I'm so sorry about this, Beth. Really I am. I should've been checking in on them. I thought Kate was down there with them."

"Oh my Lord, Peter," my mom said again, "you smell terrible." She wasn't even paying any attention to Mrs. Archer, who by that time was passing our coats to us.

My mom was pretty emotional on the way home.

"That is the last time we are ever going to that house!" she said to my dad. "I don't care if we ever see those people again. Do you think it was a coincidence that no one could make it to the party, Henry? Do you? Hmm?"

"Now Beth…"

"Don't 'now Beth' me, Henry! I don't want Peter associating with kids like that."

I was having problems sitting up because I was still so dizzy, so I lay down in the back seat, watching the streetlights as we drove by them. They seemed like stars to me.

When we pulled up to our house, I looked out the window and saw the shadow of someone in our front yard.

"It's Billy," I thought to myself. "He's come back for me."

I wanted to jump out of the car, tell him to run away, Billy, run away before they catch you. Then I realized that the shadow was only the Virgin Mary cut-out my dad and I had put up in the front yard a few weeks ago. The spotlight had gone out.

• •

When I woke up the next morning, I had an awful headache and my mom gave me an aspirin with ginger ale.

"You just stay in bed," she told me. "Better to sleep this off."

But I couldn't go back to sleep. I just lay in bed, thinking about the night before. It all seemed like a dream, like I didn't really have my hand over Billy's dink. What if he was angry at me? What if he told his mom about what happened?

"I was just lying there, sleeping. The next thing I knew, the pervert had his hand on my nuts. I think we should call the police."

But maybe he didn't feel that way. What if he knew what was happening? Maybe he was thinking about me, too. Maybe right at that very moment, he was lying in bed, listening to Def Leppard and wondering if I was okay.

I knew one thing for sure. The Virgin had used my nipples to trick me. She told them to test me to see if I was worthy of being healed. And I had failed. Now, the Virgin would never cure me. I looked down at my nipples and squeezed them hard. I hated them. Why did they make me do these terrible things?

"You wanted to do it," they said.

"I didn't," I said.

"Did too."

"Shut up!" I said and before they could say another thing, I stumbled to my closet and grabbed the roll of masking tape from beneath my sweaters and taped my nipples up good and tight.

"Take that," I told them.

"Mmph!" they said.

Before I put the tape away, I took my Yoda poster down from the wall above my bed and stuck it to my closet door.

I didn't like the Virgin staring at me anymore.

BEDTIME MOVIE #4

I'm the most famous singer in the whole world.

"You're the brightest star in the biz, kid," my manager tells me. He looks like Jameson Parker, the blond brother from the TV show *Simon and Simon*.

"I'm still the same person I always was," I tell him. I'm signing black-and-white pictures of myself. "Fame hasn't changed me."

One day, while I'm in the studio recording another

best-selling album, Jameson comes in and hands me a
letter.

"I think you should read this," he says.

"Can't it wait?" I ask.

"This one is different," Jameson says. He sounds concerned, so I take the letter from him.

It's from Mrs. Archer. She tells me that Billy is very
sick and won't take his medication. She says he's my
biggest fan and that if I could come visit Billy, he might
listen to me and take his pills.

"You're our only hope," she writes. "Billy is depending
on you. We all are."

I sigh and run my hands through my long, thick
hair.

"Book me on the next flight to Bluewater," I tell Jameson.

When I arrive at the airport, there's a huge crowd of
fans waiting for me. As I step off the plane, they start
screaming my name. I'm wearing a pair of black sunglasses and a long brown coat. I wave to my fans and stop
to pose for a couple of pictures for the *Bluewater Observer*
photographer. Then a limo picks me up and takes me to
the Archers' house.

Mrs. Archer is standing in the doorway when the limo
pulls up. She's wearing a red muumuu and looks very
worried.

"Thank God you're here," she says to me. "Billy's
downstairs. Would you like a Fig Newton before you go
down? I know they're your favorite."

I smile in a tired way and tell Mrs. Archer thanks, but
no thanks.

"Nadia, you don't get to be as good-looking as me by eating Fig Newtons all day long."

Billy is sleeping on the couch. He's wearing his red parachute pants and looks very weak.

"Billy," I whisper, "it's me. I'm here."

Billy's eyes open and I can tell how surprised he is to see me. He thinks he's dreaming.

"Is it really you?" he asks me.

"Yes, it's really me, Billy," I say. "Your mom is very concerned about you. She said you won't take your medication and that you're dying."

"I have all your albums," Billy says.

I laugh softly and say thank you. Billy asks me if I'll sit down next to him, so I do. He asks me when my new record will be in stores and do I notice a difference between my American fans and my international ones?

"I'm so glad you came," Billy says. "I feel better already."

Then he takes my hand and squeezes it. It's a bold move on his part. I'm not really sure how to react.

"You mean so much to me," Billy says. He closes his eyes. "Remember that time you were here on New Year's Eve?"

I say, "I'm not sure."

"Yes, you do. That was the best New Year's Eve ever. Remember how we listened to Def Leppard and rocked it?"

"I guess so," I say. I'm starting to get a bit nervous. I have a plane to catch in five minutes. I don't have time to listen to Billy's stupid stories.

"Remember how I made those Jungle Juices?"

I pull my hand away from his and check my watch.

Outside, the limo driver honks. He's getting impatient.

"Remember how after we drank them, you put your hand on me?" Billy asks. "Over my dink? You thought I didn't know, but I did. I wasn't sleeping."

I stand up. "Billy, I don't know what you're talking about. You're hallucinating."

"No, I'm not," Billy says. His eyes are still closed, but somehow, he finds my hand and grabs it again. "Please sit down. I haven't got much time left."

"That makes two of us," I sigh, but I sit down next to him. He *is* dying, after all.

"I wanted it," Billy whispers. "I wanted your hand on my dink. It felt good. I didn't want you to take your hand away."

"Billy, please..." I must get away. The limo honks twice. I have to get back to the recording studio.

"The only way I'll get better is if you put your hand there again," Billy says. "You don't want me to die, do you?"

"Well, no..."

"Then do it. Please. Save me."

Then Billy takes my hand and puts it over his dink. He presses my hand against the material of his red parachute pants. "Just keep it there," he says. "Keep it there until I start to feel better again. That's all I ask."

I look up at Billy. His eyes aren't closed anymore. They're open.

Then I fall asleep.

eight

I can't get Billy Archer out of my head. Every morning when I wake up, I wonder if he's waking up at that moment, too. When I come home for lunch, I wonder what he's eating that day. When I'm doing my homework at night, I think about how Billy isn't all that bright and how he could use a tutor—maybe me—to help him. And every time I put the showerhead on my dink to make sperm, I think about Billy and his parachute pants. The showerhead is evil and it makes me think things I don't want to think. Back in 7th grade, after I discovered how the showerhead could make me feel if I left it on my dink for a few minutes at just the right angle, I was the cleanest kid in Bluewater.

"*Another* shower?" my mother would ask. "You just had one this morning."

I was in the shower two, sometimes three times a day. Now when I look back on it, I'm lucky no one found out what I was *really* doing in there. Since then, I've calmed down a little bit and gotten smarter. Instead of showers, I tell my mother I'm taking baths, which makes her less suspicious. Then I use the showerhead to fill up the tub.

Anyways, I made a New Year's resolution not to use the showerhead in that way anymore, because it really is The Devil's Instrument, as Mr. Mitchell might say. And I felt like it was the one thing I could do to get into the Virgin's good books again, considering what happened between me and Billy. But I only lasted until January 3rd, which I know must've disappointed the Virgin. But I've decided I'll quit on my fourteenth birthday, which is just around the corner.

I feel very bad about what happened with Billy because my nipples were right. I had the chance to make a real boy friend and I blew it. All this month, there's been a dark cloud over my head. I almost lost my appetite a couple of times. It's that bad.

"What's wrong with you?" my mom asked me the other day. "You hardly say a word to me anymore." Then she gasped and pressed her hand against her chest. "Are you on drugs?" she whisper/screamed.

I rolled my eyes and said no. "I'm fine."

"Well, just remember. If anyone ever offers you drugs, you just walk away. Do you understand?"

I grabbed a Pop-Tart out of the cupboard and went to my room.

The trouble is that I know I will never be friends with Billy Archer. Or Andrew Sinclair. Or Craig Brown. Or any other boy in my class. And then what? I'll be the only freshman boy without a locker partner.

• •

My mother is upset at the Catholics again. Not because of

the cars parked along our street on Saturday nights and Sunday mornings, but because the students of Our Lady of Perpetual Hope High School are putting on *The Sound of Music.*

"I mean, honestly!" she said, flipping down her *Observer.* "I don't see why your sisters' school can't put on musicals. Sometimes I have to wonder if Catholics are Catholic just to make everyone else feel inferior."

Then she called to order tickets.

The day of the show, Mrs. Randall, the woman my mother planned to go with, called to cancel.

"Female problems," my mom whisper/screamed. "Now what am I going to do?"

My dad couldn't go with her, since he had to work the night shift. Something told me he was pretty relieved about that.

"I guess I could try calling Mary or Janet," my mom said, "but it's kind of late notice. There's Mrs. LaFlamme, too, but she gets so easily agitated, Henry. What if there are strobe lights?"

"Why don't you take your son?" my dad asked.

I froze.

"Peter? He wouldn't want to go out with his mom." Then she turned to me. "Would you?"

I don't like the idea of going anywhere with my mom, especially places where I might be seen. Going out in public with your parents is like screaming, "I have no friends!" And maybe I don't, but that's not the point. It's better not to be seen at all than to be seen with your parents.

But then I thought back to that morning. My mom

kept slapping the thermostat with a tea towel, screaming, "Who keeps playing with this? Who keeps playing with this?"

We all told my mom that none of us had touched it, which was the truth. But she called us liars and said that we were all plotting against her and Jesus Murphy, could somebody please open a window in here before she melts?

So I did the right thing—I shrugged and said, "I guess so."

"Well, it's a date then!" my mom said. "Me and my son. How nice is that? Maybe people will think we're a couple!"

Then she started laughing, but I didn't find it very funny. Actually, I thought it was gross. Moms shouldn't joke about things like that with their sons.

"You owe me big time," I said to my dad through a mental telepathy message.

• •

I wasn't sure what to wear to the musical, since most of my clothing has been getting tighter. I think it's the way my mom does the laundry. I ended up picking one of my favorite sweaters—a black and blue checked wool one—and my black rugby pants. I made sure I taped my nipples up good and tight and then I put on some of my dad's Old Spice for a nice touch.

"Oh my, don't you smell heavenly," my mom said. She was wearing a green dress with gold earrings.

"Ready for your date?" Christine asked. She was sitting in the living room, painting her nails.

"Shut up!" I yelled. I was still angry at Christine for what she did to me at the mall before Christmas. I had barely said two words to her since then.

"Do you kids always have to fight?" my mom asked. She was re-reading her driving route for the hundredth time. "Come on, Peter. We have to hurry up. We're running late."

We weren't late, since we still had a half hour to get to the school. But since my mom had to take every side street in Bluewater to get there, it was going to take a while.

"I always loved the theater," she said, as we turned right onto Lorne Crescent. "Especially when I was your age, Peter. I had roles in a number of school plays. Did I ever tell you that?"

I nodded.

"Never a starring role, mind you. Just scenery. Trees, mainly. But that's the wonderful thing about theater— every person's role is just as important as the next. Oh sure, I'd get jealous from time to time. The bark costumes were always so uncomfortable and talk about sore arms! But then I would think, 'Without me, the wolf would have no place to hide and then Little Miss Perfect Riding Hood would never get eaten.' That always made me feel better."

We turned right onto Wellington Road.

"You like the theater, too, Peter. You're just like me."

My mom was only saying that because I signed up for a drama class at the college a few years back. Our teacher, Mrs. Tipperwhirl, was from England and wore a red wig.

She had this thing against shoes and made everyone wear Chinese slippers to class.

"It cuts down on the clutter of your little feet," she would say, rubbing her temples.

There were about twenty kids in the class. Some of them were nice, but most were annoying. One girl named Nikki had a thing for cats. I think she thought she was one, because no matter what role we were playing, she'd purr and pretend to clean herself.

Mrs. Tipperwhirl carried around a tambourine and would bang it to get our attention. Sometimes, she had us do the dumbest things.

"You're a bird!" she would yell and bang her tambourine. We would flap our arms while she walked around us. "Let me see those big, beautiful wings riding on the wind! So proud, so free!" Then she'd hit the tambourine again and tell us we were rocks. We'd have to fall to the floor and curl into lumps. I made an excellent rock, because I would lie very still and pretend my skin was hard as steel.

"Excellent," Mrs. Tipperwhirl would say. "Such strong, silent rocks. Nikki! Rocks don't purr."

Anyways, toward the end of the course, I started gaining weight. And the idea of stepping on stage with everyone watching me freaked me out. So I didn't sign up the following year. But when I'm skinny and popular in high school, I might get back into the world of theater. You never know.

"I even dreamed of being a star one day," my mom laughed as we turned right onto East Street. "Can you imagine? Of course, I wasn't pretty enough. Or skinny enough. Or talented enough. And I knew that. But somehow, I just figured that didn't matter. Until, of course, I came to the realization it did."

I kept my eyes on the road.

"But that's the way life is sometimes, Peter. You spend all your time up in the clouds until, one day, reality decides to pull you back down." She sighed.

The parking lot at Our Lady of Perpetual Hope was pretty full by the time we got there, but we managed to find a spot and take our seats in the auditorium before the play started. It was weird being in a Catholic school and I thought about the time Daniela took me to St. Michael's. I kept looking around for the hanging lantern that lets you know if God is there, but I didn't see one.

"It smells funny in here," my mom said as we took our seats. "I thought Catholics were supposed to be clean."

The lights went down and the pianist came out. I wondered if he knew Mrs. Forbisher and how many breakdowns he'd had during rehearsals. I wasn't very impressed with the scenery on stage. It looked fake and when the nuns came out and started to sing "How Do You Solve a Problem Like Maria?" one had a voice so high that it hurt my ears. I heard someone behind me whisper, "For the love of God." As if that wasn't bad enough, another nun said her lines like a robot. I kept checking her back for the fuse box.

"It's going to be a long night," I thought to myself.

Then Maria ran onstage and changed everything.

From the minute she opened her mouth, I could tell

the actress playing Maria was different from the others. She had star quality. She was very beautiful too, and reminded me of Brooke Shields. Her blue eyes sparkled under the lights and even though she was dressed in black, she looked like an angel.

"A dark angel," I thought and sat up straighter in my chair.

When she sang "I Have Confidence in Me," I knew I was falling in love with the woman onstage. She had the best voice I've ever heard and was so sweet, spinning around with her suitcase in her hand. I knew then that whoever she was, Maria was the kind of girl that I could spend my life with. She'd never get angry or tell me what to do and would always whisper "I love you" before we went to sleep at night. Everyone would want to be her friend, because she was so nice. But she'd want to be with me and me only.

"He needs me beside me. And I need him," she'd say and smile.

Maria was the one that I'd been looking for. She was the one that could cure me of the bad things about myself. With one smile, she would heal my nipples, stop the Bedtime Movies, and help me forget all about Billy Archer. We'd run off and elope and when we got back into town, she'd show off the diamond ring to all of her friends. Maria would also get me plenty of boy friends and all of them would be jealous, because I had Maria and they didn't. They'd see that they were wrong about me all along.

When the intermission came, I read in the program

that Maria was being played by Debbie Andover. Her biography said she was a senior at Our Lady of Perpetual Hope and her favorite subject was religion. When she graduates, Ms. Andover hopes to pursue a career in either cosmetics or missionary work. Ms. Andover is thrilled to be playing the part of Maria and thanks her family and friends for their love and support.

I kept imagining my name in her biography.

"That Maria girl is good," my mom said to me as we stood out in the hall. "She has a nice voice. Better than that von Trapp fellow, anyway. Isn't he supposed to be bald? Or maybe I'm thinking of *Annie*. Is that the one where there's a ship?"

I was angry at my mom. Debbie wasn't just good— she was perfect, and one day, she would be a big movie star.

When the play ended, Debbie got the loudest applause. Someone came onstage and gave her a bouquet of roses. I wondered if she has a boyfriend and if she does, I bet he's a jerk who spends more time playing football with his friends than taking her out on dates. But Debbie would never complain. She's too classy for that. Instead, she would cry in bed each night, wishing that someone better would come along. That someone was me.

On the car ride home, I felt relieved that I'd finally fallen in love with a girl. It was something I'd needed to do for a long time. Especially since I was going to be fourteen in a couple of weeks.

That night, while I was lying in bed, I read Debbie's biography over and over again. I wondered what she was doing at that moment. Was she lying in her bed, too? Was she crying because her jerk boyfriend had forgotten about her opening night?

"What's the big deal?" he'd say to her. "It's just some stupid play."

But to Debbie, it wasn't. It was her whole life. She wanted her boyfriend to see her doing what she did best. She wanted him to see her in a way he never had before. And I knew what that felt like more than anyone else.

"I see you, Debbie," I whispered, hoping that wherever she was, she heard my voice. "I see you."

• •

My birthday is next week and I get to pick where we go for dinner. It's a tradition in my family.

"Within reason, of course," my mom said. "We can't afford to take you all to Walker's, so don't even think about it."

Walker's is Bluewater's fanciest restaurant. They have linen tablecloths and the waiters wear black bow ties. Or so I've heard. I've never been inside. Daniela went there once for her cousin Angela's wedding anniversary. She told me that they even have someone who carries around a small brush and wipes the crumbs off the tablecloth while you're eating.

"Now that's fuckin' class," Daniela said and whistled. "I bet the guy makes a hundred thousand a year just for doing that. More than my dad will ever make."

Sometimes, I feel bad for Mr. Bertoli because his restaurant isn't that busy. Daniela says her mom is worried about paying the bills. The other day, I walked by Papa Bertoli on my way to the Shop 'N' Bag and I saw Mr. Bertoli sitting at the counter. There wasn't one other person in the restaurant. He looked awfully lonely and I wondered how he'd survive. Maybe there was a way I could help him out. So when it came time to pick the place for my birthday dinner, I said what my Christian heart knew was right.

"I want to go to Papa Bertoli."

"Oh Peter, be serious," my mother said.

"I am being serious," I said. "I want to go to Papa Bertoli."

"Henry, will you please try talking some sense into your son?"

"Why? What's wrong with going there?"

"Well for one, you don't like Italian food and secondly, it's dirty."

"How do you know it's dirty?" I asked.

"Oh, you can just tell about those kinds of places." My mother shuddered.

"For the record," I said, "the Bertoli's house reeks of Lysol. So much so that you can taste it in your mouth. So I know for a fact that the restaurant would be the same."

"Lysol linguine," my mother said. "Now *that* sounds tasty."

She knew she wouldn't win because it was my birthday and she had to respect my choice. The same went for Nancy and Christine.

"Of all the restaurants in Bluewater, you pick *that* one?" That was from Nancy.

"I won't order anything." That was from Christine. "Just so you know."

I grabbed the telephone book and dialed the phone number. It rang twice before Mr. Bertoli picked up.

"Allo?"

"Is this Mr. Bertoli?"

"Yes."

"Hello, Mr. Bertoli. This is Peter Paddington."

"Who?"

"From across the street. Peter the paperboy. I'm calling to make reservations," I said proudly.

"You calla for what?"

"Reservations," I said, more loudly. "To make a reservation. For six people. Do you have a table available for Friday night? Say 5:30?"

There was silence on the other end. I wondered if he was too choked up to say anything.

"Hello?"

"Daniela?"

"Yeah. Who's this?"

"Peter."

"Why the fuck are you calling here?"

"To make a reservation at your dad's restaurant."

"A what?"

I rolled my eyes. "Look, my family will be coming there Friday night for 5:30. There'll be six of us."

"Why?"

"Because it's my birthday and I thought it would be nice."

"Oh. Well, if you want." Then she hung up.

With service like that, it's no wonder the restaurant wasn't doing too well.

• •

By the time Friday night rolled around, I wasn't sure if I still wanted to go to Papa Bertoli or not. I'd forgotten about that new Chinese restaurant on Maxwell Street. But it was too late to change plans.

"I still don't think this is funny," my mother said as we pulled up in front of the restaurant. Nancy, Christine, and I were squished in the back seat. Uncle Ed was meeting us there.

"It's not a joke," I said as we piled out of the car. Mr. Bertoli was holding the door open for us. He looked so happy.

"Atsa nice, atsa nice!" he called as each of us walked by him.

"Hello, Mr. Bertoli!" my mother yelled. "Nice to see you!"

Daniela was standing behind the counter, wearing an apron and her hairnet. I smiled at her as we sat down at the table, but she didn't even look at me, not even when she came to fill up our water glasses.

"We're expecting another person," my mother yelled at Mr. Bertoli. "My brother. He's always late, though, Mr. Bertoli." She laughed her company laugh and Mr. Bertoli said, "Atsa nice!"

Nancy gave Christine a nudge and pointed at the "Map of Italy" paper placemat.

"How are you doing tonight, Daniela?" my mother asked.

"Okay," Daniela said. "Specials are chicken parmigiana with pasta for $7.95 and meatloaf with potatoes for $6.95. Includes pie, too."

"What's in the news?" Uncle Ed came through the door. His face was as red as a tomato. "It's freezing out there. Say," he said, pulling off his gloves. "This isn't a bad place." He turned to Mr. Bertoli. "How long you been here again?"

Mr. Bertoli smiled and nodded.

"Who's this pretty young lady?" Uncle Ed pointed toward Daniela.

"That's Daniela, Ed," my mother said. "Now leave her alone and decide what you want to eat. She's just about to take our order. My goodness. I don't know where to begin." She did another fake laugh. "Everything just looks so tasty! Is the fish fresh, Daniela?"

"Fresh out of the freezer," Daniela said. "I'll be back in a couple of minutes."

In the end, everyone ordered the meatloaf except for Nancy and Christine, who both ordered garden salads.

"It's quite moist, actually," my mom whispered halfway through the meal. "I didn't think Eye-talians could make meatloaf."

I couldn't figure out what was up with Daniela. She barely spoke two words to me the whole night. And here I thought I was doing her a favor. We could've spent our money someplace else. Now, she might have a chance of going to college, thanks to me.

When we came back home, my mom brought out my birthday cake.

"Peter is a man today!" my mom said, putting the cake

down on the table in front of me. It was chocolate and covered with shredded coconut. My mom puts shredded coconut on all her cakes because she's not very good with icing.

"You're just growing like a bad weed, Peter. Your first birthday seems like yesterday. Now look at you!"

Then she pinched me really hard.

"Henry, take a picture before the candles set the house on fire."

Uncle Ed got his camera, too.

"Over here, Peter. That's it, smile nicely now."

"Ed, make sure you're centered before you take the photo," my mom said. "Honestly, you take the worst pictures."

After I blew out the candles, Uncle Ed asked me what I wished for.

"Nothing special," I said.

"Oh, I doubt that," Uncle Ed said as he shoved a forkful of cake into his mouth. He winked at me, like he knew about the secret birthday wish list I'd tucked between my mattresses last week. It was very disturbing.

I got the usual stuff for my birthday. My parents gave me a sweater, which wasn't too ugly. Christine gave me a cookie cookbook, Nancy gave me a clock-radio, and Uncle Ed gave me the Olivia Newton-John *Greatest Hits Vol. 2* album.

• •

The next day while we were sitting around watching TV, my mom said that since tomorrow was Sunday, we had to go to Springfield and visit Great Aunt Vivienne.

"It's the first Sunday of the month," she said.

"Do I have to go?" I asked. "She won't mind if I miss one visit."

I know it's not nice to say, but I hate visiting Great Aunt Vivienne in the hospital. The air smells like pee and butterscotch and everywhere you look, there are old people, just sitting around in the halls. They stare at me when I walk by. I usually try to smile at them, because who knows? Maybe they think I'm an Angel of Mercy. One time, though, I walked past this old woman on my way to the bathroom.

"Good day," I said, because that's how old people talk.

"Hello," the woman said. "Fatty."

I gasped. I couldn't understand why she would say something like that. I mean, old people are supposed to call you "dear" and serve Mint Melt-a-Ways and chocolate buttons. I tried to put it out of my mind over a cheeseburger platter in the hospital cafeteria, but the more I thought about it, the angrier I got. What gave her the right to go and call me "Fatty" when I didn't have to be nice to her in the first place? So every time I see her now, I walk by very slowly and make low moaning noises and hope she thinks I'm the Grim Reaper.

"Peter, you're not staying home," my mom said. "Aunt Vivienne lies in that bed seven days a week, three hundred and sixty-five days a year. Seeing you kids is the only joy she gets."

"Well, maybe it wouldn't be that big a deal if Peter stayed home tomorrow," my dad said. "It's his birthday, after all."

"Really?" I asked.

"Then I'm not going," Christine said.

"Count me out, too," Nancy said. "If he gets to stay home, I can, too. Besides, I'm supposed to go over to Bubbles' house."

"Peter can stay behind, but you girls are both going to Springfield tomorrow," my dad said. "I seem to remember two young ladies who didn't come with us the last time, either. I don't think it would kill you to spend the afternoon with your aunt."

"Henry, Peter can't stay home by himself all day," my mom said.

"Why not? He's a man now, after all. You said so yourself."

"Oh, I don't know," my mom said, "something could happen."

"Nothing will happen, Beth," my dad said. "We'll have to leave him alone sooner or later. And I think he's responsible enough."

"You can trust me," I said. I couldn't believe my dad was letting me stay home. Maybe he felt bad about bringing up the idea of me going to *The Sound of Music* with my mother.

"I'm still not sure," my mom said. She was twisting her hands. But I knew my dad would win. He seemed pretty determined.

I was so excited, I could hardly sleep that night. I kept thinking about what I would do the next day. I could snoop through Nancy and Christine's dresser drawers. I could play my new Olivia Newton-John *Greatest Hits Vol. 2* album as loud as I wanted to. I could make cookies from my new cookbook. I could even walk around the house naked, though I knew I wouldn't. But one thing was for sure—the day was all mine and that was the best birthday present ever.

• •

Everyone left the next day at noon. My mom handed me a list of phone numbers to call in case of an emergency.

"If worse comes to worst, you can always phone Uncle Ed," she said. "Although I don't know if he'd be much good for anything. Whatever you do, don't answer the door for strangers. Perverts are out there."

"Don't tell him that," Nancy said. "Or else he'll put a big sign in the front yard, saying 'My parents aren't home. Perverts welcome.'"

"That's not funny, Nancy," my mom said. "I had an encounter with a pervert when I was Peter's age and let me tell you, it wasn't funny in the least."

My mom got flashed one day when she was walking home from school. She tells us the story about once a year. "That was the day my innocence died," she always says, shaking her head.

When the Granada finally pulled out of the driveway, the first thing I did was lock the door. Then I sat at the kitchen table, trying to figure out what to do next. The house was so quiet! I could even hear the clock ticking in the next room. I got up and scooped myself a bowl of Neapolitan ice cream. I squirted some chocolate sauce on top and thought about calling Andrew Sinclair. But what would I say? Then I thought about Debbie Andover. I wondered if she had plans for the day. Maybe she'd like to come over for dinner. I could make teriyaki chicken for her. We'd just learned the recipe in home ec.

"Just a little something I whipped up," I'd say to her. But I didn't have her phone number. Besides, she had no idea who I was or that I was in love with her.

Then I started to panic—what if Great Aunt Vivienne was dead when my family got to Springfield? Then they'd have to turn around and come home. My whole day would be ruined! I had to act fast, so I finished off my ice cream and headed straight for the shower.

While I had the showerhead on my dink, I thought about Debbie Andover. I closed my eyes and tried to think about what her boobs looked like under her nun's dress. Were her nipples soft and puffy like mine? Or did they look like little pink berets? But every time I got close to seeing them, Billy Archer would pop up in my head, wearing his red parachute pants and asking me to touch his dink.

"You're very persistent, Billy," I said. "I'll let you do what you want, but then you'll have to let me get back to Debbie."

When I got to the point where my hand was over his dink, I got the tingly feeling in my crotch.

"Rock it, Billy! Rock it all night long!" I called as my dink made sperm.

I lay there for a bit, watching the water roll off my big belly. I was disappointed that I never got to see Debbie's nipples. I know I should've been thinking about them instead of Billy Archer. And I kept hearing Debbie's voice, saying, "I thought you loved me, Peter."

As I dried myself off, I thought about a way I could make it up to her—to prove that I still loved her. But how? Then it hit me. I went to my parent's bedroom and sat down at my mom's vanity table. I started with her beige CoverGirl foundation and rubbed it into my cheeks and forehead, making sure I didn't leave any lines around my neck. Then, I took some blush and brushed it onto my cheeks to highlight my bone structure.

"You have wonderful cheekbones," someone said.

"Thank you," I whispered.

The blue shadow I put on my eyelids made me look mysterious and the mascara darkened and curled my lashes. For the final touch, I picked the reddest lipstick I could find and carefully painted my mouth, making sure I stayed in the lines. Then I took a Kleenex and kissed it like my mom does and checked my teeth for lipstick.

After I was finished, I gave myself a good look in the mirror. "Not a bad job, Peter Paddington," I thought. "Or is that Ms. Andover?"

But I wasn't finished. I put on one of my mom's bras and stuffed a pair of socks into each of the cups.

"Stop staring at my boobs," I said to the mirror. "I have a brain, too."

Suddenly, there was a knock at the door. "Ten minutes until show time!" a voice called.

"All right!" I muttered. "Just give me a minute of peace, would you?"

I hurried to my mom's closet to find a dress, since

Christine's clothes would be too small. So would Nancy's, I thought. But I didn't want to wreck the moment thinking about that. I found my mom's black dress. It was a little tight around the waist and it was tricky getting the zipper done up in the back, but I managed to do it halfway. Then I squeezed my feet into a pair of her black shoes and found a pair of pearl clip-on earrings. The final touch was the long, black wig that Christine had in her closet. Mrs. LaFlamme had given it to her to use for a witch costume one Halloween.

Once everything was in place, I stood in front of the full-length mirror. I tossed my long black hair from side to side and laughed.

"Dark angel," a man said.

"Beware!" another said. "She'll break your heart."

But it isn't true! I don't break hearts. People just think that because I'm so beautiful. Inside, I'm sad and lonely and bored of all this attention.

I walked out to the kitchen, listening to the sharp clickety-click of my heels on the linoleum. I almost wiped out, so to be on the safe side, I tiptoed to the living room and sat down on the sofa. I crossed my legs, making sure to pull my dress up a bit to show off my long legs.

But I couldn't sit for long. The audience was waiting.

"I don't want to go on," I said to my manager. "I'm not up for it."

"The whole country is out there tonight!" Jameson said. "The public wants you. You don't have a choice. Now get out there and give them what they want."

I had almost reached the stage downstairs when I

realized I didn't have *The Sound of Music* album. What would I perform? And then I remembered my new Olivia Newton-John album, so I went to my room, grabbed it, and headed back downstairs. I put on my favorite song, "A Little More Love," and turned up the volume. Suddenly, Olivia's voice, *my* voice, filled the auditorium. The spotlight was on me as I danced and twirled around the stage. The audience was listening to my every word. Some people were even crying because my emotions were so real and so true.

I knew that Mr. Hanlan was in the audience watching me and he'd send me flowers and maybe I'd have a drink with him if he asked me. But maybe I wouldn't. And Andrew. Poor Andrew. Sitting by himself. Billy, too. All of them watching me, loving me, wanting me to be close to them, but knowing that I was a Dark Angel. If they got too close to me, I'd only break their hearts again.

And my voice was hitting all the right notes, even the high ones, and I kept twirling so fast that you'd think I'd be dizzy, except I knew the trick and that's to keep your eyes focused on one spot. So I was looking at the basement window each time I twirled. My dress and hair were flying through the air, my high heels clicking on the tiles. I could hear the people in the audience calling, "Bravo! Bravo!" and I knew that I'd be on the front page of the *Observer* the next morning. "Sensational!" the headline would read. And when I returned to my dressing room, there would be a million red roses waiting for me from my fans around the world. I'd say things like "Oh, you shouldn't have" and "For little ol' me?" And just when I was at the point where I could actually smell the roses, I twirled and saw Uncle Ed's face staring at me through the window.

I froze with my back to the window. Was it really him? Somehow, I managed to turn my head around. He was gone. I ran to the window and closed the curtains and turned off the stereo and then I raced up the stairs, slid through the kitchen and into the bathroom. I slammed the door behind me and locked it.

Was I hallucinating? I yanked off the dress and the wig and the earrings. Maybe he wasn't really there. I kicked off the shoes. Maybe it was just my imagination. But I saw him so clearly. He was wearing a yellow baseball hat and a green jacket.

I stopped and listened. There was nothing but silence. If that *was* him, he would've knocked, I said to myself. But why would he come over? He knew my parents were going to Springfield.

Unless my mom asked him to check up on me.

And then it all made sense, that Uncle Ed really *had* seen me. My mom must've called him before she left and asked him to drop by the house to make sure everything was okay. How could she do that to me? Especially after I went with her to that stupid play.

I turned to wash my make-up off and saw my reflection in the medicine cabinet mirror. I was still wearing my mom's bra. My red lipstick had smudged and my mascara was running down my face. I looked like my mom in the Conch Shell, the day she fell on her butt and cried. I heard her voice in my head.

You spend all your time up in the clouds, until, one day, reality decides to pull you back down.

I finished washing my face and put back my mom's shoes and her bra and dress. I put Christine's wig back in her closet. Then I jumped into the shower and rinsed myself clean. I didn't even look at the showerhead.

After I dried myself off, I put on my old rugby pants and taped up my nipples and pulled my sweatshirt on. Then I grabbed a Jane Parker spice cake off the kitchen counter, went to my room, and put my desk chair under the door handle.

I did something very bad. I knew it. I had let a Bedtime Movie leave my head and come to life. And I'd been caught. Uncle Ed had seen me. He had seen me and what was he thinking right now? How was I going to explain what I was doing when my parents asked me?

"See?!?" my mom would scream. "I told you we should've signed him up for Bluewater Hockey!"

"If he had taken shop class, this wouldn't have happened," my dad would cry.

"Looks like *you're* the pervert," Nancy would say.

"And we know what you do with the showerhead," Christine would say.

Worst of all, I could hear Uncle Ed telling Janice Appleby and all the rest of the donut shop girls about me.

"You should've seen it," he'd say, shaking his head and biting into his Boston Cream. "Kid's dancing around in a dress and make-up, listening to Olivia Newton-John. Shouldn't have gotten him that record for his birthday."

It would only be a matter of time before the rest of the

class found out about me. And my nipples. And what I did to Billy Archer. They'd show up in front of my house with lit torches and ropes in their hands, yelling, "Send him out! Send him out!"

"Aren't you getting a little carried away?" my nipples asked.

"No," I said. "And I don't remember asking you for your opinion."

"Don't get angry at us. *We're* not the ones who put on a pair of pantyhose."

"You think you're so much better than me, don't you?"

"Not better," my nipples said, "just smarter. Uncle Ed won't say anything. You know that."

"How can you be so sure?"

"You're both the same."

"That's not true at all! Uncle Ed and I are nothing alike. He's annoying and talks too much and wears too much cologne."

"If he tells on you, he tells on himself," my nipples said. "You'll see."

"You're crazy," I told my nipples. "You've lost your marbles."

They kept quiet for the rest of the afternoon.

I must've fallen asleep after I finished eating the spice cake because I woke up to the sound of the back door closing.

"Well, the house isn't burned to the ground," I heard my dad say.

"I smell drugs," Nancy said.

"Don't be smart," my mom said. "Peter? Are you here, dear?"

She came and knocked on my door. I was afraid to open it, but I didn't have a choice.

"Why are you in here with the door shut?"

I shrugged. "Just used to it, I guess."

"Did you have a good day?"

I shrugged again.

"Did anyone call?" my mom asked.

"No," I said. Why would I tell her the truth? Uncle Ed would give her all the details.

Later that night, I heard her on the phone to him. I stood at my bedroom door listening.

"Now Ed, I asked you to do one thing for me. Well, what do you mean you didn't have time? Oh Ed, I wish I could trust you sometimes...."

My nipples were right! Uncle Ed *didn't* tell on me. But why?

"Why did he lie?" I asked my nipples. They kept quiet. I unpeeled the masking tape to give them some air and asked them again. "Why didn't Uncle Ed say something?"

But my nipples just stared back at me from my mirror. For once, they had nothing to say.

nine

Something fishy is going on with Daniela. It wasn't just the way she acted at my birthday dinner. At first, I just figured that Daniela was having a bad day. Or she felt embarrassed about her father's restaurant. I didn't think about it too much until my first real clue came the following week.

It was Wednesday. Mrs. Kraft had asked me if I'd stay behind after school to cut heart-shaped doodle pads for Valentine's Day. I said sure, even though I wasn't all that thrilled about it. I had to get my papers delivered, but Mrs. Kraft said it wouldn't take more than fifteen minutes.

"I think you'd make a wonderful librarian," she said as we cut out our red construction paper hearts. "You'd be surprised how thrilling a career in library sciences can be, Peter."

I glanced down at her pantyhose/sandal combo.

"Well, you never know," I said. I didn't want to make Mrs. Kraft feel bad, but only nerdy people work in libraries. And I know saying that makes me a bit two-faced, but I'm not a library assistant because I *want* to be one. I'm here because I *have* to be one. But when the new and improved Peter Paddington walks down the hall on the first day of freshman year, there's no way anyone will catch him within ten feet of the library, especially at recess or after school.

Anyways, after I finished cutting up the heart doodle pads, I headed home. I was more than fifteen minutes late and knew some of my customers would be getting all nervous that something might have happened to me.

"He hasn't come yet." Mr. Hanlan would be pacing in front of the living room window. "That's not like Peter."

"Shut up!" Mrs. Hanlan would yell. "I'm trying to watch TV!"

When I got to the corner, my paper bundle was still waiting for me, which was strange because Daniela should've brought it to my house like she always does when I'm late. I had to carry it home and by the time I loaded the papers into my *Observer* bag, I was really behind schedule.

"A little late today, aren't you?" Mr. Cornish asked when I came up to his door. He grosses me out, because he has the longest fingernails I've ever seen on a man. I can't help but look when he hands me his money, even though I'm afraid I'll puke right then and there on his porch.

"I'm just running a bit late tonight, Mr. Cornish," I said.

"Yeah, well," Mr. Cornish said. He was picking at his teeth with a four-inch pinkie nail. "Cold enough for you?"

I hate it when my paper route customers ask me stupid questions, but I smiled and hurried on. I figured Daniela must've been working overtime at her dad's restaurant.

My second Daniela clue came two days later. I was in the Shop 'N' Bag treating myself to a large chocolate milk and a bag of BBQ Fritos.

"How's business?" I asked Mr. Bernard when I put my stuff down on the counter.

"Oh just fine, Peter," Mr. Bernard said and smiled in a sad way. "Just fine."

I could tell that things weren't fine, though. The 7-Eleven up the street must've been crushing the Shop 'N' Bag with its chilli dogs and shiny floors and Coke Slurpees. There was no way Mr. Bernard and his sombrero paintings could ever compete.

"Why are they doing this to me?" Mr. Bernard would cry. Every night before he made the long walk home to his small apartment, he'd grab a can of Nine Lives from the shelf for dinner. One day, someone would find Mr. Bernard, alone and broke and dead in his tiny apartment. I knew for certain that someone would be me.

"BOY FINDS BODY!" the *Observer* headline would read with a picture of me pointing toward Mr. Bernard's apartment.

"Say, your friend was in here this morning," Mr. Bernard said as he stuffed my milk and Fritos into a paper bag.

I almost said, "What friend?" but I stopped myself. I didn't want Mr. Bernard to think I didn't have any.

"Oh, really?" I asked. "Which one?"

For a minute there, I thought Mr. Bernard was going to say, "I think he said his name was Andrew. He was hoping to find you here. Wanted to take you to the movies or something."

But instead he said, "The mouthy girl. The one who

always sounds like she's got a cold. What's her name again? Her dad owns that restaurant down the way."

"Oh," I said, trying not to sound too disappointed, "Daniela."

"She bought quite a few interesting things," Mr. Bernard said. "A Valentine's Day card, some chocolate, and a tin of cinnamon hearts. Looks like she may have herself a sweetheart. Maybe you better think of getting her a little something if you want to compete."

I almost threw up. "Mr. Bernard, you have it all wrong," I said. "Daniela and I have nothing in common and to be honest, even if I was dating a girl, she wouldn't be anything like Daniela." I thought about Debbie Andover in her nun costume, strumming a guitar.

"Well, just thought you should know, Peter," Mr. Bernard said. "That'll be $1.30."

As I made my way home, I couldn't stop thinking about what Mr. Bernard had said. Daniela buying a Valentine's card? For who? If she had a boyfriend, then why hadn't she said anything to me about it? I wondered if it was Paolo Vernesse. He's in her class at St. Michael's. Daniela has had a crush on him since the beginning of the year. She says he's gorgeous.

"Great ass, great hair," she told me. "He plays on the soccer team. All the girls in my class have the hots for him, but they're too shy to do anything about it. They sit around giggling and batting their fuckin' eyelashes at him. Not me, though. I go after what I want."

For Christmas, Daniela bought Paolo a bottle of cologne.

"It's called Pino Silvestri. Comes in a bottle that looks

like a pine-comb. I got it at Rite Aid. Cost me a pretty penny, I'll tell you that much."

But when Daniela handed Paolo the gift, he gave her this weird look, said "Thanks," and walked away.

"I haven't even smelled it on him once," Daniela told me. "How's that for gratitude? What a loser. But it doesn't mean he doesn't like me. Guys can be pretty tricky to figure out. One day, they look at you like you're a piece of shit. The next day, BAM! They're all over you like a fuckin' candy apple."

I nodded, but the truth is, I don't think any guy would ever be "all over" Daniela, candy apple or not.

• •

My next clue came from Daniela herself. I ran into her outside her dad's restaurant. I was on my way to the Shop 'N' Bag again—only this time to buy more masking tape for my nipples. Mr. Bernard is going to run out soon, but I feel good knowing that my nipples are keeping him in business.

"This must be some school project," he said to me on my last tape run.

I nodded. "Masking tape animal sculptures are a lot of work," I said. "Do you have any idea how much it takes to make a life-sized elephant?"

Daniela was standing outside Papa Bertoli. She was wearing a white apron and hairnet.

"Hi," I said when she saw me. I tried to sound vague, like I'd been too busy to notice that we hadn't seen each other for a while.

"How's it going?" Daniela said and nodded. She was looking over my shoulder, scanning the parking lot.

"Aren't you cold without a jacket?" I asked.

"No."

"So, what's new?"

"Nothing." She narrowed her eyes. "Why are you asking?"

"Just asking a question," I said. "Why are you asking why I'm asking?"

"What?"

"Never mind. I heard you were in the Shop 'N' Bag the other day. Mr. Bernard told me you bought some interesting things."

"I'm always buying shit in there," Daniela said. "Big deal."

"Yeah, but Mr. Bernard said you bought a Valentine's Day card and a tin of cinnamon hearts."

"That old fucker!" Daniela said. "I should go down there and give him a piece of my fuckin' mind. Imagine, telling everyone what his customers are buying. That's an invasion of fuckin' privacy."

"Did you buy the card and hearts for Paolo?" I asked. "If you did, maybe you should return them and save your money. Remember how you bought him that cologne? You said yourself that you've never smelled it on him even…"

"*Paolo?*" Daniela interrupted. "Why the fuck would I be buying stuff for that jerk?"

"Well, you're in love with him, aren't you?"

"Please," Daniela said. "I couldn't care less about that

son of a bitch. I got a boyfriend twice as good-looking as that asshole. One that makes me sweat buckets."

I gasped. When I asked her who it was, she said she was sworn to secrecy.

"I can't breathe a word of it," she said. "A lot of lives are on the line. It's too dangerous." She checked her watch and turned to go back into the restaurant. "And don't ask any more questions, either. That goes for the old blabbermouth at the variety store, too."

That cheesed me off. I mean, it wasn't like I cared about Daniela and her stupid love life. I headed straight for the Shop 'N' Bag to load up on tape and grab a Snickers bar.

"Stay clear of Daniela," I told Mr. Bernard. "She's acting a little violent these days."

"Lover's spat?" Mr. Bernard asked and smiled.

"I thought we already went over this," I sighed. "Daniela and I aren't a couple. We don't have the same interests, we don't go to the same school. We're not even friends for that matter, Mr. Bernard. She's just someone who lives across the street from me."

"But I see the two of you together an awful lot."

"I don't plan it that way! We just run into each other."

"Well, thank you for clarifying things for me," Mr. Bernard said as he handed me my change. "I won't ask any questions next time."

"Thank you."

"But I should let you know that a box of chocolates is always a nice way to let that someone special know you care about her."

I shook my head. Mr. Bernard was really starting to bug me. I managed a fake smile, grabbed my bag and made a mental note to check out the tape selection at the 7-Eleven.

As much as I tried, I couldn't stop thinking about what Daniela had said to me. Part of me wondered if she was lying about having a boyfriend. The facts didn't add up. For starters, she said she couldn't talk about him, which didn't make sense, seeing as how she never shut up about Paolo. Secondly, her parents didn't let her date. The only boy she was allowed to be around was Gianni.

"Of course, there's you," she told me one day. "But you don't really count."

What did she mean by that? Was she saying I wasn't like other boys? What gave her the right to go and say that?

"My parents feel the same," I said. "You don't count, either."

Thirdly, how could Daniela get herself a boyfriend in the first place? What guy would want to date someone like Daniela?

But another part of me wondered if Daniela *was* telling the truth and she really *did* have a boyfriend. Maybe she was dating an escaped criminal or murderer. That's why she couldn't talk about him. Maybe she was hiding him in her basement. Then, one night, while the whole family was asleep, Daniela and her criminal boyfriend would squeeze through the basement window and steal her parents' car and drive to Mexico where they'd be in hiding for the rest of their lives.

Or what if Daniela was dating someone in the Bluewater Mafia? What if she was seeing someone related to John DeLouza, Andrew Sinclair's stepfather? Then Andrew and I could become friends through Daniela. She could introduce us at the Mafia meeting and Andrew would say to me, "Aren't you in my class at school?" and I'd say, "Oh, I'm not really sure. What's your name again?"

I didn't know what to believe. But I *did* know that Daniela didn't need me around anymore. I hardly ever saw her. Which was fine. I didn't care at all. She could spend all the time she wanted with her imaginary or real boyfriend. I was too busy with other things. Important things. Like trying to make up with the Virgin in my closet and thinking of ways I could break up the Hanlans' marriage.

• •

The next night, I was on my way to the Shop 'N' Bag. I was still cheesed off at Mr. Bernard for making all those comments about Daniela and I, but I kept picturing him eating cat food every night. He couldn't afford to lose another customer to the 7-Eleven. As I passed by Mr. Bertoli's restaurant, I looked through the window and saw Daniela standing behind the counter. She was talking to this Banger. He was skinny with long hair and zits and was wearing a red checked lumber jacket, tight jeans, and a Burger King visor. He was leaning over the counter toward Daniela. She was smiling, but seemed nervous and kept checking over her shoulder toward the kitchen.

"It's true," I thought. "Daniela has a boyfriend."

It was like I was psychic, because there are Bangers in lumber jackets all over Bluewater. Why was this one special? But somewhere, deep inside of me, I just knew. I hurried past before Daniela saw me. I was very disturbed and ended up buying three Hundred Thousand Dollar bars at the Shop 'N' Bag.

"They're for my sisters," I said to Mr. Bernard, but I don't think he cared.

I didn't want to walk past the restaurant again but I needed to get a better look at Daniela's Banger. When I looked in the window, the Banger was gone. Daniela was cleaning off a table in the corner. In the parking lot, a Thunderbird revved its engine. The radio was on full blast and the driver did a donut in the snow before tearing off. I couldn't see who it was, but I didn't really have to. I just knew he was wearing a Burger King visor. I looked back to see if Daniela was still there, but she was gone. One word flashed into my mind. That word was "Danger."

"You better watch yourself, Daniela," I whispered as I made my way home. I had already gone through two chocolate bars by the time I reached my back door.

• •

I watched Daniela from my living room window the next day. She was in her garage. I thought about going over there and saying how I saw her and her boyfriend. Then I thought, "Why let her think I'm even paying attention to what she does?" Then I thought, "But she should know that she can never keep anything from a top secret agent like myself." And then I thought, "Maybe she's too in love with her new boyfriend to even care what I know."

I decided the best thing to do was to get a confession out of Daniela herself. So I put my coat and boots on and walked up and down the sidewalk in front of my house. Daniela didn't look up once. I coughed a couple of times, but still nothing. My nose and ears started burning. Then I saw my mother peeking out from behind the living room drapes. She probably thought I was a Jehovah's Witness, so before things got any worse, I marched across the street.

"I saw you," I said. "I saw you and your boyfriend last night."

Daniela whipped around.

"You may be able to pull the wool over everyone else," I said and crossed my arms. "But you can't pull it over me."

Daniela dropped the shoe box she had in her hand and looked at me like I was a ghost.

"What the fuck are you talking about?" She ran over and yanked the garage door down.

"In the window at your father's restaurant," I said. "You were wearing a green shirt and a hairnet and he was wearing a Burger King visor. Just for the record, it didn't really go with his lumber jacket."

"Holy fuckin' shit!" Daniela whisper/screamed. "You didn't tell my parents, did you? Please tell me you didn't tell my fuckin' parents."

"No, I didn't say anything. Why are you so freaked out?"

"Promise you won't say a fuckin' thing?" Daniela asked. "I mean it. You can't tell anyone about this."

I promised and showed her my hands so she could see

my fingers weren't crossed. Daniela sat down on an empty crate and took a big breath.

His name was Phil, she said, and he worked full-time at Burger King along with Gianni. She had met him a couple of weeks ago. Gianni's car had broken down in the parking lot one night, so Phil gave him a ride home.

"My ma told him to stay for dinner. I didn't think too much of him. Just another one of Gianni's loser caker friends. But he keeps checking me out at dinner and fuckin' winking at me. By the time the spumoni was on the table, the fucker was practically drooling. When I got up to clear the table, he tells me he'll give me a hand. Then he leans over to me at the sink and asks me how old I am. I look at him and say, 'I'm forty-fuckin-seven, so get lost.' Then him and Gianni take off to the basement to whack off to *Playboy* magazines or do whatever guys do together."

Two nights later, Phil showed up at the restaurant. Daniela told him he must've been sniffing too much airplane glue—the Burger King was on the other end of town. But Phil said he'd come to see her. Daniela told him to go fuck himself.

"Then he says, 'I'm not joking. I'm serious.' I say to him, 'How much is Gianni paying you?' and he says, 'Gianni doesn't even know I'm here. He'd kill me if he knew I was asking out his little sister.' So then I kind of stop because I can see the fucker's serious and I say, 'Is that what you're doing?' and he says, 'Yep,' and I say, 'I'll think about it.'"

Since then, Phil's been trying to impress Daniela with presents. She pulled a gold chain with a shark's tooth pendant out from underneath her turtleneck.

"Do you think it's real gold?" I asked her. It reminded me of Billy Archer's necklace.

Daniela shrugged. "Probably," she said. "He'd know better than to try to pass fake gold off on me."

"So how old is Phil?"

"Seventeen. Same age as Gianni. He made it halfway through junior year and dropped out to join the work force."

"Aren't you a little young to be dating someone out of high school? I mean, you're not even in high school yourself."

"I should be!" Daniela shot back. "I'd be in high school right now if those fuckin' nuns didn't have it in for me. I should be walking around high school right now, hanging out with people my own age, going to dances and stuff. But I'm not. I'm fuckin' stuck at St. Mike's and getting child abuse from my parents."

"Even if you were a freshman, that's still too young to date. And when do you have time to do your homework if you're working *and* dating at the same time?"

"Screw homework," Daniela said. "They can fail me again for all I care. Besides, age doesn't have anything to do with it. That's what Phil told me when he gave me the necklace. He says when two people love each other as much as we do, it don't matter. Only how they feel. Isn't that fuckin' romantic?"

I said I guessed so, but I felt weird about the whole thing. On one hand, I was happy for Daniela, even though I didn't want to admit it. On the other hand, Daniela should be concentrating on graduating junior high this year, not spending time with a high school dropout Banger.

"Have you done It with him?" I asked her.

"Not that it's any of your fuckin' business, but no," Daniela said. "I've got more class than that. We dry humped in the storage room at the restaurant a couple of times, but that's about it. He says he wants to do more, though, and that it's the next step in our relationship. Thing is, it's hard to find someplace private. Phil says his parents are nosy and spy on him. But he's got this plan where I'll sneak out of the house one night and he'll meet me in his Thunderbird and we'll go somewhere really private, like under the bridge. Or maybe one of those hotels out on the Golden Mile."

"Are you going to do it?"

"Maybe," Daniela said. She was winding a piece of her black hair around her finger. "Phil told me that he can't stop thinking about me. He said I have to do It with him or else he'll go crazy. He said I'm turning his balls three shades of blue."

I made a face. "Has he seen a doctor about it?"

"He told me I'm the prettiest girl in Bluewater," Daniela said, only she was talking more to herself than to me. "No one's ever said that to me before. The prettiest girl in Bluewater. What do you make of that?"

• •

I knew Phil was Bad News with a capital B and N. And maybe I was no expert on dating, since I'd only been in love once and that was with an older woman who didn't even know my name, but I knew enough.

For starters, Daniela was too young to be dating. Even if she did fail 6th grade, she was still in junior high. And if she didn't care about school, there was no way she was going to pass this year. Plus, Phil shouldn't be making Daniela feel like she had to do It with him if she wasn't ready. And finally, Phil was a Burger King Banger who didn't even have a high school education. He made Gianni look like a rocket scientist.

I bet my bottom dollar that Phil was only after one thing. It was only a matter of time before he talked Daniela into doing something she'd regret later. I wanted to tell Daniela to stay away from Phil. But I knew that she'd never listen to me. She'd say I was jealous, which was partly true. Besides, even though I knew Phil was a loser, part of me didn't want to be the person to tell Daniela. I knew I'd be doing her a favor, but I didn't want to spoil things for her. I kept picturing her in the garage, cleaning off the tomatoes after she lost the Miss Basilico 1984 pageant. And I remembered how bad I felt that nothing had changed for her, even though she tried.

I couldn't tell Daniela's parents or Gianni about Phil because what if they killed Phil and threw Daniela out of the house? I couldn't tell my parents because my mother would make things even more messed up. And I knew I couldn't tell Phil to back off and leave Daniela alone because what if he beat me up? There was no one to help Daniela except for myself and this time, a hot oil treatment wasn't going to do the trick.

Later that night, I sat down at my desk and wrote a letter to "Dear Constance." Her column runs in the *Observer* every day, right beside the comics and the horoscopes. I think Constance is a very smart woman and I was sure she'd be able to give me some good advice.

Dear Constance, I wrote. *Help! I'm a fourteen-year-old boy. I read your column every day and think it's great. Here's a real doozey of a problem. I have a friend named Sofia (NOT HER REAL NAME). Sofia is fourteen and lives across the street from me. She's Italian. She has a lot of problems, but there are too many to talk about. Anyways, Sofia has started dating this Banger. He's a high school dropout, works at Burger King, and is trying to convince Sofia to do It with him. Constance, I know your heart must break to hear this, but please read on. Sofia's not sure if she wants to do it. I KNOW she shouldn't do it. Sofia should break up with this guy, but I don't think she'll listen to me. I can't stand by and watch a friend of mine just throw her life away!! Please tell me what you think I should do.*

Sincerely,

Theodore Sinclair (NOT MY REAL NAME!!)

I folded up the letter and was about to put it into an envelope when I realized it could be months before Constance got back to me. By then, it would be too late for Daniela. I crumpled up the letter and tried to figure out another plan. I knew the only way to save Daniela was to think like a secret agent. I needed to get evidence against Phil.

I grabbed my camera from my dresser and went into the living room. Crouching down in front of the window, I took a couple shots of Daniela's house.

"What are you doing?" my mother asked. She was sitting on the sofa, watching *Hee Haw.*

"School project," I said and got out of there before she

could ask anything else. The truth was, I wasn't sure what I was doing, either—only that it seemed important to start off my plan taking photos to use as evidence.

I sat back down on my bed, trying to figure out what pictures to take next. I knew I'd have to get a picture of Phil and Daniela together. That's the only way I'd be able to prove my case in court. But how would I get that close up to them without being spotted? There must be a better way to break them up, I thought. Then it hit me.

I grabbed the phone book from the kitchen and propped my desk chair under the door knob. I knew this wasn't going to be easy, considering how things went that last time I called Papa Bertoli, but I didn't have a choice. I grabbed one of my socks and put it over the receiver to disguise my voice. Then I dialed the phone number. I was pretty nervous. On the fourth ring, someone picked up.

"Allo?" the voice asked. It sounded like Mr. Bertoli, but I wasn't sure.

"Is this Mr. Bertoli?" I asked through the sock.

"Allo?"

"Is this Mr. Bertoli?" I asked again, only this time much louder.

"Who isa dis? Allo?"

"Mr. Bertoli, I have a very important message for you, so listen carefully." Then I took a dramatic pause. I could see Mr. Bertoli, standing there in his apron, his eyes pointing in different directions.

"Beware the Burger King Banger!" I said. Then I hung up. I thought I heard another "Allo?" as I was putting the receiver back, but I wasn't sure. In any case, I felt better knowing that the matter was in Mr. Bertoli's hands now.

• •

I kept an eye out for Daniela the next couple of days and wondered what Mr. Bertoli had done after I hung up on him. Did he start screaming in the middle of the restaurant? Did he go home and lock Daniela in the cellar? Did he call the Bluewater Mafia to make sure Phil never made another Whopper for the rest of his life?

I was scared to see Daniela, too. What if she found out it was me who called and ratted on her? What if she was planning to get revenge on me? What if Phil was looking for me at that very moment with a baseball bat? I knew deep down that I'd done the right thing. Maybe someday, Daniela would learn to forgive me. But until then, I'd just have to go on living my life.

For three whole days, there was no sign of Daniela. It was like she disappeared off the face of the earth. Whenever I walked up to the Bertoli's porch to drop off the paper, I listened for moans or screams coming from inside the house. But there was nothing, except for the smell of Lysol creeping out from under the door.

On the fourth day, I finally saw Daniela. I was never so glad to see her split ends in all my life. I was walking on the other side of the street delivering my papers when I heard someone shouting.

"For the last time, I DID clean the bathroom! Gianni just laid a fuckin' egg in there!"

Daniela was coming out of the house wearing her

Basilico uniform. Her mother was standing in the living room window, shaking her fist at Daniela. Then Mr. Bertoli came out the side door and Daniela said, "C'mon! I'm gonna be fuckin' late!"

The two of them got into the Bertoli's car while Mrs. Bertoli yelled from inside the house. Then the car pulled out of the driveway and took off down our street.

I was glad to see that everything had gone back to normal.

• •

On Saturday afternoon, I went to the Shop 'N' Bag to buy another roll of tape. While I was walking past Papa Bertoli, I looked in and saw Daniela, polishing silverware. She saw me and waved her hand for me to come inside. I was nervous about talking to her. What if she was going to yell at me?

"How are you?" I asked, trying to sound as casual as I could.

"Fine," she said. Then her voice dropped down to a whisper. "Look what Phil gave me for our anniversary."

She pulled a tiny gold ring out of her pocket.

"We've been together now for a whole month."

"You're still with Phil?" My jaw nearly hit the floor.

"Yeah, of course," Daniela said, stuffing the ring back inside her pocket. "I told you already. He's got the hots for me big time."

"Do your parents know about him yet?"

"Fuck, no! What do you think I am? Crazy?"

I knew I had to play it cool and not ask too many

questions or else Daniela might get suspicious. So I just nodded. My phone warning to Mr. Bertoli didn't work. Maybe he couldn't understand me through the sock. He probably thought I was a prank caller.

"Phil wants to take me out next weekend," Daniela said. "He says his cousin is away and we can use his apartment." She picked up a spoon and started polishing it like there was no tomorrow. "It'll be the first time we're alone. *Alone*, alone, if you know what I mean."

"That's nice," I said and smiled, even though I felt something like a bowling ball hit the bottom of my stomach. "What'll you tell your parents?"

"I'll only be gone for a couple of hours or so," Daniela said. "I'll say I'm going to the fuckin' mall or something."

While I was standing there, I saw Daniela in a way I hadn't before. I realized that even though she had a plugged-up nose and split ends and still wet the bed, she was my friend. Maybe even my best friend. But it was weird to think that because boys and girls aren't supposed to be best friends.

I thought back to when Brian Cinder was teasing me, saying that I wanted to be a girl because I was hanging around the Goody-Goody Group. I was so embarrassed. But here was Daniela, a girl and my friend and I wasn't embarrassed at all. And my friend was in a situation—a very dangerous situation, and even though she didn't realize it, she needed my help. Her virginity was on the line.

"I gotta go," I told Daniela. "I have to pick up some stuff at the Shop 'N' Bag. Do you want me to bring you anything?"

"No," Daniela said. "But remember—keep your mouth shut about me and you-know-who."

That night, I used a Kleenex instead of a sock.

"Allo?"

"Yes, is this Mr. Bertoli?" I made my voice as serious as possible. I was through fooling around. "Can you hear me, Mr. Bertoli? If you can, please say yes."

"Who isa dis?"

"Never mind, Mr. Bertoli. My identity isn't any of your business. But your daughter is my business."

"Who isa dis?"

"I told you! Never mind. This isn't about me. This is about Daniela."

"Daniela?"

"Yes, Mr. Bertoli. And Phil, the Burger King Banger."

"Burger King? You gotta wrong number."

"No, I don't!" I rubbed my temples. "Beware of Phil from Burger King. He is bad news."

"What isa bad news? Someone deys die?"

"No, there is no bad news. I mean, Phil is bad news, Mr. Bertoli. Do you remember him? He gave Gianni a ride home from work one night and had dinner at your house. He is a bad seed. Do you understand?"

"Phil? He'sa bad seed?"

"Yes, that's it, Mr. Bertoli. Now we're on the same page. Phil is a bad seed."

"Who isa dis?"

"Never mind. I don't have time to play games with you. Just listen to me. Phil is the very worst kind of seed. A Banger seed. He's after your daughter."

"Who? Who isa dis?"

"Mr. Bertoli, you are not cooperating." I tried to keep my voice down so my parents wouldn't hear, but it was getting difficult.

"Who isa dis?"

"Mr. Bertoli, just listen to what…"

"Who isa dis?"

"I'm trying to tell you something very…"

"Who isa dis?"

Then I lost it.

"GIANNI'S FRIEND PHIL WANTS TO FUCK YOUR DAUGH-TER THIS WEEKEND! DO YOU UNDERSTAND ME NOW?"

I thought I heard a gasp on the other end, but I hung up very quickly. My heart was beating a million miles a minute. A secret agent would never blow his cool like that.

"Peter, did I just hear you say what I think I heard you say?"

It was my mother, calling from the kitchen.

"No you didn't," I called back.

I sat there for a minute and waited for my heart to slow down. The telephone call was very exciting and say-ing the f-word felt kind of good. Maybe that's why Daniela uses it so much.

I wondered what was happening at the restaurant. Was Daniela there? Where was Phil? Did Mr. Bertoli finally understand what kind of danger Daniela was in? I was pretty sure about one thing, though—Phil wouldn't be coming to fuckin' dinner at the Bertolis anytime soon.

• •

Daniela was out in the garage the next day. I was still nervous that she'd know it was me who blew the whistle on her and Phil. I decided I'd avoid her for the next little while in case she was angry at me. But as I tiptoed up her driveway to deliver the paper, Daniela turned and saw me.

"I'm gonna murder that fuckin' bitch!" she yelled. "She gets it in her head that her pizella iron is in a box somewhere in the garage. Of course, she can't remember *which* fuckin' box. I'm gonna strangle her, I swear to god."

I figured it was safe. "I'll give you a hand," I said, pulling my newspaper bag from around my shoulder. My customers could wait a bit.

"Check that pile of shit over there," she said, pointing to a stack of boxes against the wall.

"What does a pizella iron look like?" I asked her as I started opening boxes.

"Like a pizella iron," Daniela said.

I knew I had to ask her about Phil, just to make sure my last phone call worked. But I had to ask it in just the right way or else I'd sound suspicious. I yawned and stretched. "Still going away for the weekend with what's-his-name?" I asked.

Daniela stopped for a second. Then she turned her back to me and opened up a shoebox.

"Phil and I are through," she said.

I was glad she wasn't facing me, because I almost smiled.

"Really?" I asked. "What happened?"

"It's too complicated to explain," Daniela said. "I don't want to get into it. Let's just say my brother is as good as fuckin' dead. Where's that fuckin' pizella iron?" She picked up another box, looked inside, and then chucked it over her shoulder. Then she sat down on a stepladder and sighed. "I'm never gonna find it. Can you tell me why I'm even looking in the first place?"

"Why don't you ask your mother to look for herself?"

"It's not that," Daniela said. "That's not what I mean. I'm not… it's just…" She shook her head. "Never mind."

I watched as she fingered one of her split ends. I got a weird feeling and I knew that if I didn't do something fast, Daniela would start crying and that just couldn't happen.

"I bet I can figure it out," I said.

"Figure what out?" Daniela looked up at me.

"About you and Phil."

"What?" Daniela put her hand on her hip.

"You dumped him, didn't you?"

She paused. Then she narrowed her eyes. "What makes you say that?"

"Because I know you," I said. "And I know that it takes a lot more than a shark's tooth pendant to impress you. Like you said yourself, you're not like other girls, batting their eyelashes over some jerk who doesn't give you the time of day. You've got too much self-respect for that."

"Self-respect," Daniela repeated, but it came out sounding like a question.

"And high standards. Did Phil cry when you broke it off?"

"A little," she said. Then she got up from the step-ladder and grabbed another box. "Actually, the fucker wouldn't stop bawling. Talk about a fuckin' baby! I tried to be easy on him, though."

I nodded slowly and then grabbed my newspaper bag. "My work here is done," I thought to myself.

"I have to get back to delivering these," I said. "If Mr. Cornish doesn't get his paper by five, he'll bust a gut."

"Okay," Daniela said. She was holding an empty box in each of her hands. "I guess I'll finish looking for this fuckin' iron."

"You'll find it," I said. "Sooner or later."

Then I went on to deliver the rest of my papers.

No one can agree on what to get my parents for their anniversary. Christine thinks we should get them a birdhouse. Nancy wants to get them electric toothbrushes. I want to get them sheers.

"That's the stupidest gift I've ever heard of," Christine said. "Who buys someone curtains for a present?"

"*Sheers,*" I said. "Not curtains. Mom's always saying how she wants sheers. Like the kind Mrs. LaFlamme has."

"I still think it's a stupid idea."

"It's no stupider than a birdhouse. There'll be bird poop all over the place. Mom and Dad don't even like birds."

"How do you know? I don't remember them ever shooting chickadees in our backyard."

"You're both way off," Nancy said. "Electric toothbrushes are the way to go. Bubbles bought a pair for her parents for Christmas and they love them."

"And what did her parents buy for her?" Christine asked. "A pair of pliers to help her zip up her jeans?"

"Bubbles has never been anything but nice to you and you don't even give her the time of day. Your attitude really sucks."

"*My* attitude? Look who's talking!"

I started to get a headache. Christine and Nancy fight all the time now. Christine says Bubbles has a single-digit I.Q. Nancy says Christine is a snob. Christine says Nancy is acting immature. Nancy says that Christine is acting like a bitch. Christine says that Nancy thinks she's better than everyone else. Nancy says that Christine thinks she's better than everyone else. It gets pretty annoying after a while.

"Do you realize that our mom wears dentures, Nancy?" Christine asked. "If you can explain to me the benefit of giving an electric toothbrush to someone with false teeth, please tell me."

"What? Like she can't take them out and brush them?"

"I still think sheers are the only way to go," I said.

"Shut up, Peter!" Nancy and Christine yelled.

"Why don't both of you just shut up!" I yelled back. It was like a bomb went off inside of me, I was so angry at them. "You're both acting like complete losers!" I turned to Nancy. "If Bubbles is such a nice person, then why did she only talk to you *after* you broke up with André? And Christine, I don't care how mean you are to everyone. I wouldn't tell you to 'go away' if *you* were the one being chased by a bunch of Bangers in Bluewater Mall. I'd still let you in the store, Peoples policy or no Peoples policy."

I turned around and stormed down the hall. I couldn't even bear to look at them anymore.

"What's *his* problem?" I heard Nancy say to Christine.

That just made me want to turn back and scream, "*You're* the one with the problem, Nancy! *You're* the one with the birth control pills in your dresser drawer!"

But I didn't because then Nancy would ask me what I was doing in her dresser drawer in the first place and how could I tell her that I was looking for her copy of *Playgirl*? So I closed my bedroom door and put my desk chair beneath the doorknob and tried to remember back to the way things were before—before Nancy turned into a sister who has sex before marriage and hangs out with people named Bubbles. Before Nancy dumped André.

Before Nancy was thin.

• •

I guess things started to go wrong last fall, around the time I hung up on John DeLouza. Up until then, everything was the same as it had always been. Nancy would go off to work her weekend shift at Dunkin Donuts and come back with a bag of day-olds. Suzanne's flyers would come in the mail and Nancy would hide them. On Sunday afternoons, she and André would sit at the kitchen table with the Sears catalogue and pick out the things they'd need once they got married.

It was pretty clear to me that André loved Nancy, even if he was a loser. I'd find cards from him in Nancy's drawer. "To my little bunny," one said. "I wuv you." That made me want to puke. Did he really call her that? Another time, I found a card that said, "You rock me like a hurricane, babe," which was pretty tacky, if you ask me.

One time, though, I found a whole letter from André in Nancy's bottom drawer. It was written on lined, three-hole paper and smelled like cologne. There were a lot of spelling mistakes, which proved that André was dumber than I thought.

"Nancy, I was thinking about last nite and what you said," it said. "I know there are certian people that think you could do better than me (i.e. your parents) but they don't know how much we care abot each other. We're good together, babe and I promise I'll take care of you. I'll get a good job, we can by a house and start a family. It'll be like all our dreams came true. I promise you, it'll hapen, so please don't go! I don't know what I'd do if you ever leave me. I love you so much. xoxo André."

What did Nancy say to him? Did she tell him she wanted to break up? Did she say that they came from different worlds? Did she tell him to walk away, André, just walk away and never look back, no matter how much it hurt? I folded the note up and put it back in Nancy's drawer. Whatever she said to him, she must've changed her mind, because Nancy kept on ordering appliances and hand towels from Sears.

"What on earth is going on here?" my mom asked one day after Sears called to tell Nancy that her new Kenmore six-speed blender was ready for pick-up. "Nancy, this has got to stop."

"What are you talking about?" Nancy asked. She was flipping through the Consumer's Distributing catalogue.

"Well I don't see why an eighteen-year-old girl needs a blender. And besides, Nancy, don't you think André should find a job before you start stocking the cupboard?"

Nancy licked her thumb and flipped the page. "Give the guy a break, would you?"

"Look, Nancy," my mom said. "I understand that you care for André a great deal and I know it isn't easy for a girl like you, but that doesn't mean you should settle for the first…"

"What do you mean 'a girl like you?'" Nancy interrupted.

"Pardon?" my mom asked. A phony smile spread across her face.

Nancy stood up from her chair and crossed her arms. "You heard me. I asked you what you meant when you said 'a girl like you?'"

"What I meant was," my mom said slowly. "What I meant was that I know how difficult it must be for someone special like you to find someone just as special."

"That's not what you meant at all and you know it," Nancy said. She was so angry, her face was turning purple. I thought I saw smoke coming out of her ears. "Why can't you let other people be happy without trying to ruin it all the time?"

"Nancy, I don't know what you're…"

"Why can't you just be normal and say, 'That's great, dear' or 'I'm glad for you' or 'I trust you?' Why do you have to be so freaking miserable all the time? Why do you have to be such a bitch?"

I gasped. No one had ever called my mom a bitch before. At least not to her face. I was waiting for my mom to start screaming, but before she could do anything, Nancy stormed out of the kitchen, went to her room, and locked the door.

My mom stood there for a moment, looking like she was trying to catch her breath. She took her glasses off, held them up to the light, and squinted. "*I* don't even have a blender," she said to her glasses.

The next day, Nancy came home with her new Kenmore blender. She made banana milkshakes for herself and André, but no one else was allowed to have one.

• •

Anyways, what happened last fall was this: The afternoon of my mother's birthday dinner at the Conch Shell, Nancy and André decided they were going to have their picture taken in the park. The photographer was André's cousin. His name was Jean-Paul. He had a studio in his basement, which I thought was kind of creepy and I wondered if he ever took perverted pictures.

I don't know why Nancy and André wanted to have their picture taken. Maybe they were planning to run one of those cheesy engagement notices in the *Observer*. Nancy was wearing a peach dress that she'd bought at Suzanne's and André was wearing a white dress shirt with a pair of Orange Tab Levi's. Jean-Paul was getting them to stand in different poses and then he said something about needing a wide-angle lens to fit them both into the picture and Nancy started crying and made André drive her to the Conch Shell in his crappy car.

• •

That was six months ago. Now it's the middle of April and Nancy has a best friend named Bubbles, dyes her hair blonde, and spends all evening in front of the mirror. She has lost 40 pounds. I thought going through The Change with my mom was hard enough.

"What do you think of this new lipstick?"

"Mo-*ther*! Please don't tell me you put my new suede skirt in the dryer!"

"Donuts should be illegal. I'm completely serious. Donuts and potato chips. Oh, and pepperoni."

I've never heard Nancy talk so much in my entire life. It's like her volume switch has been turned on high. No one really knows what to think about the new Nancy. My mom thinks she's been brainwashed.

"You have to wonder, Henry," she said to my father. "I wouldn't be surprised if she starts going out to those cult meetings under the tent on Highway 7."

"I think you're getting a little carried away."

"Henry, you can't stick your head in the sand about this. The other day, she started crying because I put margarine in the broccoli without telling her. She told me she never felt so betrayed in her life."

"So she's a little emotional. Hardly seems out of place in this house."

"What's that supposed to mean?"

My mother also thinks Nancy is on drugs. She pulled me aside the other day and asked me if I'd ever smelled anything "funny" on Nancy.

"You know what I mean," she said. "Funny. As in 'drug-funny.'" She crinkled her nose.

"What does 'drug-funny' smell like?" I asked.

"A little like oregano," she said.

I shook my head.

"I feel terrible about asking," she said. "But it's just that Nancy's so, well, *different* than she was before. And I don't trust that Bubbles character. I think she's a bad influence."

Even though I'd never admit it to her face, I had to agree with my mom about Bubbles. That's because Bubbles isn't very smart, uses Lee Press-On nails, and wears jeans so tight she has to lie on her bed every morning and pull up the zipper with a coat hanger.

"I've got one pair I can't even sit down in," I heard her tell Nancy. She sounded proud. "I wear them for 'standing room only' events."

Bubbles has feathered blonde hair and freckles and is always chewing gum. I wonder if she ever goes to bed with gum in her mouth. You shouldn't do that or else you'll wake up with gum in your hair the next morning. I know.

Nancy and Bubbles started hanging out together in November. They're in the same homeroom class and talk on the phone for at least an hour every night.

"She sits right behind me," Nancy said. "I thought she didn't like me. Just goes to show that first impressions can be wrong."

"That's right," Bubbles said, smacking her gum. "I used to think Nancy was a total loser."

"Shut up!" Nancy laughed and hit Bubbles on the arm. "You didn't really think that, did you?"

"Well what'd you expect? You never talked to anyone and were always glued to André's side. Don't even get me started about *that* loser. I totally don't get what you saw in him."

"Neither do I," Nancy sighed. "He was a complete jerk-off. I guess that's what having zero self-esteem does to you. Right?"

At that point, I had to leave the room because I thought I was going to puke. And I was angry about what Bubbles and Nancy had said about André. I mean, maybe he wasn't the coolest guy and maybe he was a bit of a loser. But that didn't give them any right to talk that way about him.

I think Bubbles was the one who told Nancy to dump André. I found a card from him in Nancy's drawer shortly after she started hanging out with Bubbles.

"I don't care what your friends think about me," he wrote. "We're good together, babe. Don't let other people's opinins matter! Remember all the good times we use to have? Don't let the majic die."

But the truth was, Nancy and André had started fighting as soon as they left Jean-Paul standing in the park. I'd put my ear to the furnace vent and listen to them argue in the basement.

"Why aren't you supporting me?"

"Because it's time you dropped this dieting shit. You don't need to lose weight."

"Yes I do. And stop thinking of yourself for a change."

"Hey, don't start with me, Nancy. *You're* the selfish one. *You're* the one who went all weird just because of what Jean-Paul said. I told you—the guy's an idiot."

"It wasn't just what *he* said. It was eighteen years of stupid comments. And I'm tired of hearing them."

"What are you talking about?"

"Never mind. You wouldn't understand."

"Well maybe I would and maybe I wouldn't. But I'm at the end of my rope. I mean, we can't even go to McDonald's anymore, Nancy. How fucked up is that?"

But no matter what André said to her, Nancy didn't stop. She kept eating grapefruit for breakfast and salads for dinner. She exercised to her Jane Fonda workout record. She called Suzanne's and told them to take her off their mailing list.

It wasn't long before Nancy gave André the boot. He got pretty weird after that and would park his car outside of our house, waiting for her to come home from school or work.

"Do you think we should call the police, Henry?" my mom asked.

"I don't know," my dad said.

But when they asked Nancy about it, she said not to. She told them that André never said or did anything. He just pulled away when her Chevette turned onto our street. He hasn't been around for a couple of months now, so maybe he's finally given up.

• •

We ended up agreeing to get my parents a brass mailbox for their anniversary. It wasn't as exciting as sheers, but they needed a new one.

"Pick one up at Swenson's next time you're working," Nancy said to Christine.

"Nancy, I can't go shopping if I'm working."

"You work in a mall! Go after your shift is done."

"I don't work 'shifts.' There's a difference between Peoples Jewelers and Dunkin Donuts."

"What's that supposed to mean?"

"You're the one with a car," Christine said. "Why don't you pick it up the next time you and Bubbles are out skipping around?"

"Why don't you?"

"Why don't you?"

I rolled my eyes and plugged my ears with my fingers. In the end, Nancy and I drove to Swenson's the next night to get the mailbox.

"What's up Christine's butt, lately?" Nancy asked.

"I don't know," I said. I wanted to ask Nancy what was up *her* butt, but I bit my tongue.

"She's just being a total bitch, lately. Do you think she's jealous?"

"Of what?"

"Of her not being the only skinny one now."

I shrugged and pretended to be interested in something we were passing.

"Because if that's what her problem is, she's going to have to deal with it. There's no way I'm going back to the way things were before."

After we picked up the brass mailbox, Nancy and I were walking through the Food Court on our way to the exit when we heard someone behind us say, "Nancy!"

We turned around to see a good-looking guy wearing a tight blue T-shirt and coral necklace.

"Oh, hi Rick," Nancy said.

"How's it going?"

"Not bad, not bad."

"Are you coming to the game this weekend?"

Nancy flicked her head to one side. "I might."

Was this the guy she bought the birth control pills for?

"Well, maybe I'll see you there."

"Maybe." Nancy giggled. I wanted to throw up.

"See you."

"Bye."

"Who was that?" I asked. I didn't like him at all.

"Only the most popular guy in school," Nancy said. "I can't believe he talked to me! Bubbles is going to die when she hears about this!"

I wondered what André would think of Rick.

On our way home, we had to stop at a gas station so that Nancy could fill up. She got out of the car and I tilted her rearview mirror so that I could pop a couple of zits while I waited.

The sun was just going down. The days were getting longer, which meant that summer was around the corner again. People would stop wearing jackets soon and start wearing shorts and T-shirts. Freshman year was only a couple of months away and I still hadn't started working on the new Peter Paddington. The year had gone by so quickly. Underneath the tape, my nipples twitched.

I moved up closer to get a better look at a big zit on my forehead and caught Nancy's reflection in the mirror. She was wearing dangly silver earrings that flashed in the sunlight and a new pair of jeans and a pink cashmere sweater that she'd bought at Suzy Shier. All this time, I pretended not to notice Nancy. In my head, she was still the same Nancy. But now, for the first time, I really saw how thin she was. I could see her collarbone sticking out from underneath her skin and I realized that I'd never seen Nancy's collarbone before. Nancy's pretty now. She's thin and she's a whole new Nancy Paddington. And I understood what André was waiting for those nights he parked in front of our house. He was waiting for the old, fat Nancy to come home. I was waiting for the same thing.

eleven

Every May, the trees along our street blossom with little pink flowers. They're very pretty, even if they only last a couple of weeks. Mr. Mitchell told us the flowers are God's gift to us and we should all sit underneath the trees and write poems. He's been on this kick lately. It started with him reading us a Robert Frost poem about a cow. Then, for English period, he had us write haikus.

"Remember: five syllables in your first line, then seven, and back to five again!"

I wrote my haiku about a pencil:

Long, slender, yellow
Sharp lead point writing things down.
Mistake? Eraser.

Mr. Mitchell only gave me a B+ on it, which shows you how much he knows about good poetry. I guess I got bitten by the poetry bug a bit, because I've started writing haikus about everything: newspapers, grass, grocery stores, TV shows, you name it. My best one so far is the one I dedicated to Mr. Hanlan:

Strong man with brown eyes.
Happy birds sing. Why not you?
"Evil wife must die."

The last line Mr. Hanlan says, not me. I don't think
Mrs. Hanlan is evil enough to kill. But I do think she's
too evil to deserve someone as good and kind as Mr.
Hanlan. But Mr. Hanlan doesn't see that since he's so
good and kind in the first place. She's got him trapped.

But maybe there's a way I can let him know. Maybe I
can break the Hanlans up the same way I did Daniela and
Phil, the Burger King Banger. I went to grab the telephone book.

"Do you really think this is a good idea?" my nipples
asked from underneath their bandage. I got smart
recently and found the elastic bandage my mom had
wrapped around her ankle after her Mary Kay fall. I figured it beat buying tape all the time. Every morning, I
wrap it around my chest twice and fasten it in place with
a safety pin.

"I'm not asking for your opinion," I said, opening the
book to "H."

"Doing this isn't going to change anything," my nipples said. "Mr. Hanlan doesn't like you. Not in the way
you want him to, anyway. The only thing you are to him
is the paperboy."

"That's not true!" I said. "Besides, why should I listen
to you in the first place? You've been nothing but liars
since the day you popped out."

"We're the only ones telling the truth," they said.

I couldn't concentrate, so I closed the phone book before finding the Hanlans' number. My nipples were jealous of me, plain and simple. They were afraid I wouldn't need them anymore when things started to change—once I broke up the Hanlans, once I lost weight, once I got a boy friend, once I became the person I knew was inside of me, just waiting to get out.

• •

The next day at school, we were out in the field, playing soccer. Well, maybe I shouldn't say "we." It was Craig Brown and the other boys from the Athlete Group who were really playing. The rest of us were standing there, pretending to look ready if the ball came our way. I was talking to Margaret Stone about Mr. Archill, the organist at St. Paul's Methodist.

"I always smell whiskey whenever he's around," I was saying. "I bet he's an alcoholic."

"Well, I'm not sure about that," Margaret said, but I could tell by the look on her face she thought the same thing, too. Since she's a minister's daughter, Margaret can't say anything bad about anyone. It's hard being a Christian.

"People! Let's move it!" Mr. Nunzio yelled, clapping his hands. He was staring over at Margaret and me. "You have to go to the ball, people. The ball will not come to you."

Mr. Nunzio is always calling us "people."

"People! It's time to motivate yourselves!"

"Sports are like life, people. You can stand on the side-lines or you can get in the game."

"The only exercise you people seem to get is by flapping your gums."

I had Mr. Nunzio for 7th grade last year. But this year, he teaches gym to my class while his class takes geography with Mr. Mitchell.

Mr. Nunzio is short and always red in the face, especially when he's yelling. He doesn't yell because he's angry. He's just one of those people who does it without thinking, like when Daniela Bertoli uses the f-word. I asked Daniela if she knew Mr. Nunzio, since I thought he might be Italian. She says all Italian people know each other.

"It's the shits," Daniela told me. "Everyone's always sticking their noses into your business."

But Daniela said she's never heard of Mr. Nunzio, so I guess he's something else.

Mr. Nunzio is balding, but he's very hairy everywhere else. He has a bushy red mustache and the furriest arms I've ever seen. When Mr. Nunzio is teaching gym, he wears short-sleeved shirts, so I really notice just how big and hairy they are. He wears blue gym pants, too. Sometimes, I can see his dink poking out.

Mr. Nunzio has a picture of his wife and two kids on his desk. His wife is all right looking, I guess, but she should get a perm. Her hair is long and straight and parted in the middle. I think Mr. Nunzio could do much better. Mrs. Nunzio is probably very demanding and tells Mr. Nunzio he isn't making enough money.

Mr. Nunzio's first name is Al. I know this because I overheard Mr. Mitchell call him that once. It's weird when you hear teachers call each other by their first names. It's like they're friends or something.

Anyways, Mr. Nunzio is always telling me that I should exercise more.

"You've got to have confidence," he says to me. "Confidence in everything you do. That includes sports, Peter."

I know that when Mr. Nunzio tells me to exercise, he isn't being mean. It's like he sees something in me that I don't see myself. He cares about me, even though he doesn't come right out and say it.

Sometimes, though, I wish Mr. Nunzio would lay off, especially when other people are around. I mean, the Indian kids never do anything in gym class, but he never yells at them.

Anyways, so Mr. Nunzio tells Margaret and me to "get in the game, people." And part of me was kind of angry, because I wanted to talk to Margaret more about Mr. Archill, but another part of me said, "He's only saying that because he cares about you, Peter."

So while I'm standing there, thinking about all this, something hits my foot. I look down and it's the soccer ball. It takes me a few seconds to realize what it is, because I've never seen one that close up before. And the next thing I hear is Mr. Nunzio yelling, "Run, Peter, run! Take it to the net!"

And I see Craig Brown and his goons heading toward me, so I start kicking the ball and running with it. And I hear Mr. Nunzio say, "The other way, Peter! Go toward *the other net!*" But I don't care, because it feels kind of good and my heart is beating fast, and I'm thinking how proud Mr. Nunzio must be and he'll go home tonight with a big smile on his face and tell his demanding wife how I came through for him today, just like he knew I always would. Maybe he'll even start to cry.

And just as I was getting to the part where I could see Mr. Nunzio's tears, everything went black.

• •

When I woke up, I was in Mrs. Terribone's office. She's the nurse at Clarkedale and works on Tuesdays and Thursdays. Once a year, Mrs. Terribone goes around to all the classrooms, checking people's hair for lice using toothpicks. It's very embarrassing.

Mrs. Terribone smokes, too. I've seen her pull out of the parking lot after school, sucking on a cigarette like it was the end of the world. That tells you what kind of nurse she is.

"HOW MANY FINGERS AM I HOLDING UP?" she was yelling at me. I could smell the smoke on her breath. "WHAT YEAR WERE YOU BORN? WHAT IS YOUR ADDRESS?" She kept snapping her fingers in my face. It was very annoying.

"I'm fine," I told her, but I was still a little groggy. I couldn't figure out how I got there with crazy Mrs. Terribone yelling at me. Then, I started to remember.

Running in the field, kicking the soccer ball, Mr. Nunzio telling me to turn the other way, turn the other way. Then, nothing.

"Did I faint?" I asked Mrs. Terribone. I was pretty excited. Fainting is very dramatic. I wondered how I looked when it happened. Did I put my hand to my fore-head? Did my knees give out? Did Mr. Nunzio carry me off the field in his arms?

"Oh, you passed out all right," Mrs. Terribone said. "Hit the ground like a ton o' bricks, Peter. The whole kit and caboodle."

I was kind of mad when Mrs. Terribone said that. It didn't sound very graceful.

"It must've been my heart," I said. "It's very weak."

Maybe I had a disease. I'd have to go to the hospital and Mr. Nunzio would come to visit me. He'd feel so guilty.

"It's all my fault, Peter," he'd say. "If only I hadn't pushed you so hard."

"It wasn't your heart," Mrs. Terribone said. She yawned and I could see all the fillings in her molars. "It was this."

And then Mrs. Terribone held up the elastic bandage that I had wrapped around myself that morning before school. I closed my eyes and thought I was going to die. I put my hands on my chest. My nipples were free under my sweatshirt. They'd start talking any minute and how was I going to explain that?

"This came undone, Peter. You tripped on it. Now, do you want to tell me what this is about?"

I couldn't speak. All I kept thinking was what if my sweatshirt had gone up around my neck when I fainted? What if everyone had seen my stomach, or even worse, my nipples? What about Andrew Sinclair and Mr. Nunzio and everyone else?

"It's for my ribs," I said quietly. "I sprained them a while ago. They're very delicate."

"Peter, you didn't sprain your ribs," Mrs. Terribone sighed. "Now, why don't you try telling me the truth?"

I don't hate many people because it's not very Christian. But at that moment, I hated Mrs. Terribone more than I hated anyone ever. All I wanted was to be invisible and go back into unconsciousness where it was black and no one asked me questions I couldn't answer.

"My head hurts," I said. "I think I need to rest some more."

Mrs. Terribone said that my mom was on her way and that she'd be back in a minute.

"I gotta get something out of my car," she said and grabbed her keys. I knew that meant she was going for a smoke.

I lay there in the cot, staring at the holes in the ceiling. I thought about running away. There wasn't a window in the nurse's office, but if I could sneak down the hall and into the boy's washroom, maybe I could climb up and out one of the windows. Then I remembered how small the windows were and the last thing I needed was for someone to find me stuck in a window frame.

I wondered where my class was. Were they still out in the field, playing soccer? How much time had passed since I fainted in the field? Wherever they were, I'm sure everyone was laughing at me. How could I do something so stupid?

"We were wondering the same thing," my nipples said. "Serves you right for squishing us down with that stupid bandage."

"I wouldn't be wearing that stupid bandage if you were

normal nipples," I said, "so it's more your fault than mine."

"If that's what *you* say. But you might as well get used to us because we're not going anywhere."

"Why are you being so mean to me?" I asked them.

"We know everything about you. You can keep chasing soccer balls all you want. But you can't run away from us."

It wasn't long before my mom came barging through the office door.

"Oh my lord," she said when she saw me lying on the cot. "What on earth?"

"He'll be all right, Mrs. Paddington," Mrs. Terribone said. She smelled like smoke and Scope. "Just a little fainting spell, that's all."

Mrs. Terribone told me to wait outside while she spoke to my mom.

While I was standing in the hall, Brian Cinder came walking by. I pressed myself as far back as I could against the wall and prayed that just once, just this one time, he wouldn't say anything.

Brian stopped in front of me. "Are you okay?" he asked.

I looked up at him and nodded. I couldn't believe he asked me that.

"You fell pretty hard."

"Did I?" I tried to smile. "I don't really remember it."

"Oh yeah," Brian said. "Really hard. So hard, there's a big hole in the field in the shape of your ass. They're bringing in a dump truck tomorrow to fill it in." Then he started laughing and walked away.

• •

"We're going to have to tell your father when he gets home," my mom said. She put the elastic bandage on the coffee table and had just hung up the phone after making an appointment with Dr. Luka. She'd stopped crying by that point, but her eyes were still puffy and red. "You're going to have to tell him about what happened this after-noon."

The good thing is that my mom doesn't know about my nipples. When she asked me why I'd wrapped the bandage around myself, I told her that I did it to look thinner.

"My stomach is too big," I said. "I thought the band-age would be like a girdle. Like the kind Grandma Paddington wears."

I figured it was better to tell her that than tell her the truth.

"But why would you do something like that?" my mom asked. "Why?"

"Because," I said. "I already told you. My stomach is too big."

"Peter, you're being ridiculous," my mom said. She made a snorting sound. "You're just a bit on the chubby side, that's all."

"Chubby side? Mom…"

"Is Nancy behind this?"

"No."

"Then why would you *do* something like that? I don't understand, Peter."

"You're not listening —"

"I don't want to talk about this right now, Peter. We'll

have to wait until your father gets home."

I rolled my eyes and sat back into the sofa. I can't understand how she could be so two-faced. She wants me to give her an answer. So I do—which isn't the real answer, but it's real enough. But then, that answer isn't the right one for her, so I don't know what she wants me to say.

We sat in the living room, waiting for my dad. Neither of us said anything. The only sound was the ticking of the living room clock. My dad was out buying a new lawn mower. After a while, the car pulled into the driveway and then the back door opened and I heard my dad come up the stairs.

"Henry, your son has something he needs to tell you," my mom said as soon as my dad came into the living room.

He turned from me to her and then back to me. "All right," he sighed and sat down. The look on his face was the same as when he sat in the bleachers, watching me try to play softball. That was two years ago. I signed up because I thought it'd make my dad happy. I figured he could make friends with the other fathers while they watched the game from the bleachers and my dad could yell things like, "Go, go, go!" or "Did you see my son catch that ball? He's heading straight to the majors, wait and see" instead of sitting in the den, listening to his country and western tapes while I practiced calligraphy in my room.

But it didn't take long to figure out that my dad could-n't yell things like "Go, go, go!" because I never went anywhere. I struck out most times. And as far as catching anything, that didn't happen either. I got put in right field and I was afraid of the ball hitting me in the face, so I stood and watched the other boys run after it while the coach yelled at me. I couldn't look at my dad, sitting there in the bleachers. He couldn't look at me, either. After a few games, he stopped coming. And I stopped playing. And neither one of us talked about baseball after that.

"Did you get a new lawn mower?" I asked.

He nodded. "I got one on sale at Swenson's."

"You're stalling, Peter," my mom said.

"We have to go see Dr. Luka again, dad," I said.

• •

"Now, Peter," Dr. Luka said, closing the file and sitting down across from me. "How are ve doing?"

"Fine," I said. I was trying to hold my breath because the old person smell in Dr. Luka's office was super strong.

"Vhat's new?"

"Not much."

I still wasn't sure what I was going to tell Dr. Luka. My dad was in the waiting room, reading an old copy of *Reader's Digest*. He didn't say too much when I told him about the bandage, other than he was sorry that I felt I had to do something like that. I'm not sure what he meant.

"Now, Peter," Dr. Luka said again. I was breathing through my mouth by this point. "Your mother is very concerned about you. She is very vorried."

"Dr. Luka, pardon me for saying so," I said, "but air makes my mom worry."

Dr. Luka started laughing his head off when I said that. I thought he was going to choke and die right on the spot. Then I'd really be in trouble.

"BOY COMMITS MURDER TELLING JOKE!" the *Observer* headline would read.

"That's very funny, Peter," Dr. Luka said after he had calmed down. "You're a very clever boy."

"Really?" I asked.

"Your mother said that you had an accident at school the other day. She said you fainted in the schoolyard. Can you tell me vhat happened?"

"Certainly, Dr. Luka. You see, my nipples popped out last fall. I didn't want anyone to notice them, so I taped them down every morning. About a week ago, I moved on to an elastic bandage because buying all that tape got to be expensive. Plus, I could tell Mr. Bernard at the Shop 'N' Bag started to get suspicious because really, who ever heard of masking tape animal sculptures? Anyways, the elastic bandage came undone the other day in gym class and I tripped on it and conked out. That's what happened. Did I mention that my nipples also talk to me?"

Dr. Luka sat there, waiting for me to answer. I noticed a booger in his right nostril that kept popping out every time he exhaled.

"Tell him," my nipples whispered from beneath the masking tape. I had to go back to the old way of doing things since my mom hid the elastic bandage. "Tell him."

I froze. My nipples had never spoken while someone else was in the room.

"Did you hear that, Dr. Luka?"

"Hear vhat?"

"The voices. Did you hear them?"

Dr. Luka narrowed his eyes and twisted up his mouth. "Mmm hmm," he said, opening my file again. "Can you tell me how long you've been hearing voices, Peter?"

"Tell him," my nipples said.

I stared at Dr. Luka, hoping he heard that time. But by the way he was scribbling in my folder, I knew he hadn't. I had to think fast or else Dr. Luka was going to send me away to a crazy hospital.

"Sorry," I said. "It must've been Mrs. Luka I heard. I think she's on the phone. She's quite a talker, isn't she?"

"Yes, you could say that," Dr. Luka sighed.

"How long have you been married?"

"Thirty-seven years."

"Wow. Has it been a good relationship?" I figured the more questions I asked, the better my chances of Dr. Luka forgetting about me. "Where did you meet? Was it love at first sight?"

"Stop it," my nipples said. "Tell him."

Dr. Luka shook his pencil at me. "You are a very curious boy, Peter. Maybe next time, I'll answer your questions. But about you, now. Can you tell me vhat happened?"

I was backed into a corner. "The truth is…" I started.

"Tell him."

"The truth is that…"

"Go on."

"The truth is that I'm out of shape, Dr. Luka. I was running after the soccer ball and I got short of breath and I tripped and I think I need to lose some weight."

"Coward!" my nipples hissed.

"Yes!" Dr. Luka yelled and clapped his hands.

"Vhat is it?" I heard Mrs. Luka call out from her desk.

Dr. Luka was smiling at me like I'd just won the jackpot. "That's very good, Peter! Very good! I am so glad to hear you say that because you are the von that has to lose the veight, you see? You are the von who must decide, yes! I vant to be healthy! Yes! I vant to be in shape! Yes! I vant to have energy! You see?"

I nodded and tried to smile, but Dr. Luka was making me nervous. I'd never seen him so excited before.

Mrs. Luka was standing in the doorway. She had a monkey arm in her hand. "Vhat's going on?" she asked. I wanted to die, I was so embarrassed.

"Peter vants to lose veight!" Dr. Luka said.

"That's vonderful!" she exclaimed. "Vonderful!"

The next thing I knew, my dad was standing beside Mrs. Luka.

"What's all the commotion about?" he asked.

Dr. Luka smiled and told him that I vanted to lose veight and vasn't he proud of me? My dad looked at me with this half-grin on his face.

"Is that true?" he asked me on the ride home.

I shrugged. "I guess so," I said. "Maybe if I lose weight, I can play baseball this summer." I think I managed to sound excited. It was the least I could do for him.

"You don't like baseball, do you Peter?" my dad asked. We were stopped at a red light.

I sighed and shook my head.

"Then why do you want to sign up?"

"Because you like it."

"I don't like baseball."

"You don't?"

"No!" my dad said. "I can't stand it. Never could."

"What about golf?" I asked.

"Love golf," my dad said. The light turned green.

I figured I could live with that.

My mom let me stay home for the rest of the week.

"It's better if you just take it easy for the next little while," she said. "You could have suffered some brain damage from the fall, so I don't want you to exert yourself in any way."

We spent the mornings watching *The Price Is Right* and in the afternoons, we watched *Another World.*

"I don't want you to think that this is what I do all day while you kids are in school," my mom said, sitting down in the armchair with a glass of Pepsi. "Taking care of a household is a lot more demanding than some people might think. Every now and then, I just have to take a break and relax. Peter, will you look through the *TV Guide* and tell me who's on *Donahue* tomorrow?"

We got along pretty well for the most part, except when she got on the topic of dieting.

"I don't trust that doctor. I'm sorry, but I don't," she said to my dad when we first got back from seeing Dr. Luka. I was listening to them from behind my bedroom door. "I suppose he has some magic diet pills he wants Peter to buy now?"

"You're overreacting," my dad said. "Peter was the one who brought it up. Not Luka."

"I just don't approve of making a fourteen-year-old go on a diet. It's not fair to him."

"It's not fair for him to wrap bandages around himself, either, Beth."

That must've got my mother thinking because the only response I heard was the sound of her nose honking into a Kleenex.

She tried to get me to change my mind when we were alone.

"Are you sure about this?" she asked me during a *Price Is Right* commercial break.

"Yes," I said. To be honest, I hadn't really thought about it too much.

"You don't really want to eat grapefruit all the time, do you? They don't taste very good."

"Who says I have to eat grapefruit?"

"Oh, I don't care," she said. "Do whatever you want. I'm sorry if you kids don't feel you were raised right." She reached for the box of Kleenexes.

"Mom…"

"And I'm sorry if I wasn't Miss Perfect Mother all the time. But you were all so persistent. Always at me for a cookie or a chocolate bar or a donut. And sometimes, it was just easier to give you what you wanted than to fight, fight, fight all the time." She took off her glasses and wiped her eyes. "Maybe I should have been more strict with you kids. I don't know. But you never had the time for me unless I had something sweet in my hand. Do you know what that felt like?"

The TV audience cheered as someone on *The Price Is Right* got called to "Come on down!"

"Your father is right," my mom sighed, holding up her glasses before she put them back on, "I can't keep these clean to save my life."

• •

The Sunday night before I went back to school, I tried to get on the Virgin's good side again. I needed her help more than ever. There was no way I could go back to school and face everyone again. I took my Yoda poster down. It was disrespectful of me to put it up there in the first place. I lay on my bed and sent telepathic messages to her. I twisted my nipples with my fingertips, like they were dials on a radio. I figured I might get better reception that way.

"Peter to Virgin," I whispered and slowly turned my nipples to the left. "Come in Virgin."

"Ow!" my nipples yelled. But I ignored them.

I lay there as still as I could, rolling my eyes back and making my body as stiff as a board. That's what happens when people go into religious trances. It's very dramatic.

Anyways, while I was in my trance, I waited for the Virgin's voice to come through. I was expecting her to give me some kind of riddle that I'd have to solve, like the world was going to explode, only she'd say it in Pig Latin.

But after what seemed like forever, I gave up. Maybe the Virgin was still cranky at me for covering her up in the first place. I sent her a telepathic message, telling her that I was sorry.

I had a hard time sleeping that night because I kept hearing everyone's laughter in my head. How would I ever face anyone again?

"You should've told the doctor the truth," my nipples said.

"I *did* tell him the truth. I *do* need to go on a diet."

"You didn't tell him about us, though. Why not?"

"Because no one can ever find out about you. Besides, you'll go away if I ignore you long enough. All you want is attention."

"Do you really think we're going away?" my nipples asked.

"Of course," I said. My head was starting to hurt. I wanted my nipples to shut up, but they had a mind of their own. I thought about the smell of orange pop on Andrew's breath and my hand over Billy's dink and the way Mr. Hanlan looked at me when he asked if I wanted big or small marshmallows in my hot chocolate.

"Do you really think we're going away?" my nipples asked again.

Why wouldn't they be quiet? It was 11:32 at night and I had to get up for school! I closed my eyes and tried to concentrate on falling asleep, but it turned out to be a very long night.

• •

I was so afraid the next morning, but in the end, no one said anything to me, except for one person. I got to school just as the bell was ringing. I stood in line like everyone else behind the yellow line spray-painted on the asphalt. Lisa Miller was in front of me. She was whispering something to Michelle Appleby. At first, I thought she was saying something about me, but then Michelle reached into her purse and put a tampon in Lisa's hand. Lisa gave Michelle a dirty look and said, "Not here!" Then Lisa stuffed the tampon in her jean pocket.

Behind me, Jessica Lewis, one of the Goody-Goody girls, was trying to make a sticker deal with Julie Tilson.

"The Coke smell is so strong," Jessica said and held the sticker up to her nose. "It smells soooo good—just like a real Coke. Are you sure you don't want to trade?"

Behind them was Andrew. He was reading a science-fiction book.

"He looks so sophisticated," I thought, even though I didn't dare look at him for too long or else he might catch me.

When Mr. Mitchell came out, he was wearing his usual brown pants/white shirt/blue tie combo.

"All right class," he called out, "single file. No talking or pushing."

I kept my eyes on the floor while I walked to the classroom. I couldn't take any chance of being noticed. I was so afraid that Mr. Mitchell was going to say something when we took our seats.

"Students, I'd like you to welcome back Peter Paddington. You may remember that Peter had an unfortunate fainting spell last week due to an elastic bandage he had wrapped around himself to hide his deformed nipples."

So I was relieved when Mr. Mitchell pulled out *Christian Tales for Modern Youth*. I'd never been so happy to hear one of his stories in my whole life.

At recess, I went to the library as usual. Mrs. Kraft said she was glad to see me.

"We missed you around here. Say, I need to get these shelves sorted out by school's end. Do you think you can start on the far wall?"

While I was working my way through the Judy Blume books, I looked out the window. It was warm and sunny outside. Most of the students were wearing T-shirts and shorts. The Athlete Group boys were playing a game of touch football. The Indian kids were standing in a circle behind the gym. The Slut Group girls were talking to some of the members of the Banger Group. The Goody-Goody girls were sitting in the field with their photo albums of stickers. The Short Group boys were playing horse. Eddy Vanderberg was yelling, "No spiking or dribbling!" Off the far edge of the tarmac, the Geek Group was passing around *Fangoria* magazines. Andrew Sinclair was looking over Sean Dilworth's shoulder.

"Oh, Andrew," I whispered to myself. Then I looked down at my hand and saw I was holding a copy of *Blubber*. I put it back on the shelf.

"H-h-h-hi P-Peter."

I turned around to see Jackie Myner standing behind me. She was wearing a wrinkled green track suit and red shoes. A piece of masking tape was wrapped around her right shoe, holding it together. She had a *Tiger Beat* magazine in her hand and I noticed it was folded open to a picture of Adrian Zmed in his *T.J. Hooker* police uniform.

"Are y-y-y-you feeling b-b-better?" Jackie asked.

"Yes, I'm fine," I said and looked around. The last thing I needed was for someone to walk in and see me talking to her.

"Th-th-that's good," Jackie said. "I d-d-didn't know if you were in th-th-th-th-the hospital. When M-M-Mr. Nunzio and Mr. M-M-Mitchell carried y-y-you off the field on th-that stretcher, I th-th-th-thought you w-were a g-g-goner."

I looked over Jackie's shoulder and tried to smile. "Well, I have a weak heart."

I wanted Jackie gone. At any moment, someone could walk into the library and see us. I glanced out the window again at the Athlete Group, the Short Group, the Goody-Goody Group. I had spent the whole week worrying about what people were going to say about me. But no one had said anything. It was almost like no one noticed I was gone at all. They were out there and I was in here so what made me think that anyone would care if I was talking to Jackie? I *was* Jackie Myner.

"Wh-Wh-When you were unconscious, d-d-d-do you think you d-d-died? D-d-did you see your body lying in the f-f-field?"

I hadn't thought about that. It was true that I could-n't really remember what happened between the time I passed out and when I woke up with ugly Mrs. Terribone yelling at me. But what if I *did* die? What if I *did* have a near-death experience? I mean, I had an image of my body lying in the field, but that's because I was nervous about what I must've looked like. Or so I thought.

"I think the answer to your question is a definite maybe," I said. "The chances are pretty good that I did die for a couple of seconds. Maybe over time, more will come back to me. I'll probably remember a tunnel and seeing my dead grandma, telling me to 'Go back, Peter! Go back!'"

Jackie gasped. "Th-That's really sp-sp-spooky. You m-m-must feel very lucky to have c-c-c-c-c-c-come back from the dead."

Outside, I heard Craig Brown yell "Touchdown!"

"In some ways," I said.

BEDTIME MOVIE #5

Mr. Nunzio asks me to stay after school. He says he needs help washing down the blackboards.

"Thank you for coming," he says when I walk into the classroom. He's wearing a white T-shirt and blue gym pants. I can see his dink poking out, but I pretend not to notice.

Mr. Nunzio hands me a cloth.

"I have to make a phone call," he says to me. "Will you excuse me for a moment, Peter?"

I say sure and he leaves. Though he doesn't tell me, I know he's gone off to the staff room to call his wife. He tells her that he's running late and not to stay up waiting for him.

"All you do is work!" Mrs. Nunzio yells into the phone. She's combing her straight hair. "I'm sick of it! I should have never married you!"

When Mr. Nunzio comes back into the classroom, I can see he's upset. I put down the cloth.

"What's wrong, Mr. Nunzio?" I ask him.

"Oh nothing, Peter," he says, looking at the picture on

his desk. But I can tell he wants to tell me. He needs someone to talk to. No one understands how hard he works. No one except for me.

"Hey," I say quietly and sit down in the chair next to him, "it's me you're talking to."

Mr. Nunzio smiles in a sad kind of way.

"You're too mature for your age, Peter," he says. "How did you get to be so wise?"

Mr. Nunzio says that he's not getting along with his wife, that she's angry with him and is going to leave him. I tell him not to worry. He's better off without her.

"You need confidence, Mr. Nunzio," I tell him. "Confidence in everything you do."

"Call me Al," Mr. Nunzio says. It feels weird, but it's what he wants me to do.

"You'll survive, Al," I say. "You're one of the tough guys."

"And what about you, Peter? I know something about you, too."

Then, dark terror spreads across my face. I can't let him know anything about me. It's too dangerous.

"I have to go," I say and pick up my knapsack.

"No!" Mr. Nunzio says and grabs my arm tightly. I can see the muscles moving beneath his hairy arms. "I know why you fainted the other day."

"Al, please." I must get away, away from him, away from everything. "Let me go."

"Why are you doing this?" Mr. Nunzio asks. "Let me see them."

"No," I say. "I can't."

"If I take off my shirt, will you take off yours?"

I stop to think for a bit. "Maybe," I say. "But no promises."

Mr. Nunzio lets go of my arm and pulls off his white T-shirt. His chest is hairy and muscular and I see his nipples peeking through like two raisins.

"Now it's your turn."

I shake my head. "I've changed my mind," I say.

"Don't play games with me, people!" Mr. Nunzio yells. I see the look in his eyes—the look that speaks of his man-hunger. Terrified, I break free and run out into the hallway, screaming for help, but everyone has gone home. I try the doors, but they're locked. Mr. Nunzio is close behind. I run into the staff room. It's a bad move on my part. I'm cornered.

"Please don't," I plead, but he's too fast. With one loud "RIP!" my T-shirt is torn in half. I've never been this naked in front of anyone before. The next thing I know, he's unpeeling the elastic bandage from around my chest.

"Stop," I say and this time I really mean it. But it's too late. I'm spinning and spinning and I can't slow down. "Stop," I say again, but no one's listening. And I know the trick to stop from getting dizzy and that's to keep your eyes focused on one spot. So I'm looking at the basement window each time and suddenly, I'm not wearing any bandages at all. Uncle Ed winks at me from behind the glass.

Then I fall asleep.

twelve

If I was going to get skinny in time for freshman year, I had to act fast. There was no time to lose. I knew enough about dieting from watching Nancy and Christine, so I just copied whatever they ate, which usually was salads, grapefruit, cottage cheese, melba toast, chicken broth, and sometimes, a piece of fish. It was awful at first because I was always hungry and grapefruit is terrible without any sugar on it. But every time my mother asked, "Are you sure that's all you're going to eat?" or "Anyone for a Ding Dong?" it only made me stronger. If Nancy and Christine could do it, so could I.

But exercising is something I'll *never* get used to.

I knew I needed to do it, but it had been so long since I last exercised that I wasn't sure how to start. I thought about taking walks in the evening, but that sounded boring. Besides, I already walk enough for my paper route. Then I thought jogging might be good, because it's fashionable. I asked Christine if she had an extra headband I could borrow. She goes jogging three times a week.

"For what?" she asked.

"For when I go jogging," I said.

"Are you serious?" She looked at me as if I'd just stepped off a space ship.

"Forget I asked," I said. "I'll buy my own."

"Don't do that," Christine sighed. "I've probably got something you can have. But who are you going jogging with?"

"Myself."

"You shouldn't do that. At least not in the beginning. I'll go with you."

"Are you sure I'm not going to *embarrass* you? Someone from Peoples might see us together."

Christine bit her bottom lip and stared at me for a few seconds. "You don't embarrass me," she said. "So don't think that. And be ready at seven sharp."

When the time came, Christine came bouncing out of her room, wearing her "When God made man, SHE was only joking" T-shirt and a pair of black tights. Her hair was tied up in a bun and she was wearing lipstick and eye shadow. I was wearing a sweatshirt and a pair of rugby pants.

"You'll die in that," Christine said and tossed me a white headband.

"Isn't your make-up going to run?" I asked.

"Look, don't feel you have to compete with me. This isn't a race. So just start off at your own pace and if you start feeling dizzy or not able to breathe, then stop."

I knew Christine was just saying that because she was afraid that I'd pass her and take the lead.

"Thanks for the tip," I said. "But I don't think I'll need it."

Christine and I started by walking to the corner and

then we picked up the pace. I was doing pretty good, but my stomach and boobs were jiggling. I swore the neighbours were watching me from their living room windows.

"Remember to keep breathing," Christine said.

That was easy for Christine to say, considering she didn't have masking tape wrapped around her chest. Suddenly, I felt a sharp pain in my left side.

"My appendix burst," I thought. "Someone, call a doctor!"

I told Christine to go on. "Something's gone wrong," I panted. "I need to sit down for a bit."

Christine went ahead and I walked the rest of the way to our house, trying to catch my breath. My nipples were sore from all that shaking. Jogging was stupid, I thought. Just as I reached my front yard, I heard someone calling my name. I looked across the street and Daniela was standing in her garage with a broom in her hand. She yelled at me to come over.

"What do you want?" I panted. My lungs were burning.

"What the fuck were you just doing?" she asked, crinkling her nose.

"Jogging," I said.

"Well, I'd suggest some deodorant." She waved her hand in front of her face. "At least you're killing all the fuckin' flies."

"Very funny," I said and walked away.

• •

The next day, I asked Nancy about her aerobics class. She and Bubbles go twice a week.

"You can come if you want," Nancy said. "It's fun and the instructor is really nice."

I was nervous about going because I was afraid that someone might see me. Or even worse, someone in the class might know me. But Nancy told me not to be such a spaz and that the class was all women so that made me feel a little better. On Tuesday night, after my dinner of plain tuna and a bowl of salad, Nancy told me to get ready. She was dressed in her latest Suzy Shier outfit—a pink tank top with matching pink shorts, pink leg warmers, and a pink headband.

"My lord," my mom said when she saw Nancy. "Are you going to an exercise class or the senior prom?"

I was planning to wear the usual—black rugby pants with a sweatshirt—but once I saw Nancy, I felt retarded. If only I had a matching headband, too.

"No one will care what you look like," Nancy told me. "Everyone wears jogging pants and T-shirts anyway."

Then Bubbles showed up.

"Hey, that's great you're coming with us!" she said. She was wearing a blue tank top with matching blue shorts, blue leg warmers, and a blue headband.

"What are you two, twins?" Christine asked them.

"You never know!" Bubbles said and smacked her gum.

"Be careful!" my mom yelled as we were walking out. "Nancy, you keep a close eye on your brother. And Peter, if you start feeling pains in your chest or anything, you come right home."

The aerobics class was held in the basement of St. Paul's

Church, so I felt better knowing where I was going. When we went down the stairs, there were eight women standing around, talking. All of them were thin. I felt very fat.

"C'mon," Nancy said. "I want to introduce you to the instructor. She's really nice."

Nancy led me over to a purple butt. At least, that's all I could see, since the woman was bent over at the waist.

"Tracy, I want to introduce you to my brother, Peter. He's checking out the class tonight."

The woman straightened up and turned around. I gasped. It was evil Mrs. Hanlan!

"Well, hello there, Peter," Mrs. Hanlan said and smiled. "It's nice to see you without that paper sack over your shoulder."

"Yeah." I could hardly talk.

"You two know each other?" Nancy asked.

"Your brother's my paperboy," Mrs. Hanlan said, "and a very good one at that. Dan says he's never seen a kid so punctual."

Did Mr. Hanlan really say that? I almost asked, but I knew better. I didn't like the way she called him by his first name, like she knew him better than me or something.

"I didn't know you were a teacher," I said.

"Just a couple nights a week," Mrs. Hanlan said. "It helps me stay in shape."

"Tracy used to be fat, too," Nancy said.

"You were?" I looked at her toothpick arms.

Mrs. Hanlan laughed. "During my teenage years, I was. C'mon, let's get started." She put her hand on my shoulder. "If you start feeling short of breath, Peter, just slow down. And don't feel that you have to keep up with everyone. Just take it at your pace."

I still couldn't believe that skinny Mrs. Hanlan used to be fat.

"Okay, let's get started everyone!" Mrs. Hanlan called out and put a tape in the ghetto blaster that was sitting on the floor.

Mrs. Hanlan had us march in place for a little bit to get warmed up. "That's it!" she said, over a Loverboy song. "Now swing those arms!"

It was pretty easy and I wasn't getting any pains in my side like when I went jogging. I was thinking that this wouldn't be so bad, after all, even if it was Mrs. Hanlan standing in front of me. I made a point to keep my stomach sucked in so she wouldn't notice and tell Mr. Hanlan about it.

"Now, jumping jacks!"

Everyone started jumping up and down and flapping their arms. I was starting to sweat a little bit by then, but not too badly. My nipples were bothering me, though. I didn't tape all the way around my chest because I knew it'd be too hard to breathe. Instead, I went back to my old Scotch tape star trick. But the tape wasn't holding very well and my nipples were burning. They started to hurt and I was getting frustrated.

"Now windmills!"

All the women started waving their hands in the air. I was losing my rhythm and looked over at Nancy to see how she was doing. She was in perfect time with Mrs.

Hanlan. Bubbles was, too. She was even smacking her gum to the beat.

"That's it! Take it at your own pace," Mrs. Hanlan called out.

She was looking right at me when she said that. I could tell she was trying to wear me out, but there was no way I was giving in.

"Now do-si-do!"

And then everything started getting very complicated and the class was skipping into the middle of the circle and skipping back out, like we were all at a square dance. I tried to do the same, but I ended up skipping into the circle when everyone was on their way out.

"Now sugar shack!"

I didn't even know what a sugar shack was and by watching Mrs. Hanlan, I still couldn't tell. She was waving her toothpick arms in the air and everyone was jumping around like they had ants in their pants. I couldn't stand the embarrassment anymore, so I mouthed the words "bathroom" to Nancy and jumped my way backwards until I was outside the door.

I sat down on the front steps at St. Paul's. I felt so embarrassed. I couldn't jog. I couldn't do-si-do. I couldn't do anything. I could just hear Mrs. Hanlan telling Dan all about it. How was I ever going to face them again? Ninth grade was only two and a half months away and I'd never be anyone different than I was at that moment—fat, boy friendless, taped-up Peter Paddington.

I headed straight for the Shop 'N' Bag to see the one person I could count on—Mr. Bernard. I hadn't been by to visit him since I started my diet. He must've thought I'd died or something.

"Well hello, stranger," he said when I came into the store. "Long time no see."

"I've been away on a trip," I lied. I couldn't tell him that I'd been avoiding his store on account of my stupid diet. He'd probably be hurt. "Europe, mostly."

Mr. Bernard smiled and said, "Of course. I can only imagine."

I grabbed a Snickers and a Hundred Thousand Dollar bar from the shelf and told Mr. Bernard to ring me up.

"Vhy have you betrayed me?" Dr. Luka asked.

"I knew you wouldn't last," Mrs. Hanlan said.

"I thought you loved me," Debbie Andover cried.

I paid Mr. Bernard, shoved the chocolate bars into my back pockets, and hurried out of the Shop 'N' Bag.

"Dirty chocolate," I whispered to myself. But I couldn't wait to get home and tear into them.

As I was walking past Papa Bertoli, I looked in and saw Daniela sitting on one of the bar stools. There was no one else in the restaurant, so I decided to go in.

"What's new?" I asked her.

"I think I'm gonna fuckin' fail this year," Daniela said, picking at the scabs on her knees. She didn't even turn around to look at me.

"Are you sure?" I sat down beside her. If Daniela failed 8th grade, that would put her behind *two* years. By the time she graduated high school, Daniela would be older than the teachers.

Daniela nodded. "Sister Louisa told me that unless I passed all my fuckin' projects and tests next month, she was going to keep me behind. I've done okay so far. I got a D- on my book report, which is like a fifty-three or something, I think. And I got twenty-six out of fifty on my math test. But today, I got back my book report and there was this big fuckin' F on it."

"Why did you get an F on it?"

"I don't fuckin' know!" Daniela shot back. "I copied it word for word from my copy of *Cosmo*."

"You shouldn't have done that," I said. "Copying things out of magazines is illegal. You could go to jail. Why didn't you just write your own?"

"Because I didn't have any fuckin' time, okay?"

I kept my mouth shut because Daniela was getting loud. She had already picked off four scabs.

"They've won," she said.

"Who?" I asked.

"Everyone," she said. "My parents. Gianni. My teachers. Everyone who told me I couldn't fuckin' make it. They've won and I might as well just sit here for the rest of my fuckin' life and watch everyone walk by the window."

It was weird, but for once, I knew exactly how Daniela felt. Even though I never served tables or had a nun for a teacher, I felt like "they" had won in my life, too. "They" were the people that thought Daniela and I were losers. "They" thought they were better than us, just because they were thin and had normal nipples and didn't wet the bed.

But did "they" ever enter a beauty pageant, even though

there was no chance of winning? Did "they" ever save one of their friends' virginity from a Banger? Did "they" ever have the Virgin Mary appear to them in their closet? Who did "they" think they were, anyway? And why did Daniela and I always let them beat us? I was so angry, my nipples started to vibrate beneath the masking tape.

"Daniela, we've got to take control of our lives," I said and slammed my palm down on the counter.

"What are you talking about?"

"I need to lose weight," I said. "And you need to get a job. A real one. Just imagine if you were working *and* making money. Your *own* money. Then you could save up, buy a house and the only driveway you'd have to shovel would be your own. Of course, by then, you could probably hire someone to come and do all your house-work for you. Can you imagine if you placed a Help Wanted ad in the *Observer* and Paolo Vernesse showed up at your door? You'd just look at him and say, 'I wanted someone to take out the trash. Not bring it to my doorstep.' Then you'd slam the door in his face and Paolo would go home and take out his bottle of Pino Silvestri and cry."

"What the fuck are you talking about?"

"What I'm talking about is you getting a real job."

"How am I going to do something like that?"

"What if you took over my paper route?"

Daniela's eyes bugged out. "Are you kidding me?"

I shook my head, even though I was still a little surprised myself. But how could I change anything about myself if I didn't start somewhere? Maybe it was time to say goodbye to Mr. Hanlan, even though he'd be upset. "You can't hold on to me forever," I said to him in a telepathic message.

Besides, I'd be starting high school in a few months and by then, I'd be thin with plenty of boy friends and have football practice after school.

"But if you take over my route," I said to Daniela, "you have to be professional. You have to get the papers out to people on time. And you have to watch what you say to them. People will expect you to be nice to them, whether you feel like it or not."

"Hey, don't fuckin' lecture me about being a pro," Daniela said. "I've spent the last fourteen years of my fuckin' life working like a slave."

Then she flicked one of her peeled-off scabs across the bar. I gave her the chocolate bars I had in my back pockets. They were a bit mushed up, but I told her they were still edible.

Daniela grabbed them. "I hope you didn't fuckin' fart on these or anything," she said, sniffing the Hundred Thousand Dollar bar.

"I'll talk to you later," I said.

I was going to head home but then I figured I'd go back to the Shop 'N' Bag and tell Mr. Bernard that he might not be seeing me for a while.

"It's not you," I'd tell him, "I'm just going through some big changes in my life right now."

I just hoped he wouldn't take it too hard.

Just as I was coming up to the door, I looked in and saw Uncle Ed. He was standing on the other side of the counter, talking to Mr. Bernard. At first I thought, "That can't be right. That's not Uncle Ed." But one look at the Hawaiian shirt told me it couldn't be anyone else. Why was he in there, talking to Mr. Bernard? How did they know each other? I started to get angry. Why couldn't Uncle Ed just leave me alone? Why couldn't he stop embarrassing me? He must've been following me, going to the same places I went, telling everyone things about me. Private things. Things he shouldn't know about. If he pulled my picture out of his wallet, I'd never talk to him again.

Mr. Bernard was smiling at Uncle Ed in a way I hadn't seen him smile before. It was weird. It seemed like they knew each other.

Then there's the other thing. For some reason I thought of what my mom had said when I asked her why Uncle Ed never married.

"What thing?" I'd asked her.

I noticed the way Uncle Ed was leaning into the counter toward Mr. Bernard, the same way Phil the Burger King Banger leaned toward Daniela in the restaurant.

What thing?

Mr. Bernard laughed at something Uncle Ed said.

Somewhere, a car horn honked. I turned around and walked home as fast as I could.

••

I finally found a way to exercise that didn't make me feel retarded. I was snooping through Nancy's room the other day, looking to see if Nancy had used up all her birth control pills, when I came across her Jane Fonda workout album. I looked at the picture of Jane on the cover. Her hair was pulled back and she was wearing a gray leotard. She was smiling right at me, as if to say, "I've been waiting for you, Peter Paddington." And it was the strangest thing, but the more I looked at Jane, the more I realized how much she looked like the Virgin Mary in my closet door. It was almost as if God had made me go snooping in Nancy's room to find Jane.

"Ave Maria," I whispered and crossed myself.

Now, Jane and I are best friends. Every night, I go downstairs and spend an hour with her. We stretch, we jog, we do sit-ups, and we firm up our buns. Every time that Jane says, "You can do it!" I know she's talking directly to me.

Sometimes, I pretend to be Jane and I mouth the words she's saying. I make believe that *Entertainment Tonight* is filming me for an upcoming television special called "Behind the Scenes with Hollywood's Biggest Stars." The ratings for the show will be very high.

"You can do it, America!" I smile at the camera and squeeze my buttocks high in the air.

Jane has taught me to take things slow. I'm still on the Beginners side. I don't think that I'm ready for the Advanced just yet. But with Jane's help, I'll get there.

"You can do it!" she says.

I always make sure I keep the basement curtains closed. The other day, while Jane and I were doing our buttock squeezes, I made a list in my head of all the things I'd changed about myself since the beginning of the year. The first is that I had actually started a diet and lasted more than three days. I think I've lost a couple of pounds because my finger doesn't go into my belly button quite as far. The second thing is that I'd given up my paper route. I started training Daniela the other day. It's going pretty well for the most part, but she scares some of the older people on my route. The other day, Daniela whipped the paper at Mrs. Guutweister's door and nearly broke the glass. Mrs. Guutweister came running out, as if a bomb had just gone off.

"You'll have to be patient," I whispered to Mrs. Guutweister. "God isn't finished with her yet."

The third thing is that I saved Daniela's virginity all by myself. A fourth thing is that I hardly ever think of Billy Archer anymore, except when I'm in the shower. A fifth thing is that I plan to take football lessons this summer so I can join the high school team in the fall. And the sixth thing is that I'm on my way to becoming someone new; someone I always knew I was, but no one could see.

I guess the only thing that hasn't changed are my cherry nipples. They're still there, puffy and red. Every morning, I wrap them up and every night, I set them free. In some ways, I'm starting to get used to them. I wonder if they'll ever go away. I ask them, but they never talk to me anymore. Sometimes, I think they're silent because they're angry at me. And other times, I wonder if they ever talked in the first place. It's weird how your mind can make you believe things that aren't really true. Especially when it comes to yourself.

BEDTIME MOVIE #6

I'm walking down a crowded high school hallway. I hear lockers opening and closing. A bell rings and a girl laughs. But I know she's not laughing at me. No one laughs at me anymore.

I'm thin and muscular and wearing a white T-shirt tucked into a pair of blue jeans. I'm also wearing deck shoes. My hair is long and hangs down over my forehead. It covers my eyes so that no one ever knows who or what I'm looking at. That's part of my mystery.

Inside, I feel very powerful. Everyone wants something from me. People want me to join their clubs at school. They want me to sit at their table in the cafeteria. They invite me over to their houses on the weekend. They ask me to help them with their homework, even though they don't really need it.

I don't really mind, even though sometimes, I get annoyed. But I can't really blame them, either. It's like there's something magical about me that no one can really describe.

Andrew Sinclair is up ahead, waiting by his locker. He sees me coming and thinks, "I should have called him. I should have asked him to the movies while I still had the chance."

"Poor Andrew," I think. He hates his life.

I pass the drama classroom. Debbie Andover is there, rehearsing for her next musical. I smile to myself. One of my new boy friends says that Debbie likes me.

"You should ask her out," he tells me. "Every guy in this school would kill for the chance to date Debbie."

"I'll think about it," I say.

I turn the corner and see Christine standing at her locker. She's wearing her "I'm Peter Paddington's sister" T-shirt.

"I thought we talked about this," I sigh. "That T-shirt is embarrassing."

"Is it a crime to be proud of you?" she asks me.

Nancy walks over to us.

"Mrs. Hanlan was arrested for murdering another aerobics instructor yesterday," she says. "They say she's gonna get the death penalty for sure."

I shake my head. "I'll have to give Dan a call tonight to see how he's doing." I turn the corner and head down the hallway toward the shop classes. That's where all the Bangers hang out. Most students are afraid to walk by them. They're afraid the Bangers will beat them up. But I'm not.

"Hey Peter."

It's Billy Archer. He's standing outside his locker with a bunch of thugs. They all nod at me. Billy's wearing his parachute pants. I feel a little sexy, but I don't let Billy know that.

"Hey Billy," I say. "Take your pills today?"

The other Bangers laugh. Billy tells me to screw off. But he's not angry. He's laughing when he says it. We have that kind of relationship.

After school, I have a very important championship football game.

"We're all counting on you, Paddington," Mr. Nunzio says.

"Back off, man!" I say and flip my hair. I'm very temperamental, but that's to be expected. As captain of the football team, I'm under a lot of pressure. "I'll do what I got to do."

Out on the field, my team and I warm up. "This is it, people," I say. "You can stand on the sidelines or you can get in the game."

Craig Brown nods, but he's secretly jealous of my popularity and good looks.

A whistle blows. The game is about to begin! I look over toward the stands and see familiar faces. My mom is there, misty-eyed. My dad is sitting beside her. He's yelling, "Shake it off, Petey!" in a very loud voice. I've never heard him yell like that before. On the field in front of them, Daniela is shaking a pair of pom-poms. I made sure she got onto the cheerleading team.

"Go team!" she yells and shakes her pom-poms. "Go fuckin' go!"

Suddenly, something catches my eye. It's the football. This time, I know what to do. I grab the ball and start running in the right direction. If I score this touchdown, I'll break the high school record. The crowd is on their feet. I can hear their screams and clapping.

I keep running, passing all the players from the other team. They all look like Brian Cinder.

"Eat dust!" I yell as I race by.

Then I start to get the feeling that I'm not running *to* something, but running *from* something. It's true that the other players are close behind me, but there's something else. It's bigger, faster, and darker and it's something that I know already, something that I try not to think about too often. It's been following me for a long time now. And if I stop for one second to look behind me, it will trip me and ruin everything. So I don't look behind and I don't stop running.

My heart is crashing into my rib cage and I'm scared that the masking tape around my chest will break and then my cherry nipples will come popping out and then they'll know.

Everyone will see the fruit I'm trying to hide.

I look up to see how far I have left to run and spot someone in the distance, standing between the goal posts.

"What's in the news?" he asks.

Then I fall asleep.

Insights,
Interviews
& More . . .

About the author

2 Meet Brian Francis

3 Brian Francis and His Esteemed
Writing Career

About the book

5 Why This Book Is "For Dad"

7 Brian Francis Talks to Dan Savage

Read on

14 Canadian Fruits v. American Fruits

16 Battle of the Chocolate Bars

Meet **Brian Francis**

Kathryn Gaitens

BRIAN FRANCIS has worked as a freelance
writer for a variety of magazines and
newspapers. In 2000 he won the Emerging
Author Award, presented by the Writers'
Union of Canada. He lives in Toronto. *The
Secret Fruit of Peter Paddington,* previously
published under the title *Fruit,* is his first
novel. ☙

Brian Francis
and His Esteemed Writing Career

WHEN I WAS in sixth grade, growing up in Sarnia, Ontario, I decided that I wanted to be a writer. It was during that year that I wrote my first book, a cheery little ditty called *If I Die Before I Wake*. It was the happy tale of two childhood friends, one of whom dies of leukemia at the end.

I never did find the right publisher for it, so it never went anywhere.

When I was in high school, I got back into writing and wrote a short story about a guy who kills himself on his parents' front lawn and a poem about worms on a sidewalk.

I never did find the right publisher for them either, so they never went anywhere.

When I was studying English at the University of Western Ontario, I wrote poems that incorporated Latin phrases, none of which I was able to translate and all of which were lifted from other poems. But they made me seem intelligent. I also wrote a short story about a six foot Judy Garland impersonator.

I never did find the right . . . well, you get the idea.

After a few rocky years of postgraduation, I eventually found myself living in Toronto and working in the magazine and newspaper industry, trying to find the time to write in between the day job, grocery shopping, and episodes of *The Golden Girls*. I wrote a ▶

> 66 After a few rocky years of postgraduation, I eventually found myself living in Toronto and working in the magazine and newspaper industry, trying to find the time to write in between the day job, grocery shopping, and episodes of *The Golden Girls*. 99

Brian Francis and His Esteemed Writing Career *(continued)*

short story about a boy who grows breasts. That led to another story and another. Eventually the breasts turned into nipples (because really, who ever heard of talking breasts?). Within a couple of years, I had something that actually looked like a book. And guess what?

I found the right publisher and something I wrote actually went somewhere. ∾

66 Eventually the breasts turned into nipples (because really, who ever heard of talking breasts?). 99

Why This Book Is "For Dad"

I'M OFTEN ASKED how autobiographical *The Secret Fruit of Peter Paddington* is, and while Peter isn't me, I did base a lot of his relationship with his father, Henry, on my own experiences. Like Henry, my dad was a quiet man. He never bullied me or made me do things I didn't want to do. But I can't help but think what a mystery I must have been to him as a child. What must it have been like to watch your son bypass the Tonka trucks and head straight for the Barbie dolls? What kind of logic could be found from a kid who wanted to dress as Marilyn Monroe for Halloween? (Yes, that part is true.)

As I grew into my adolescence and began to see myself in relation to other boys, I realized how different I was—and I began to see myself through my dad's eyes. More than anything, I wanted to make my dad proud of me. But every attempt to be a "normal boy" ended in failure. I sucked at sports, I went shopping with girls instead of dating them, and I kept my distance from other boys. As a result, my own frustration and the disappointment I was sure my dad felt drove a wedge between us. Being around him reminded me of all the things I aspired to be, but wasn't.

When I came out to my parents at twenty-three, my dad had little to say. In many ways, I saw my homosexuality as the final nail in the coffin. But when I turned to leave the room, my father walked over and hugged me. I couldn't remember the last time I'd been that physically close to him. ▶

> 66 What must it have been like to watch your son bypass the Tonka trucks and head straight for the Barbie dolls? What kind of logic could be found from a kid who wanted to dress as Marilyn Monroe for Halloween? 99

Why This Book Is "For Dad" *(continued)*

Shortly after that, my parents helped form a support group for parents of gay and lesbian children in my hometown. My dad even walked with me in the city's first Pride parade. And he came to accept me in a way I couldn't have imagined. Perhaps in a way he never could have, either.

I don't want to sugar coat this or turn my relationship with my dad into some kind of Hallmark card. We were still emotionally strained around one another, not unlike a lot of fathers and sons. My mom used to make us hug good-bye—something we did with no small amount of awkwardness. But I'm glad we did it.

My dad died before the book was published. He never got a chance to read it. I often wonder what he would have thought about it.

But I think I can safely say he would have been proud of his son.

I'm proud of him too. ∾

> 66 Shortly after that, my parents helped form a support group for parents of gay and lesbian children in my hometown. My dad even walked with me in the city's first Pride parade. 99

Parents, Families, and Friends of Lesbians and Gays (PFLAG) promotes the health and well-being of gay, lesbian, bisexual, and transgendered persons, their families and friends through: support, to cope with an adverse society; education, to enlighten an ill-informed public; and advocacy, to end discrimination and to secure equal civil rights. PFLAG provides opportunity for dialogue about sexual orientation and gender identity, and acts to create a society that is healthy and respectful of human diversity. For more information please visit www.pflag.org.

Brian Francis
Talks to Dan Savage

DAN SAVAGE is an internationally syndicated sex-advice columnist of "Savage Love," read by millions of people every week. He has written "Savage Love" for more than ten years and it runs in more than seventy newspapers in the United States, Canada, Europe, and Asia. Savage is also the editor of *The Stranger,* Seattle's weekly newspaper, and he is the author of *Savage Love,* a collection of his advice columns; *The Kid,* an award-winning memoir about adoption; and *Skipping Towards Gomorrah,* a collection of essays. His new book, *The Commitment,* will be released in September 2005. Dan Savage recently sat down with Brian Francis for a conversation about gay adolescence, the tedium of weddings, and the enduring appeal of red Speedos.

Dan Savage: *All adolescents feel a sense of estrangement from their own bodies during puberty. For gay adolescents, that sense of estrangement is made more intense by feelings of betrayal—"How could my body be doing this to me!" I think that's the animating idea of your novel. As a gay man, what was your reaction when your body informed you that, like it or not, you were going to be gay when you grew up?*

Brian Francis: My body and I always made better enemies than friends, so when it told me I was going to be gay, I was like, "Whatever, bitch." From a young age, I was engaged in this emotional—and sometimes physical — ▶

66 My body and I always made better enemies than friends, so when it told me I was going to be gay, I was like, 'Whatever, bitch.' 99

tug-of-war with myself. Ah, the quest for normality! It kept slipping through my chubby adolescent fingers! I survived by doing the one thing that gay adolescents do best—avoided thinking about the issue and focused on my hair.

DS: *Do you think gay men ever fully recover from that sense of betrayal? So many of the social pathologies that plague the gay community appear to be some sort of subconscious effort on the part of gay men to punish their bodies: the smoking, the abuse of recreational drugs —for the record: not all drug use is abuse—and the physically and emotionally damaging extremes that some gay men carry promiscuity to. And then there's the chest waxing, eyebrow plucking, and tanning. What's the deal?*

BF: I'm sorry, I was just coming out of a K-Hole. What was the question again?

DS: *Most fiction about closeted, gay adolescents seems to be about—how best to put this?— fantasy figures. Closeted jocks, closeted presidents of the student council, closeted semi-professional surfers. Basically adult fantasy figures. I don't think I've ever seen a book about a gay teenager who was so repulsive—funny as shit, of course, but repulsive. It seems to violate some unwritten rule of gay fiction: "1. Closeted gay kids have to be hot, hot, hot." Was it an act of bravery creating a character who, like a lot of gay*

66 I survived by doing the one thing that gay adolescents do best—avoided thinking about the issue and focused on my hair. 99

kids, is lonely, fat, and lives in a fantasy
world?

BF: It wasn't bravery so much as it was
liberation. I was at the point of frustration.
I knew that I was never the closet jock or
the student council president or the semi-
professional surfer. Call it "Revenge of the Fat
Gay Kid,"—grab your Twinkies and
CHARGE!!!— but I was itching to give
someone like Peter Paddington a voice. It was
one I hadn't read before and more
importantly, it was a voice I felt needed to
be heard. And for the record, I don't think
Peter is repulsive. Pimply legs can be quite
pretty, given the right lighting.

> **For the record,
> I don't think
> Peter is repulsive.
> Pimply legs can
> be quite pretty,
> given the right
> lighting.**

DS: *Why do you think most gay men prefer
to forget about their actual adolescences and
focus on fantasy versions? Are they too painful?
Or just too banal?*

BF: I think it's a combination of the two.
There's a lot of pain, but there's a lot of
boredom during those years too. Fantasies
are really about escapism, and whatever
your motivation—boredom, pain, control,
acceptance—they really all serve the same
purpose.

DS: *How much of this story is autobiographical?
You're a slim, attractive gay man living in the
big city and you've got a boyfriend. You're not
a Peter Paddington—now, at any rate. Were
you ever?*

▶

Brian Francis Talks to Dan Savage *(continued)*

BF: Let me put it this way—I didn't have to job-shadow any fat paperboys in the name of research. But I was more of an extrovert than Peter. I was the typical funny fat kid— the one who went out and bought dirty joke books for material at recess. I used my humor as a distraction. The difficult thing about being overweight is that there's simply no place to hide. You're out in the open, waiting for someone to target you. So you try to stall people in whatever ways you can. But when all is said and done, no matter where I live, or how much I weigh or what I look like, I'll never disown that fat kid. He acts as my compass in the world.

DS: *Hey, you're a gay Canadian with a boyfriend. Any plans to turn that boyfriend into a boy-husband?*

BF: It's an option, but it's not a pressing one. To be honest, I can't really visualize what my gay wedding would be like. I mean, I'd give my left nut to have *The Facts of Life* girls as my bridesmaids, but I doubt it will happen. And does my mom walk me down the aisle? And do we wear matching tuxes? And which one of us wears the garter? Part of it is my own exhaustion with the whole wedding spectacle too. I've given up a fair number of precious Saturdays—and eaten my fair share of chicken breasts in mushroom sauce—to watch couples I barely know declare their undying love for each other. And part of me just doesn't get it. I think your relationship

> **❝** To be honest, I can't really visualize what my gay wedding would be like. I mean, I'd give my left nut to have *The Facts of Life* girls as my bridesmaids, but I doubt it will happen. **❞**

should be private. Your love should be private. But hell, if it means getting a new washer/dryer, slap on the garter.

· ·

DS: *Bedtime Movies: I think a lot of us when we're young and gay fantasize about scenarios in which same-sex love, more so than same-sex sex, is, if you'll pardon the expression, thrust upon us. Guys show up at our houses and need something to wear and all we can find is a red Speedo, or the attractive adult male husbands of neighbors fall in love with us, through no fault of our own, and we wouldn't want to hurt them so we reluctantly return their affections. We're the victims/heroes in these fantasies. Peter's fantasies are almost as cinematic as they are hilarious. Why do you think this kind of fantasizing is so common among gay men?*

BF: Whenever I allowed myself a gay fantasy, whether it be sexual or romantic in nature, there was always some kind of catch. Like, I had to be bullied into it. Or it was what *all* the guys did after football practice. Or I happened to look like Heather Locklear. That was the only way I could rationalize my desires. Of course, a teenaged guy wanting to look like Heather Locklear isn't the most rational thing in the world, but I digress. The bottom line was there were too many horrific implications in permitting myself to openly feel desire for another male. It went against every rule I was taught as a kid. So I think a lot of gay youth create worlds where that desire is natural and permissible. And that's the catch—the fantasy worlds ▶

> ❝ Whenever I allowed myself a gay fantasy, whether it be sexual or romantic in nature, there was always some kind of catch. Like, I had to be bullied into it. Or it was what *all* the guys did after football practice. ❞

Brian Francis Talks to Dan Savage *(continued)*

created are ultimately more satisfying than reality. It's only when you start calling yourself "Heather" that you could be in trouble.

....

DS: *When I was a gay kid, I used to tell my mother I wanted to be a girl when I grew up— which I'm not now, of course, and I don't have any desire to be. But I knew at age five that I wanted to have the kind of relationship with a man that I saw my female relatives had with their husbands. So I thought, well, I guess I'll just have to be a girl when I grow up. How else will I get what I want? I guess this isn't really a question, just a stroll down memory lane.*

BF: Thanks for sharing, Dan.

....

DS: *What makes straight women and gay men so compatible—emotionally speaking? It has to go beyond lusting after boys, don't you think?*

BF: It's the shoes. It's all about the shoes.

....

DS: *Why the hell do you hate Italians so much?*

BF: Are you high? Daniela Bertoli is the only character with balls in this book! For the record, I'd like to state that my partner is Italian, so however Italians come across in the book is his fault entirely. Actually, the truth of the matter is that I've always been jealous of Italian culture—the food, the theatrics, the freedom to say "fuck" in front ▶

> " For the record, I'd like to state that my partner is Italian, so however Italians come across in the book is his fault entirely. "

of your mother without getting your ears boxed. Atsa nice!

....

DS: *I can say "fuck" in front of my mother—and she's Irish.*

BF: My mother's idea of swearing is "Jesus Murphy." 'Nuf said. To wrap this up, I think it's only fitting to turn the tables, Mr. Savage. As I mentioned, *The Facts of Life* girls would be the ultimate celebrity bridesmaids at my gay wedding. Who would be yours?

DS: *The Finnish Men's Synchronized Diving Team, of course, in red Speedos.* ∽

Canadian Fruits v.
American Fruits

The Secret Fruit of Peter Paddington was originally published under the title *Fruit* in Canada in Spring 2004. When I got the call about an offer for United States hardcover rights, I was thrilled. Then I was told by my Canadian editor that the American publisher would want to make changes to the manuscript. Fearing a rewrite of the book, I prepared for the worst.

As it turned out, the changes the American publisher wanted to make were minimal, but surprising ones. I never realized how many subtle differences there are between Canada and the United States. While there were plenty of cultural references in *The Secret Fruit of Peter Paddington* that remained unchanged—Mary Kay Cosmetics, *The Love Boat,* and Adrian Zmed to name a few—there were a fair number of references that *were* changed. For example, the Canadian Peter Paddington is in grade eight at Clarkedale Elementary School. The American Peter is in eighth grade at Clarkedale Middle School. The principle of the Canadian school is Mr. Grey, not Mr. Gray. Every morning, Canadian Peter sings *O Canada!,* rather than reciting the "Pledge of Allegiance." He also attends the United Church, not the Methodist Church. Peter's sister, Nancy, works at Tim Hortons instead of Dunkin Donuts. Peter's neighbor, Mrs. Bertoli, wears a Blue Jays toque in Canada and an Orioles cap in the United States.

Some other notables: Canadians have Cheezies. Americans have Cheez Doodles.

> " I have to admit my shock that you Americans don't have the same chocolate bars as your neighbors to the North. "

Canadians have Fudgee-O cookies. Americans have Oreos. (Okay, we have Oreos too, but Fudgee-Os are better!) And Canadians eat Wagon Wheels whereas Americans eat Pinwheels.

And while we're on the topic of food, I have to admit my shock that you Americans don't have the same chocolate bars as your neighbors to the North. No Crispy Crunch? No Sweet Marie? No—gasp!—Mr. Big? My heart goes out to you!

I thought it might be a fun idea to do a taste test between the chocolate bars listed in the Canadian version of *The Secret Fruit of Peter Paddington* and the American chocolate bars that replaced them to determine which bars reigned superior. I managed to assemble a few (impartial) coworkers one day to do the testing. (Yes, it was tough getting people to agree to a chocolate bar taste testing, but I prevailed.) Results follow on the next page. ▶

> 66 Canadians have Cheezies. Americans have Cheez Doodles. Canadians have Fudgee-O cookies. Americans have Oreos. (Okay, we have Oreos too, but Fudgee-Os are better.) 99

Battle of the
Chocolate Bars

Chocolate Bar	Sell line	Judge's comments	Champion
PayDay ★	"Peanut Caramel Bar"	Salty, like a stale peanut butter cookie.	
Sweet Marie 🍁	"Lots of fresh roasted peanuts."	Right amount of sweetness, moist, and hint of coconut.	✔
Milky Way ★	"Rich chocolate, creamy caramel, smooth nougat."	Good taste, delicious caramel, and chewy-riffic!	✔
Mars Bar 🍁	"Energy Bar" (Yeah, right!)	Dry, stale, and with an inferior chocolate coating.	
100 Grand ★	None	Caramel-y, great texture, buttery.	
Mr. Big 🍁	None	Great crunch and chew factor, perfect combination.	✔
Butterfinger ★	"Crispety, crunchety, peanut-buttery."	So bad it makes a Big Turk bar look good, burnt toffee taste.	
Crispy Crunch 🍁	"Peanut candy wrapped in milk chocolate."	Delicious, perfect texture, flakey, and buttery.	✔

Overall rankings of chocolate bars:
1) Crispy Crunch 2) Milky Way 3) Mr. Big and 100 Grand (tie)
4) Sweet Marie 5) Mars Bar 6) PayDay 7) Butterfinger

🍁 indicates Canadian bar
★ indicates American bar